AMANDA HAZARD MYSTERY

DEAD IN THE DIRT

CONNIE FEDDERSEN

KENSINGTON/1-57566-046-6/CANADA $5.99/US. $4.99

Nick Thorn surveyed the victim from every possible angle and then announced his conclusion. "It appears that Will Bloom was knocked down by his overeager livestock and trampled. With an open feed sack in his hand, he couldn't get up. It looks as if he caught several hooves in the head and thorax."

"That's the way it *looks*," Amanda said as she climbed over the fence, snagging her pantyhose in the process. "But that's *not* what happened."

"I knew you'd have your own suspicious theory," Nick grumbled. "Just what is it this time, Chicken Little? Did the sky fall in on Will Bloom?"

Amanda glared branding irons at Thorn, unamused by his droll sense of humor. "Of course I have a theory. Will Bloom must have been clubbed with a blunt instrument and then dragged into the corral to make his death look accidental."

Nick crossed his arms over his massive chest. "And what, Hazard, or dare I ask, led you to that conclusion? Did you arrive on the scene to see the assailant drag the body into the corral?"

"No." Amanda bared her teeth. "But I did see the swath of grass wiped clean of morning dew."

"Dew?" Nick glanced at the corral gate. "All I see are dirt and hoofprints. You realize this *vanishing dew clue* won't hold up well in court, especially since there is no sign of it at the time of discovery."

"The dew was *sparklingly* apparent at the time of *my* discovery," she huffed. "And after you take a look inside Will's house, you're going to agree that something very fishy has been going on around here."

Thorn cocked a dubious brow. "I am?"

"You are," she confirmed. "Follow me, Thorn . . ."

BIG MIKE MYSTERIES
BY GARRISON ALLEN!

ROYAL CAT   (1-57566-045-8, $4.99)

More than mischief is afoot when the less-than-popular
retired teacher playing The Virgin Queen in the annual
Elizabethan Spring Faire is executed in the dark of night.
Her crown passes to Penelope Warren, bookstore owner
and amateur sleuth extraordinaire. Then the murderer
takes an encore, and it's up to Penelope and her awesome
Abyssinian cat, "Big Mike," to take their sleuthing behind the scenes . . . where death treads the boards and
a cunning killer refuses to be upstaged.

DESERT CAT   (0-8217-4503-4, $3.99)

Meddlesome, mean spirited Louise Fletcher was high on
everyone's least-liked list. An expert at backstabbing, she
is found with a knife between her shoulderblades and a
death grip on a bright new penny. Everyone in Empty
Creek, Arizona, has a motive. So, it's up to Penelope
Warren and her feline partner Big Mike to sniff out the
victim's secrets, paw through her past—and pounce on
a killer.

*Available wherever paperbacks are sold, or order direct from the
Publisher. Send cover price plus 50¢ per copy for mailing and handling to Penguin USA, P.O. Box 999, c/o Dept. 17109, Bergenfield, NJ 07621. Residents of New York and Tennessee must
include sales tax. DO NOT SEND CASH.*

DEAD IN THE DIRT

CONNIE FEDDERSEN

KENSINGTON BOOKS
KENSINGTON PUBLISHING CORP.

This book is a work of fiction. The names, characters, and incidents are either products of the author's imagination or are used fictitiously. Any resemblance to locales, events, or persons, living or dead, is entirely coincidental.

KENSINGTON BOOKS are published by

Kensington Publishing Corp.
850 Third Avenue
New York, NY 10022

Copyright © 1996 by Connie Feddersen

Kensington and the K logo Reg. U.S. Pat. & TM Off.

First Kensington Paperback Printing: June, 1996
10 9 8 7 6 5 4 3 2 1

Printed in the United States of America

This book is dedicated to my husband Ed, and our children Christie, Jeff, Jill, Jon, and Kurt, with much love . . .

One

Amanda Hazard, CPA, nearly leaped out of her skin when the blare of the phone reverberated off the metal file cabinets and concrete block walls of her office. The abrupt sound caused her to poke her finger against the wrong key of her calculator. Rather than *subtracting* a debit from Thatcher's Oil and Gas accounts she had accidentally *added* it. Before Amanda could correct the error, the phone shrieked at her again.

"Alright already," Amanda muttered, snatching up the phone.

It had not been a productive week—too many interruptions to keep Amanda's analytical mind clicking at its customary competent pace. First thing Monday morning her secretary, Jenny Long, had called to say that her young son had come down with chicken pox. Amanda, who had grown accustomed to having a secretary field incoming calls and file tax forms, found herself up to her eyebrows in bookwork.

Irritable did not adequately describe Amanda's disposition. She was as cross and cranky as a junkyard dog.

"Hazard Accounting Agency," Amanda said crisply.

"Hi, doll, it's Mother."

Amanda gnashed her teeth. "Hello, Mother."

"I'm at the end of my rope!" Mother yowled into the phone.

"Aren't we all?" Amanda quipped.

"You've got to do something with your grandfather," Mother raved on. "That old goat is driving me batty. I can't take it anymore!"

Amanda broke into a devilish smile. Pops—as Amanda affectionately referred to her paternal grandfather—was the only one in the Hazard family who gave Mother the *bad time* Mother gave everybody else. Amanda had secretly admired Pops's techniques for years.

"I have never been able to do anything to please that man," Mother yammered. "Now that he's moved in with us, it's gotten worse! I've got to get away for some rest and relaxation before I go crazy!"

In Amanda's opinion, Mother didn't have far to go.

"You've got to let Pops stay with you while your daddy and I take a cruise to the Caribbean."

"Mother, as much as I would love to have Pops here in Vamoose with me, I'm behind in my work—"

Mother interrupted by clearing her throat. "For heaven's sake, doll. This is family, and family should always come first. Your daddy promised me a cruise for our anniversary. It's bought and paid for."

"If family comes first, why are you sailing off on a cruise and abandoning Pops?"

"Don't use that sarcastic tone with me," Mother snapped, as only Mother could. "I'm the one who's been putting up with that cantankerous old codger since your daddy decided Pops shouldn't be living alone.

"I need a break, and I certainly can't leave Pops with your brother and that lazy wife of his, not when they already have those two spoiled brats I call my grandchildren to contend with. If your brother would take control of those kids, and insist his wife do something besides twiddle her thumbs, his household wouldn't be in such an uproar."

Amanda drummed her fingers, checked her wristwatch, and listened to Mother yackety-yak about her daughter-in-law's failing graces.

Mother finally cleared her throat again and swerved back to the previous topic of conversation. "Besides, Pops always liked you best. He's ready and willing to come to Podunk City for a few weeks."

"That's Vamoose, Mother," Amanda said through her teeth.

"Hicksville is Hicksville," Mother said dismissively. "The point is, Pops needs a change of scenery and so do I. You can have your cop boyfriend drive Pops around in his squad car. I doubt that Thorn fellow has much else to do in that one-horse town anyway."

Visualizing Mother's neck, Amanda put a stranglehold on the phone. Mother didn't have a clue that sexy country cop Nick Thorn was busy with his part-time farming and ranching operation, plus policing the area. Thorn's workload was as strenuous as Amanda's, though no amount of explanation could convince Mother of that. Mother was hell-bent on having her way, as usual.

"You can pick Pops up tomorrow morning." It was a direct order from headquarters. "I'll have his suitcases packed. Since you live on that rented farm, you'll have plenty of room for Pops to tinker around, repairing all those antiques he's nuts about—probably because he's an antique himself."

Amanda mentally listed the tasks she needed to perform so her elderly grandfather would have the available space to do what he loved best—rebuild and restore antique clocks and furniture. It was his true calling in life.

The wooden granary inside the barn at Amanda's farm would make an ideal workshop for Pops, but renovations were needed. A carpenter had to be hired to convert the granary.

Amanda made a note to contact Buzz Sawyer ASAP. The local carpenter owed Amanda a favor. He had yet to pay his yearly fees for figuring his taxes and keeping accounts updated for his business.

"Your daddy and I will be catching a flight from the City to Miami at seven o'clock in the morning. Pops will be waiting for you to pick him up. *Bon voyage,* doll."

The line went dead.

"Well," Amanda said to herself, replacing the receiver, "think of it this way. You got the better end of this deal. *You* get Pops, but *Daddy* is stuck with Mother."

Shoving the tax forms aside, Amanda jotted down the approximate dimensions of the granary in her barn. New plywood walls and flooring would have to be installed to provide acceptable work space for Pops to pursue his favorite pastime.

In less than five minutes, Amanda had calculated how many 4 x 8 sheets of three-quarter-inch plywood would be needed to complete the project. Two windows would have to be installed for proper ventilation. She couldn't have Pops getting high on paint stripper and varnish fumes!

Amanda picked up the phone and dialed Pronto Lumber and Supply Company. When Delbert Smiley answered, Amanda rattled off the list of needed lumber and requested a tabulation of the cost of nails and wood.

"Can you have the supplies delivered to my farm this afternoon?" Amanda asked.

"Sure thing, Amanda," said Delbert. "I'll have my son haul it up to you after lunch. Where do you want the lumber unloaded?"

After Amanda gave Delbert the necessary information she looked up Buzz Sawyer's number. It was obvious that Buzz kept his cellular phone with him at all times, for when he answered Amanda's call, she could hear the rhythmic strike of a hammer serenading her.

"Buzz Sawyer here. Have hammer will travel."

"Buzz, this is Amanda Hazard."

The hammer taps halted abruptly.

"Um . . . I was going to put your check in the mail this very afternoon, believe it or not."

Amanda chose not to believe it. "I'm going to swap services with you," she announced. She was also going to use Mother's tactic of making demands rather than requests. "I need you to do some remodeling in my barn. I've already ordered the lumber from Pronto, and it will be delivered this afternoon. You can start right after lunch."

"I'm in the middle of—"

"This project shouldn't take more than a couple of days," Amanda cut in. "When you're finished, we'll call it even. After all, we're among friends here in Vamoose. I wouldn't want to have to send a collection agency out to recover the outstanding fees you owe me. Some of those bruisers can be very intimidating. I wouldn't want you to wind up with a broken arm."

"Me, either," Buzz mumbled.

Amanda then proceeded to give Buzz the dimensions of the granary and details of what she wanted done to accommodate her grandfather in his new workshop. When she had extracted a promise that Buzz would arrive that afternoon, Amanda hung up the phone.

"Finally!" she said with a gusty sigh.

Amanda dragged the stack of tax forms back in front of her. In profound concentration, hoping to complete the updates for Thatcher's accounts, her fingers flew over the calculator keys. She had tallied only a fourth of the expenditures and debits when the phone jingled again.

Damn it! Where's Jenny when I need her?

"Hazard Accounting. Hazard speaking," she said briskly.

"Amanda, this is Will Bloom. We need to talk . . . *now.*"

Amanda frowned at the edgy undertone in her client's voice. Will Bloom, a small-time farmer, had requested her services only two months earlier. For the life of her Amanda had not been able to figure out why. There was nothing complicated about Will's tax returns. As it was, he was on the verge of qualifying for welfare. Will Bloom wasn't in debt, and he had no wife or children to support on his meager income or to claim as deductions. So why did he need Amanda's immediate services for simple calculations?

"Let me pull your file," Amanda suggested, scooting her chair toward the metal cabinets.

"That isn't necessary," Will insisted. "I have a few things I want you to pick up from my farm—for safekeeping."

Amanda's hand stalled in midair. "Oh? What things?"

"Just come by my place. I want you to have this stuff . . . just in case . . ."

In the background, Amanda heard the clang of a doorbell. Someone had obviously arrived at Will's home.

"Well, damn," Will muttered. "Get here as fast as you can, Amanda. I'm counting on the reputation you've developed around Vamoose. Meet me down at the barn. After I get rid of my uninvited guest, I'll be down there, feeding my livestock."

"Will, what's this all about?" Amanda questioned, concerned by his apprehensive tone.

"Meet me at the corral. I'll explain it to you then."

The hum of the dial tone indicated that Will Bloom had raced off to answer his doorbell.

Amanda stared down at the uncompleted files and then glanced at her watch. She had arrived at her office forty-five minutes earlier than usual to begin work. Now it was 8:15 and she had nothing to show for her efforts.

It was a twenty-minute drive—down washboarded country roads that Commissioner Brown never graded—to reach Bloom Farm. By the time Amanda drove to and from the farm, and had her conference with Will Bloom, the morning would be shot all to hell. And then there was Buzz Sawyer to deal with, before picking up Pops the following morning, Amanda reminded herself.

The way Amanda had it figured, the day was going to be a *dead loss*.

Muttering, Amanda plucked up the Thatcher Oil and Gas file and tucked it under her arm. She would have to cancel the rendezvous she had planned with Nick Thorn so she could work through the night. As usual, family responsibility and business obligations were shoving her love life into the backseat—figuratively speaking.

And damn, Amanda thought as she whizzed out the door. Thorn had indicated there was something important he had wanted to discuss with her this evening. *Wouldn't you know, this is the first night we had planned to spend alone together in more than three weeks and I have to postpone it!*

Amanda slid behind the steering wheel of her Toyota and cranked the engine. The car growled to life. Amanda switched on the wipers to clear the new layer of dew that had formed on her windshield.

Autumn had arrived in Vamoose, glazing the world like a frosted mug, turning leaves a dozen different shades of red, orange, and brown. Unfortunately, Amanda was too busy to appreciate the change of scenery.

As usual, she was burning both ends of her candle trying to keep up with her workload. Having received much acclaim, after solving three murder cases that Thorn had been certain were accidents, Amanda was in great demand. Practically everybody in Vamoose—except Thorn—had entrusted her with their tax work. Amanda appreciated all the votes of confidence, but her schedule was grueling.

Ah well, she consoled herself. *It's the price competent, efficient businesswomen pay for success.*

Waving at the passersby who were headed to the Last Chance Cafe for their customary morning coffee and conversation, Amanda zipped down the highway. She didn't have time to dawdle over a cup of coffee. Instead, she was on her way to meet a client who had sounded upset. About what Amanda didn't have a clue. What could be wrong in the simple, uncomplicated world of Will Bloom?

She swore inventively when the right front tire of her car dropped into a rut the size of the Mariana Trench. Curse Commissioner Brown! It wouldn't hurt him to send out a road-grading crew every few months, would it?

Since this was an election year, Amanda vowed to campaign against that do-nothing clown and ensure he was ousted from office.

What Vamoose County needed was an efficient, competent *female* commissioner. For a moment, Amanda considered running for election, but she simply couldn't spare the time. A woman could only do so much to correct the problems in this world.

In a cloud of dust, and a hearty "Hi-Ho, Silver," Amanda zoomed up the hill to see Will Bloom's run-down, two-story farmhouse nestled among a cluster of cedar trees. Morning sunlight glistened like diamonds on the frost-coated green shingles of the house. Grass sparkled like streamers of tinsel.

Amanda stepped from the car and fastened her jacket to ward off the crisp autumn chill. She would have preferred to hold this conference in the house, dilapidated though it looked to be. Why Will Bloom insisted on meeting her at the barn she couldn't imagine. But come to think of it, Will had never invited her into his home, not even two months earlier—the first time he had asked her to come by to pick up his accounting receipts.

Amanda supposed Will was self-conscious about inviting guests into his home. She knew for a fact that he couldn't afford to remodel the place. As it was, he could barely make ends meet on his meager income.

However, Amanda thought as she glanced back at the house, *it wouldn't kill Will to pry money loose from his wallet to buy some paint, would it? A fresh coat of paint would do wonders for the outward appearance of his home.*

A bellowing cow caught Amanda's attention. She rounded the corner of the barn to see the livestock penned in a small corral. Two large red bulls, a dozen cows, and several young calves collided as they milled around the pen, loudly crunching on cattle cubes that had been strewn in the dirt.

Amanda glanced toward the opened barn door. "Will?"

No answer, except the bawling of calves that searched for their mothers in the congested herd.

Muttering, Amanda circled around the barn rather than tramp through the corral filled with cattle. "Will? Yoo-hoo!"

Stepping inside the barn, Amanda noted several sacks of cattle cube supplement stacked against the wall beside a pyramid of square bales of prairie hay.

But no Will Bloom.

"Will! It's Amanda Hazard," she yelled.

Her voice echoed through the barn and then died in silence.

Amanda ventured back outside, wondering where Will could have gone. Just as she took a huge breath to shout Will's name again, she saw him.

Or rather his boots . . .

Amanda gulped hard and then darted toward the corral fence. A sense of impending doom settled in her bones as she clambered up the fence to stare down into the corral.

The cattle, having consumed their daily ration of cattle cubes, were scattered around the pen munching on sprigs of grass. There, sprawled facedown in the dirt, with an open feed sack beside his outstretched arm, lay Will Bloom. Dirty hoofprints dotted the back of his flannel shirt and faded blue jeans. A baseball cap, flattened by hungry, stamping cattle, lay beside him. Trickles of blood oozed from the wound on the back of his head.

Amanda grimaced. She had the unshakable feeling that she would be filing Bloom's first—and final—tax return for the IRS. If she wasn't mistaken—and she rarely was—Will Bloom was dead in the dirt.

This, Amanda realized regretfully, was the fourth corpse she had stumbled upon in the small rural community of Vamoose. As had become her custom, Amanda carefully scrutinized the scene of the accident, making note of the exact number of cattle penned in the corral, the crinkled brown paper feed sack, and the position of the corpse in the dirt. . . .

Amanda's thoughts stalled when she glanced from west to east. As the sun beamed across the grass, Amanda made a shocking discovery. Morning frost and dewdrops sparkled everywhere—except on a narrow swath of ground leading into the corral.

Amanda's sharp, analytical mind immediately cried foul play. From all indication, Will had been dragged into the corral and left to be trampled by his own livestock. She suspected that the average Joe was supposed to believe Will Bloom had been knocked down and stepped on by his hungry cattle.

Amanda Hazard was no average Joe.

She was willing to bet her life savings that the scene of the *supposed* accident in the corral had been purposely staged. The tracks in the morning dew left telltale signs, assuring Amanda that things weren't what they seemed.

Casting a cautious glance at the cattle, Amanda swung one leg over the top rail. Had she known she would be scaling fences to survey a crime scene, she would have dressed appropriately. Her three-piece silk business suit cramped her investigative style.

When the curious cattle converged on her, Amanda flapped her arms in expansive gestures, shooing the livestock out of her way. She squatted down beside Will to check for a pulse in his neck.

Will Bloom didn't have one.

Amanda had been pretty sure that would be the case. Will Bloom was definitely dead in the dirt.

Damn.

Once again, Amanda surveyed the path of grass that had been wiped clean of morning frost and dew. Yep, she confidently assured herself. Will Bloom had been dragged into the corral by an unknown assailant. Judging by the path in the grass, she suspected the actual assault had taken place beside the barn. The smudged indentation of a bootheel indicated someone other than Will might have been in the corral.

Without disturbing the area more than it had already been by milling cattle, Amanda retraced her steps and climbed the fence. Circling the gargantuan barn, Amanda headed to the house to contact Officer Nick Thorn.

Getting word to Thorn wouldn't be easy, Amanda predicted. Between keeping the police beat around Vamoose and planting his fall wheat crop, Thorn had been meeting himself coming and going. He was not going to appreciate the interruption, and Amanda could already hear him scowling and snorting when she informed him that another murder—not a seeming accident—had taken place in Vamoose!

Amanda wiped her wet blue pumps on the mat in front of the door before she barged into Will's run-down house. Why she bothered, once she noticed the thread-bare carpet, she didn't know. Habit, she supposed.

The living room was sparsely furnished with an antique couch and love seat. An outdated vinyl recliner sat across the room from a thirteen-inch TV set. Amanda could not imagine why anybody would want to do Will Bloom in. He had nothing anyone could want.

Amanda sniffed the air, detecting a hint of smoke. She glanced around the room once more, searching for ashtrays. There were none. She swore she smelled the lingering odor of cigarette or cigar smoke, but there was no physical indication that Will Bloom indulged.

Amanda took one last sniff and frowned thoughtfully. It was cigar smoke, she decided.

Since there was no phone in the room, Amanda strode down the hall and veered into the kitchen. She stumbled to a halt when sunlight reflected off the chrome-plated, state-of-the-art microwave oven and ultramodern stove. Amanda felt as if she had walked through a time machine when she crossed the threshold. Brand-new carpet covered the kitchen floor, and shiny oak cabinets lined the walls.

Amanda made a beeline toward the cordless phone that sat on the bright orange Formica countertop. In a matter of seconds she reached Thorn's police dispatcher to relay her message.

"I need to contact Thorn," Amanda announced, surveying the remodeled kitchen in astonishment.

"Thorn is off duty this morning. Would you like to speak to Deputy Sykes?"

No way, thought Amanda. *Benny Sykes is too much the rookie for this kind of police business.* Deputy Sykes's forte was speeding tickets—period. Although

Benny could rattle off police jargon to beat the band, and he had memorized the official handbooks forward and backward, he was no Nick Thorn, not even on Thorn's bad days.

"No one but Thorn will do," Amanda insisted. "Send Deputy Sykes to locate Thorn. He's probably planting wheat on the old Jolly place that he rents from me."

"Well, I'll try but—"

"What's the code for emergency and request for assistance?" Amanda quickly interrupted.

"Code 3," the dispatcher informed her.

"That's what I've got here," Amanda declared. "Tell Thorn to haul butt over to Will Bloom's farm. Tell him Hazard is waiting at the house."

Amanda dropped the receiver into place and glanced around. Since she had some time on her hands, she decided to make a thorough inspection of the house.

Will Bloom's living room was a modest, but deceptive front. For what? Amanda had no idea! But if the remodeled kitchen was anything to go by, Will was living far beyond his means . . . and the rest of the world was none the wiser.

Except for whoever had left Will Bloom dead in the dirt.

Amanda tramped off, finding herself in the spacious den situated at the back of the house. Her jaw dropped when she noticed the big-screen television bookended by shelves lined with priceless antique clocks . . . clocks that her grandfather would love get his hands on!

In another corner of the room sat an expensive CD player, amplifiers large enough to blast eardrums, and a hi-tech VCR. A plush leather couch was situated near the bay window that overlooked a scenic view of rolling pastures and a wooded creek.

Damn, Will had concealed a veritable mansion inside this supposed shack!

Her curiosity fully aroused, Amanda scaled the steps leading to the second story. There she made several more startling discoveries about the state of Will's financial affairs. No expense had been spared in decorating the master bedroom. The man had spent a small fortune on the four-poster bed, marble-top dressers, and walnut end tables. The room looked like something Abraham Lincoln might have slept in. Talk about priceless heirlooms! Wow! Amanda had never seen the likes! Her grandfather would go bonkers if he took a gander at this place.

"You were a devious rascal, Will," Amanda muttered. And here she had given Will a discount for handling his tax accounts. So much for wasted sympathy and generosity.

What in the blazes had Will been doing? Stealing heirlooms, pawning stolen goods? Although he projected the facade of a down-on-his-luck farmer trying to scratch out a living, Will Bloom lived pretty damned high on the hog!

A quick inspection of the other upstairs rooms indicated that Will had been spending money that never appeared as income on his tax returns. He had amassed a baffling combination of priceless antiques and modern conveniences—including a Jacuzzi bathtub.

Amanda could visualize Will sprawled out on his leather recliner, the remote control to the big-screen TV in one hand and the control to his VCR in the other, quietly smirking at the world outside his seemingly modest home. He had obviously pulled the wool over the eyes of his neighbors and his new accountant.

That would explain why Will had made a habit of changing accountants each year. Amanda had considered that a bit odd when she noticed Will's previous income tax returns had been filed by a variety of companies. Now she knew why Will Bloom wanted no one to become too familiar with his business.

Too bad for Will Bloom that someone had discovered his secret cache or buried treasure—whatever. If Will had lived, he certainly couldn't have ratted to the police about the assault without explaining the source of funds that purchased so many modern conveniences and the collection of antiquated valuables. If Will had lived, he would have had to stand trial for tax evasion. But he was dead and it was up to Amanda to ascertain who had knocked the blossoms off Will Bloom—permanently.

Dressed in faded blue jeans and a well-worn shirt, Nick Thorn hoisted the metal grain auger onto his broad shoulders and aimed it toward the seed drill attached to his Allis-Chalmers tractor. The auger churned, groaned and sucked wheat seed from the dump truck and spit it into the drill.

Nick muttered when seed clogged in the auger, forcing him to switch off the mechanism before the overload burned up the electric motor.

It seemed he had been going around in circles for days on end, planting wheat to provide winter forage for his cattle. Now that he was renting the property Amanda Hazard had inherited from Elmer Jolly, Nick was twice as busy as usual at planting time. Between the farmwork and cruising in his black-and-white he'd had little time for relaxation. He could use a break.

A wry smile slid across Nick's lips. He was anticipating a quiet evening alone with the blond bombshell accountant he had been dating. He was the envy of everything in pants since he and Hazard had become an official item in Vamoose.

Nick intended for this evening to become a new milestone in his relationship with Hazard. There were things they needed to discuss—in depth . . .

Nick's thoughts scattered like a flock of ducks when he heard the blare of a siren and saw the flashing lights of the approaching squad car. Deputy Benny Sykes was coming on like gangbusters, leaving a cloud of dust behind him. *No telling what Benny has going,* Nick thought to himself. The gung-ho deputy had a tendency to get excited over little or nothing.

When the patrol car skidded to a halt and gravel flew like buckshot, Nick switched off the auger he had just turned back on. "Got a problem, Sykes?"

Benny bounded off the car seat like a jackrabbit and shoved his mirrored sunglasses against the bridge of his nose. "The dispatcher called," Benny reported. "Amanda Hazard has a Code 3 and she wants no one but you."

Nick frowned, glancing expectantly at Benny.

"The dispatcher told Amanda you were 10-70D," Benny continued. "But you know how your girlfriend is, Chief."

Yes, Nick definitely knew how his girlfriend was—right down to each delicious and intimate detail. What he didn't know was what kind of trouble Hazard had embroiled herself in this time.

Wheeling around, Nick strode toward his black four-wheel drive truck—the one with the hay fork protruding from the bed.

"Do you want a backup, Chief?" Benny called after him.

"No, get back on patrol. I'll handle Hazard's supposed emergency . . ." Nick pulled up short and half turned to see Benny sliding onto the seat of the black-and-white. "You forgot to tell me where Hazard's emergency was."

Benny's lean face turned the color of raw liver. "Sorry, Chief," he mumbled. "She's at Will Bloom's farm with a top priority emergency."

"Bloom's?" Nick repeated, baffled.

What is she doing out there? He supposed there was only one way to answer that question: Ask Hazard.

Nick shifted his truck into gear and sped off.

He sincerely hoped Hazard hadn't tripped over another dead body. Her insistence on all-out investigations was always a source of conflict between them.

So much for anticipating a quiet, romantic evening, Nick thought. He had the unmistakable feeling that Hazard, who envisioned herself as the female answer to crime fighting in small-town America, was gearing up for a brand-new investigation.

TWO

Amanda surged onto the front porch of Will Bloom's home the moment she heard the roar of the truck heralding Thorn's arrival.

"An emergency, Hazard?" Nick asked.

Amanda strode off the porch, gesturing for Thorn to follow her. "I found Will Bloom dead in the dirt," she reported grimly. "A victim of foul play."

"Now, Hazard—"

"Don't *now, Hazard* me, Thorn," Amanda muttered as she tramped toward the barn. "The clues are laid out in such an obvious fashion that even your skeptical male mind—"

Amanda's voice dried up when she rounded the corner of the barn. To her thorough disgust, the morning dew had evaporated. Thorn had not arrived before the evidence vanished.

Annoyed, Amanda watched Thorn casually swing a long, muscled leg over the wooden fence rail to take a closer look at the position of the victim. She knew what he was thinking. She could almost *hear* him thinking it!

After Thorn had surveyed the victim from every possible angle, he announced his conclusion. "It appears that Bloom came down to the barn to feed supplemental cubes to his cattle. He was knocked down by overeager livestock and trampled."

Nick pivoted toward the brown paper feed sack that lay beside Bloom's outstretched arm. "Will must have been blindsided by one of his bulls, or maybe even one of the cows. Once he was down, with an open sack in his hand, he couldn't get up. It looks as if he caught several hooves in the head and thorax."

"That's the way it *looks*," Amanda said as she climbed over the fence, snagging her pantyhose in the process. "But that is *not* what happened."

"I knew you would have your own suspicious theory," Nick grumbled. "Just what is it this time, Chicken Little? Did the sky fall in on Will Bloom?"

Amanda glared branding irons at Thorn, unamused by his droll sense of humor. As crazy as she was about Tom Selleck's clone—minus the mustache—it always infuriated her when Thorn failed to take her instincts and suspicions seriously.

"Of course, I have a theory," she said. "Will Bloom must have been clubbed with a blunt instrument and then dragged into the corral to make his death look accidental—which it was not!"

Nick crossed his arms over his massive chest. "And what, Hazard, or dare I ask, could possibly have led you to that conclusion? Did you arrive upon the scene to see the alleged assailant—or assailants—drag the body into the corral?"

"No, but—"

"Did you witness a vehicle leaving the scene at excessive speeds or find a possible murder weapon lying around?"

"No." Amanda bared her teeth. "But I did see the swath of ground wiped clean of morning dew."

"Dew?" Nick strode around to stand at Bloom's feet, gazing toward the corral gate. "All I see are dirt and hoofprints. You realize this *vanishing dew clue* won't hold up in court, especially since there is no sign of it at the time of discovery."

"The dew was *sparklingly* apparent at the time of *my* discovery," she huffed. "I also know that an unexpected guest arrived at Will's home while he and I were speaking on the phone. He called to insist that I meet him at the barn—pronto. I heard the doorbell ring before he hung up. And after you take a look inside Will's house, you're going to agree that something very fishy has been going on around here."

Thorn cocked a dubious brow. "I am?"

"You are," she confirmed. "Follow me, Thorn."

Amanda retraced her path over the fence and around the barn. "When I went to the house to call for your assistance, I made several shocking discoveries."

Thorn made a sound that could have meant anything as he followed in Amanda's wake. She allowed him to wallow in his usual skepticism as she led him through the meagerly furnished living room and into the recently remodeled kitchen.

Nick pulled up short when the glaring sunlight flashed against the newly installed stainless steel sink.

"Not what you expected, either?" Amanda took grand satisfaction in asking. "There's more, Thorn. You ain't seen nothin' yet."

Nick detoured to the phone to contact the medical examiner. After giving precise directions to Bloom Farm, Nick strode down the thin carpet of the hall to join

Amanda in the den. Sure enough, Nick blinked like a disturbed owl when he spied the electronic gadgets and expensive furnishings that filled the oak-paneled room.

"I don't know what side business Will Bloom was into, but I know for a fact that the income reported on his tax returns couldn't have paid for all these luxuries," Amanda declared. "Surely you can't argue with the fact that his sparsely furnished living area appears to be the smoke and mirrors that concealed the secret life Will Bloom led . . . Thorn?"

Amanda studied the strange, unfamiliar expression that captured Thorn's handsome face. His black diamond eyes had narrowed to slits. His sexy smile had turned upside down.

"Thorn, are you okay?"

"There's more, I suppose," Nick muttered.

Amanda nodded and then spun on her heels to mount the steps. Thorn said not one word as Amanda led him from one upstairs room to the other, pointing out the combination of valuable antiques and expensive modern furnishings that told their own suspicious tale.

"It's obvious to me that someone knew of Will's secret wealth, or that an unknown accomplice decided to dispose of him. Then there is the possibility that Will could have been blackmailing someone. Or maybe he was part of the witness program and had been stashed in Vamoose for safekeeping. Holy smoke!" Amanda burst out. "The possibilities are endless! This case is going to require a formal investigation."

Nick wheeled around, pinning Hazard with a hard stare. "Whatever has been going on here, you are going to stay out of it, Hazard," he demanded.

"Stay out of it?" she hooted, staring incredulously at

him. "I'm a witness to what I suspect to be a well-staged murder. I'm certainly not going to stay out of it. For better or worse, Will Bloom was my client, and it is my civil and moral duty to—"

"Civil and moral duty? Bull!" Nick snorted. "Tell it like it is, Hazard. You've stumbled over a few dead bodies in the past and now you perceive yourself as Vamoose's version of Sherlock Holmes. If I decide to open an investigation, then I will. That is, after all, what I have been hired to do. In the past, I have ordered you not to nose around in police business, but you've ignored me. This time I mean business, Hazard. I want you to back off. Understand?"

"But—"

"Butt out, Hazard. I said I'll handle this."

Amanda blinked at Thorn's commanding tone and ominous expression. "You can hardly expect me to—"

Her voice trailed off when she heard the crunch of gravel on the driveway. Spinning about, Amanda headed for the steps to confer with the medical examiner. Before she could lead the way, Thorn zipped past her, leaving her to bring up the rear.

"Go back to work, Hazard. I'll handle this. We'll discuss it tonight."

"Tonight is off," Amanda informed him.

He wheeled around to stare up at the woman who stood two steps above him on the stairs. "Why? Because I refuse to let you play amateur sleuth in this case?"

"No, because Mother called to say that I'm in charge of my grandfather while she and Daddy are cruising around the Caribbean. I have arrangements to make and bookwork to do before I pick up Pops in the morning.

Whatever you had planned to discuss with me tonight will have to wait."

Nick nodded his raven head and took the steps two at a time to intercept the medical examiner.

Frowning, Amanda stared at Thorn's departing back. She wondered if Thorn intended to take her suspicions seriously—for a change. Usually it took a considerable amount of argument to convince Thorn that a supposed accident was a murder. The laid-back country cop, who usually took the Andy of "Mayberry RFD" approach, never got very excited about much of anything.

Well, she amended with a wry smile, there *were* a few things that got Thorn very excited.

Amanda's thoughts evaporated when she halted in the shabby living room. She noticed the accounting ledger Will had mentioned to her. The notebook was tucked on the bottom shelf of an antique end table. Beneath the antique oak clock that sat on the top shelf was a note that read: For Amanda Hazard.

Will Bloom was giving Amanda one of his valuable antique clocks? As supposed payment for services rendered perhaps? As if he couldn't pay in cash, she thought with a snort. Bloom had been devious to the bitter end.

He was also trying to tell her something, Amanda decided. Bloom had indicated that there were things he wanted her to pick up for safekeeping—just in case. Bloom claimed Amanda had a reputation for ensuring things got done correctly, and he had needed her expertise.

To Amanda, that indicated Bloom was anticipating trouble. He must have known disaster was about to strike. And it had, before Amanda arrived to intervene. Yes, Amanda convinced herself. Bloom had gotten himself into a fix and he had called her, hoping she could save the day. Unfortunately, she arrived after the fact.

Amanda scooped up the ledger and then carefully placed the intricately carved clock in the crook of her arm. When she collected the items for safekeeping, she was also accepting the assignment Bloom had in mind for her—whatever that might have been. Finding Bloom dead demanded her commitment. Although she had not been able to answer his cry for help, she would see justice served.

Surely Thorn didn't believe that Amanda could keep her nose out of *his* investigation. This was *her* fourth case, after all. Investigation had become second nature to her. Besides, she rationalized as she headed for the door, crime solving was something she had in common with Thorn.

"That's really weak, Hazard," Amanda murmured softly to herself. "You and Thorn have plenty in common without dreaming up flimsy excuses. You're crazy about that sexy cop. You just can't resist dabbling in detective work when opportunity arises."

When one of Amanda's clients fell victim to a crime, she was compelled to do whatever necessary to solve the case. It was as simple as that. As busy as poor dear Thorn was these days, he would thank her for scaring up as many facts as possible to assist him.

Later, Thorn would thank her for her contribution to solving the most recent crime in Vamoose, Amanda tried to reassure herself.

Maybe . . .

With practiced efficiency, the coroner squatted down to examine the body. "Skull fracture," he diagnosed. His gloved hand swept down Bloom's spine. "Shattered vertebrae. Numerous bruises."

"Your best guess?" Nick prompted as he leisurely propped himself against the corral gate.

"From the look of things," the coroner said as he rose from his crouch, "the victim was knocked down and trampled by his own cattle. The empty feed sack indicates the livestock didn't stop tramping all over him until the last of the pellet feed was consumed."

"Is that your conclusion?"

"Isn't it yours?" the coroner questioned.

Nick stared at the cattle that huddled in the far corner of the lot. "Cattle can smell feed long before they can see it. Once they are accustomed to eating range cube supplements, they can—and they will—run you down to get to it. I've had a few narrow escapes from similar disasters myself. Even being young and fleet of foot, a rancher can get his business in bad shape real quick."

"I can't argue with that. Obviously, Mr. Bloom can't, either," the medical examiner inserted.

"Will Bloom was forty, and not as quick and agile as he needed to be in this instance," Nick continued. "If the cattle—especially those two bulls that each weigh a ton—caught Will from behind, he would have found himself in serious trouble. Cattle think nothing of knocking each other out of the way to get at feed cubes. Humans are no exception when it comes to devouring feed."

When the coroner turned away, Nick added quietly, "But I want you to place paper bags over the victim's hands, run a liver test for the time of death, and make routine checks for a possible homicide."

Owl-eyed, the coroner spun around. "I thought you said this looked to be accidental."

"I did. That's what your report will read."

The coroner studied Nick for a long, ponderous moment. "Are you asking me to bend the rules here?"

"I didn't say that."

The coroner snorted. "You haven't said much of anything. What's with you, Thorn?"

Nick pushed away from the fence, carefully avoiding the area around the body. He strode up beside the coroner, his expression grim. "I want this incident kept under wraps until I have a chance to investigate thoroughly. I don't want that pack of press hounds sniffing around here. You know how they can obstruct justice when they think they might have a chance at a fast-breaking story. If this turns out to be homicide, I don't want this case broadcast through the media, sending the assailant underground, making it impossible for me to track him down."

"So you want me to give Will Bloom the full benefit of my expertise and keep it under my hat?"

Nick nodded somberly. "This is just between you and me, off the record. Call me with the results of this accident, as soon as you can."

"I don't suppose you plan to tell me what you think is going on," the coroner grumbled as he strode off to retrieve the paper bags.

"Nothing is going on," Nick insisted.

"Right. I'm just running possible homicide testing for practice."

"Right . . ." Nick murmured as he assisted the coroner with his official duties.

* * *

After the coroner drove away, Nick wandered around the barn. He inspected the area carefully, searching for evidence that supported Hazard's theory of brutal attack followed by a staged accident. Nick found no sign of a blunt instrument that might have been used as a weapon.

He hadn't really thought he would.

Question was: How was Nick quietly going to conduct this investigation without Hazard poking her nose into it? If the niggling feeling that dogged Nick's footsteps proved accurate, there was no way in hell that Nick would let Hazard within a hundred yards of this case. And when he said to back off, he damned well meant it!

Nick strode back into the barn to inspect the brown paper feed sacks that had been stacked against the north wall. A frown puckered his brow when he noticed the label that had been stamped on the sacks. Why would Will, who ran a small-time farming operation, haul cattle cubes from a warehouse in Rawhide, Texas?

Old instincts, finely honed from years in OKCPD, hounded Nick. The Bloom scenario had a familiar and unpleasant odor to it.

Nick impulsively grabbed the pliers he had stashed in the back pocket of his jeans and made a beeline toward the pyramid of hay bales. He clipped the baling wire that held the compacted straw in place. Blocks of hay cartwheeled off the pyramid, sending up a fog of dust . . . revealing several Ziploc bags.

"Well, I'll be damned," Nick muttered as he scooped up the concealed containers. "Right here in my own backyard."

Nick aimed himself toward the stack of range cubes packaged in brown sacks. He slit the nearest sack open, watching pellets tumble to the straw-lined floor. And sure enough, several small plastic bags had been concealed inside the cattle feed, too.

Tucking the bags inside his shirt, Nick jogged toward the house. If his instincts proved correct, he had serious trouble on his hands in Vamoose. The kind of trouble that required the assistance of knowledgeable experts, not his amateur sleuth girlfriend and a rookie deputy.

Nick's mind reeled as he surged through the modestly furnished living area of Will Bloom's home. He had arrangements to make, dozens of them. He also had a stage to set if he intended to crack this case. The stage did not include Hazard, Nick firmly reminded himself.

Flashbacks of painful memories assailed Nick as he veered into Will's refurbished kitchen. Memories of the hectic, gritty lifestyle that Nick had walked away from several years earlier suddenly flooded over him. He closed his eyes and grimaced when the gruesome scene from his past flared in his mind.

Diana . . she had become the innocent victim of a ruthless, vengeful criminal who had retaliated when Nick applied pressure. Nick had been young, foolish, and too damned daring for his own good. He had been caught up in a world where polite society's rules didn't apply.

His former girlfriend had been the price he paid.

But not this time, Nick vowed as he reached for the phone. This time he was going to play by hell's own rules if he went up against the devil himself. And Hazard, bless her gorgeous hide, was not going to be sacrificed to see justice served.

Nick was taking Hazard out of the game before it even started. Hazard's connection to Nick could become her deadly curse. Hazard was not—repeat not, with great emphasis!—going to end up like Diana.

"OSBI. May I help you?" came the feminine voice over the line.

Nick jerked himself from his bleak thoughts. "I need to talk to Richard Thorn," he insisted.

"I'm sorry, Rich is working a case at the moment—"

"Page him," Nick demanded impatiently. "This is his brother of Vamoose PD. And this is top priority."

Nick rattled off the number where he could be reached and then hung up. Like a man possessed, he began a quick but highly efficient search of Will Bloom's home. Wearing his leather work gloves, Nick rummaged through every trash container in the house and plucked up every opened envelope in sight. He rummaged through every drawer and cabinet in the kitchen, looking for notes and information that Will might have tucked away for safekeeping.

With precision-honed care, Nick inspected the home from top to bottom. By the time the phone rang he had a stack of phone bills, bank accounts, and feed bills as thick as his fist.

"Thorn here," Nick said as he snatched up the receiver.

"Thorn here, too. What's up, little brother?"

"I need your help, Rich," Nick insisted. "I think I've uncovered a scam in Vamoose like you wouldn't believe. I need to tap into OKCPD and OSBI's hi-tech information system. This is going to be damned tricky. I need to operate in top secrecy."

"Holy Shit, Nick, what have you got cooking in our sleepy little hometown?" Rich questioned.

"Come find out for yourself and bring your forensics

experts with you. And whatever the hell you do, don't come tramping out to the family farm in your professional business suit and tie. I'd rather you and your staff look like transient farm labor. I have no intention of spooking the Vamoosians. You know how fast news travels in a close-knit town. News of your arrival will beat you to Vamoose if you swarm in here like a SWAT team."

"Give me a break, Nick," Richard Thorn grumbled. "I'm working a homicide with the FBI. I can't just—"

"If this turns out to be what I think it is," Nick cut in quickly. "I'll need a court order for wiretaps and a veteran team for surveillance and stakeouts. Bring our old friends with you."

"Damn, Nick, nothing big goes down in Vamoose. I ought to know, I was raised there."

"Things change, Rich. I've got to go underground, and I need you to go with me."

There was a noticable pause from the other end of the line.

Finally, Rich said in a bleak voice. "Just like the old days? Same gut instincts? Same bad vibes?"

"The very same," Nick grimly affirmed. "And don't forget to come packing fancy hardware. I don't plan to stop at simply seining for tadpoles in this case. I intend to reel in some big fish while I'm at it. We'll make our farm headquarters for this operation."

"I assume you've already devised a plan," Rich murmured.

Nick stared at the stack of receipts and bills that he had clamped in his gloved fist. "I've got a plan, all right. I just need the right players—real pros—to pull it off."

Rick snorted sarcastically. "You aren't putting on a

spectacular show to impress that new girlfriend of yours, are you?"

"No, I'm only trying to keep her alive long enough so you can make her acquaintance. Be here this afternoon, Rich, and bring all the necessary party favors."

"For God's sake, Nick, I told you I'm working a case—"

Nick slammed down the phone. He was in no mood for excuses. He had places to go and things to do—PDQ.

Amanda stationed herself by the granary door, directly beside the stack of plywood delivered from Pronto Lumber and Supply Company. Her foot tapped impatiently as she watched Buzz Sawyer's pickup cruise past her house toward the barn.

He was an hour late.

"I got here as fast as I could," Buzz said when he noticed Amanda's annoyed expression.

Amanda surveyed the local carpenter. His shoulder-length hair was the color of sawdust. When he smiled apologetically, Amanda decided his jagged-edged teeth reminded her of the blade on a Skilsaw. The top portion of the pinkie on Buzz's left hand was missing. His thumb was also black and blue—probably because he had accidentally hit the wrong kind of nail.

The bed of Buzz's truck was a mobile carpenter shop. Tape measures, levels, saws, nail guns, and paint cans filled the vehicle to capacity. Buzz Sawyer was prepared for everything—except arriving at a work site or paying his bills on time.

Pushing away from the side of the barn, Amanda turned her attention to the granary. "I have visions of converting this area into a workshop for my elderly grandfather who dabbles in repairing and refinishing antique collectibles. Since he ambulates by means of a walker, he needs room to turn around without bumping into or falling over things. He also requires wide windows for light and proper ventilation, plus a worktable and stool."

"No problem," Buzz assured her. "I'll use my air gun to nail up the plywood. That will speed things up. I'll have this project completed in nothing flat."

"Good, my grandfather will be here tomorrow. Knowing him, he won't want to waste any time before pursuing his favorite hobby."

"I suppose you heard the bad news about Will Bloom," Buzz commented as he hoisted up a sheet of plywood. "Officer Thorn said Bloom met with an untimely accident in his corral."

Amanda jerked up her head. Accident? *Accident!* She was hoping she had convinced Thorn otherwise. If Thorn had written Bloom off as an accident victim, so he could finish planting his wheat crop, she'd skin him alive!

"Have you ever done any remodeling jobs for Will?" Amanda couldn't stop herself from asking, when the investigative bug bit her.

Buzz set the plywood in place and grabbed his air gun. "As a matter of fact I did. I helped Will put up oak paneling in his den. But being a jack-of-all-trades, Will is a fair carpenter himself. I only worked with him for a few days. He was able to finish up the project without my help."

Amanda beetled her brows and listened to the whack-thump of the air gun. "A handyman?"

Buzz stood up to retrieve another sheet of plywood.

"Will has been doing odd jobs around the community since he bought the old Tarbutton Farm four years ago. It probably kept him afloat when the farming business got lean."

Kept Will afloat? Amanda silently smirked. Considering the secret fortune Will had amassed, he had more than likely been *afloat* on a fancy yacht he had stashed out of sight. The IRS would have rubbed their hands together in gleeful anticipation if they had gotten wind of Will Bloom's unreported income.

"Will even nailed up the tin on this very barn for your landlady when a storm ripped it off a few years ago," Buzz reported offhandedly. "Yep, he was willing to do about anything to earn a few extra bucks."

Anything? Including stealing from or blackmailing someone? It made Amanda wonder.

After Amanda had indicated where she wanted the windows installed in the granary, she headed toward the house. Since Thorn apparently intended to look the other way in this case, Amanda would have to take it upon herself to contact Vamoose's most reliable source for background information.

If there were skeletons rattling around in Will Bloom's closet—secrets that might have gotten him killed—Velma Hertzog could point Amanda in the right direction. Velma, a gum-chewing beautician, had her pudgy finger on everything that moved in Vamoose—and some things that didn't.

Amanda dialed the phone number from memory and heard the familiar crackle-pop of Velma's chewing gum when she answered.

"Velma's Beauty Boutique." Chomp.

"Velma, this is Amanda Hazard."

"Hi, hon! Long time no see."

"I was wondering if you might be able to work me in for a trim sometime soon."

"Is this afternoon soon enough?"

Amanda smiled in satisfaction. "Perr-fect."

"Come by at two-thirty," Velma requested. "I'll fix you right up, hon."

Amanda replaced the receiver. Before the sun set on the small rural community of Vamoose, Amanda should have a list of possible suspects. Thorn was going to be thoroughly ashamed of himself for writing Will Bloom off as an incidental dead blossom. When Amanda completed her investigation, Thorn would have to take her suspicions seriously.

Amanda wouldn't rub Thorn's nose in it—much.

Deciding to make good use of her time, Amanda plunked down at the table to pore over Thatcher's tax returns before she sped off to keep her hair appointment. Her concentration scattered like the four winds when she noticed the payment received for a fuel bill delivered to Will Bloom's farm.

Will Bloom had been wearing out the pavement, if the excessive gallons of gasoline he had purchased was anything to go by. According to the report from Thatcher's service station, Will had not only purchased an amazing amount of fuel, but he had paid his bills in full.

Although Amanda was itching to double-check the expenditure with the ledger she had picked up at Will's home, she had to complete the forms for Thatcher's accounts. The quarterly reports and income statements were due at the end of the week, and the IRS frowned on unnecessary delays.

Amanda set to work with industrious zeal, her fingers

flying over the calculator keys, wasting not so much as a second. Efficient though she was, it would still take her half the night to complete her paperwork. And furthermore, sometime before seven the following morning she was going to have to rearrange her home to accommodate her grandfather and his walker. Throw rugs and mats would have to be removed to prevent tripping Pops up. Furniture would have to be moved to provide extra space for him to maneuver around.

When, Amanda asked herself, was she going to find time to do that?

For exactly one hour and fourteen minutes, Amanda whizzed through the credits and expenditures. Swiftly, she listed the entries on the income statement. A quick glance at her watch indicated she barely had enough time to zoom into town to keep her appointment at Velma's.

This fact-finding mission had damned well better be worth sacrificing my hair, Amanda thought to herself. She had suffered through one too many bad hair days after Velma's cosmetic experiments turned sour. It had taken weeks before the lavender dye had finally washed out of Amanda's blond hair, before frizzy curls could be tamed with a curling iron.

No experimental dyes, Amanda vowed as she sped off. *Just a trim—two millimeters, tops.*

Three

"Hi, hon! How are you and our hunk of a police chief getting along these days?"

Amanda pulled up short when she spied the new addition to Velma's beauty salon. Amanda took one look at the younger version of the Amazon beautician and inwardly groaned. Unless she missed her guess, the new beautician was related to Velma. The busty, barrel-shaped female with black Shirley Temple curls dangling around her plump face had to have hatched from the same nest.

"This is my niece," Velma proudly introduced as she motioned Amanda into The Chair. "Beverly Hill, meet Amanda Hazard, CPA."

With grim resignation, Amanda parked herself in The Chair, behind which Beverly loomed in eager anticipation.

"Bev is fresh from beauty school in the City," Velma reported as she cracked her chewing gum.

Wonderful, thought Amanda. *A rookie beautician. I'm doomed.*

"I've heard all about you and our handsome cop," Beverly said, scooping up her scissors. "Aunt Velma says, like, you and Nick are like Vamoose's most famous couple. Like, the ideal couple, in fact."

When Beverly Hill grinned, her eyes practically disappeared in the cavern above her chipmunklike cheeks—quite a feat, considering the half-moon eye shadow that was thickly caked between her fake lashes and thinly plucked eyebrows. And if Amanda wasn't mistaken, that Marilyn Monroe mole on Bev's face was as fake as her lashes.

Amanda made a meager stab at conversation while Bev took brush in hand and practically yanked out Amanda's hair by the roots.

"How long have you been working for Velma?" Amanda questioned.

"Like, you're my first official customer," Bev announced.

Amanda silently groaned and clamped her fingers around the arms of The Chair.

"I called Aunt Velma yesterday and I went: Could you, like, use some help in the salon? And she went: You can start tomorrow if you want to. And I went: Cool! I'll be there at noon. And, like, here I am!"

Amanda rolled her eyes in dismay. Bev's adolescent-level vocabulary was going to take some getting used to.

"I knew you wouldn't mind letting Bev take a whack at you," Velma said as she retrieved a basket of pink plastic rollers from the cabinet. "It will give me a chance to spiffy up the shop and set Bev up with her own stockpile of supplies."

Bev cupped her beefy hands around Amanda's jaws, pensively staring at the reflection in the mirror. "You're gonna love the new style I have in mind for you," she said. "It was, like, all the rage at beauty school. This is one hairstyle that makes a statement."

"I'm in the habit of speaking for myself—"

Amanda's voice trailed off into a silent wail when Bev took a snip with her scissors. A clump of blond hair dropped to the floor. Bev had whacked off Amanda's hair so short that her left earlobe was clearly visible. Amanda hadn't worn her hair this short since she was in diapers!

While Velma puttered around the salon, equally dividing up rollers, perm solution, combs, and brushes, Amanda practiced deep, controlled breathing. But Bev's high-fashion, statement-making style got steadily worse. Before Amanda recovered her powers of speech, Bev had chopped off her bangs into pointed scallops. God have mercy! Amanda's forehead looked like the jagged teeth of Buzz's Skilsaw!

"I guess you heard about Will Bloom's stroke of bad luck," Velma commented. Her mascara-caked eyelid dropped into a wink, and her full jowls wrinkled like folding doors. "There will be a lot of widows and divorcées around Vamoose who are going to miss the perfected skills of that jack-of-all-trades."

"Oh?" It was the best Amanda could manage at the moment. Her gaze was transfixed on her reflection in the mirror. Beverly Hill was whacking away in fiendish pleasure, making Edward Scissorhands look like a novice.

Amanda couldn't begin to hide this cosmetic disaster under a bad-hair-day hat. She would have to buy a wig to conceal the damage.

"Too bad about that Bloom fella," Bev put in, between a flurry of snips and whacks. "Like, it must have been a real bummer to be trampled by cattle."

Once the shock of seeing herself scalped wore off, Amanda concentrated on luring Velma into divulging every scrap of information about Will Bloom. "What do you mean about widows and divorcées missing Bloom?"

Velma chomped on her chewing gum and then snickered mischievously. "I mean that Will was known to accommodate everyone who was willing and able—before, during, or after he repaired a leaky faucet, mowed a lawn, or adjusted the tension on storm doors. Will may not have been as great-looking as Nick Thorn, but the members of Vamoose's Lonely Hearts Club often take whatever they can get—if you know what I mean." Snap, pop.

Unreported income with fringe benefits? Interesting, thought Amanda.

"I don't know about the older generation of men," Bev said with a shake of her curls. "If my boyfriend was, like, fooling around all over town, I'd be tempted to take after him with a butcher knife. That Bobbitt woman might have had the right idea after all."

Someone might very well have taken after Will Bloom, Amanda mused. She was convinced that Will hadn't ended up dead in the dirt by accident.

"Keep this under your hats, girls, but there were a few married woman tripping the light fantastic with Will, too," Velma murmured. "Will Bloom played the entire field."

Amanda ignored her disastrous haircut and focused undivided attention on Velma's broad reflection in the mirror. "He was having affairs with married women?"

Velma nodded. "And some of them were a good ten years older than Will. A few were less than half his age. And if word ever got out, there would be some wild scandals around Vamoose."

"Like who?" Bev demanded, all ears.

Amanda was also all ears. Hers were now poking out from the sides of her head, thanks to Bev's dramatic scalping.

Velma glanced solemnly at her niece and then at Amanda. "Promise you won't breathe a word of this?"

"Like, my lips are zipped," Bev promised.

"Ditto," Amanda chimed in.

Velma inched closer, her eyes twinkling with the thrill of conveying juicy tidbits of gossip. "Does the name Georgina Green ring any bells?"

Beverly's hands stalled above Amanda's head. "You've got to be kidding, Aunt Velma! Georgina is only three years older than I am. She's married to that hot-shot attorney who joined his daddy's firm in the City. Daniel Green's family is, like, megarich."

Amanda quickly filed the information in her computer-like brain. While Velma explained how she had stumbled onto the information, a possible scenario was forming in Amanda's mind. Georgina's jealous, humiliated husband could have paid Will Bloom a visit early this morning, possibly on his way to work. The upscale lawyer was probably outraged to discover his wife was screwing around, and with a man whose lowly existence could not begin to measure up to Daniel Green's fashionable and successful lifestyle.

"I heard Daniel's daddy has been grooming him for politics," Bev said, adding her two cents' worth. "If news of Georgina's affair leaked out, it might ruin Daniel's chances of holding office. The media would jump all over it like hungry tigers."

No kidding, thought Amanda. The press thrived on stories like that. Sometimes the junior high school mentality of the media could be nauseating. They could dig up dirt faster than dogs buried bones.

Amanda's analytical mind shifted into overdrive. What if it was *Georgina* who had bumped Will Bloom off to keep him quiet? What if Will had been demanding hush money to keep the affair under wraps and Georgina had gotten tired of paying? That would certainly explain one source of funds that provided the ultramodern conveniences that filled Will's home.

In Amanda's book, the information Velma and Bev had conveyed cast serious shadows of suspicion on Georgina and Daniel Green. Both Greens had ample motive to want Will silenced—permanently. Will must have known his scheme was about to backfire. Hence, he had called Amanda.

"It doesn't sound as if Georgina has cleaned up her act much since she graduated high school," Bev added with an unladylike snort. "She may have been voted prom queen, but she is still a loser in my book. Like, she never could keep her head on straight."

Before Amanda could request further elaboration, Velma's tongue was off and running again. "And word is that Bobbie Sue Hampton was doing the horizontal two-step with Will Bloom while Buddy was hauling his prize racehorses back and forth to the tracks."

"You mean Billy Jean Baxter's—the famous country singer's—sister?" Bev's eyes rounded and her ruby red mouth dropped wide open. "Whoa! Like, that blows my mind!"

Bev broke into another flurry of whacks and snips. Blond hair flew as fast as the words poured from Bev's mouth. "My gosh, Aunt Velma, if Buddy ever found out, he'd go ballistic. He thinks Bobbie Sue hung the moon—

or so Mama says. Mama used to clean house for Bobbie Sue for extra spending money. She claims Buddy treats his wife like royalty."

Amanda decided, there and then, that Beverly Hill was going to fit in splendidly at Velma's Beauty Boutique. What Velma might not know about the younger generations of Vamoosians, Bev could—and would—supply.

If Velma's and Bev's gossip was right on target, Amanda had two sets of suspects to question. Both prominent families could have been blackmailed by Will Bloom. The local Casanova handyman could have been silenced when he became too expensive.

The gossip definitely bore checking out, Amanda decided.

"You missed a spot," Velma pointed out, still cracking her gum. Her fuchsia-colored acrylic nail tapped against the crown of Amanda's head. "Amanda has a cowlick you have to contend with here."

Amanda cringed when Bev grabbed the clump of hair and took another quick snip. When Bev released the tuft of hair, it stood at attention like Alfalfa's of the Little Rascals.

Good Lord, thought Amanda. *Thorn is going to take one look at this hairdo and know for certain that I went to Velma's in search of investigative clues.*

And furthermore, Thorn did not like cropped-off haircuts. When he was feeling amorous, he liked to tangle his fingers in long, lustrous strands. This new style would hamper his seductive techniques.

"I prefer to wash after I cut," Bev announced as she spun Amanda around to dunk her head in the sink.

"I think I'll put this in the annual Vamoose garage

sale." Velma hoisted up a god-awful looking vase that she had made in her pottery class last spring.

"Mama already has a bunch of stuff stacked in the shed for the community flea market," Bev said while she towel-dried Amanda's hair.

"Can anyone participate in the event?" Amanda asked. "I have several items I need to discard."

"Like, sure," Bev spoke up. "Everybody in town is welcome to haul their stuff to the park pavilion and trade junk. You know what they say: One person's trash is somebody's treasure."

"All you have to do is bring your items to the park and put the prices on them." Chomp, snap. "Everybody sets up their booths and unloads their junk on Friday night. The sale begins at eight o'clock Saturday morning. Officer Thorn and Deputy Sykes patrol the area to make certain no one tries to swipe anything before the sale starts."

By the time Bev had blown Amanda's hair dry, Velma had two cardboard boxes crammed full of garage sale items. Amanda had intended to circle back to the topic of Will Bloom, but adjusting to the sight of her new hairdo demanded her full attention. She looked like a pixie with her ears sticking out, a tuft of hair standing straight up on top of her head, and her bangs in pointed clumps—glued against her forehead with enough hair gel to choke Vidal Sassoon.

Thorn was going to throw a ring-tailed fit!

When Bev clamped a can of hair spray in her meaty fist, Amanda sucked in a quick breath. Sticky spray fogged the salon and ripped another hole in the ozone layer.

"Like, you look terrific with your new do, Amanda," Bev bubbled. "Don't you just love it?"

Amanda peered at the pixie that was staring back at her from the mirror and manufactured a smile. "Like, sure."

Velma lumbered over to survey her niece's creation. "Everybody in town will be asking for the cut and style Amanda is wearing." Crackle, pop.

Amanda managed to hold her composure until she had paid Beverly and exited from the salon. Tears streamed down her cheeks as she drove home. Amanda and the ostriches would have to bury their heads in sand for several months.

The price she was forced to pay for information!

Buzz Sawyer staggered back a pace when Amanda answered his knock at her front door. Her astounding new hairdo momentarily stunned him.

"Um . . . I thought I'd stop by to tell you that I nailed up the plywood in the granary. I'll be back in the morning to install the windows."

Amanda watched the carpenter stare at her scalped head for as long as she could stand it. "Go ahead and say it, Buzz. I look like hell."

Buzz crammed his hands in the pockets of his red coveralls and smiled awkwardly, displaying his uneven teeth. "Well . . . um . . . it just takes some getting used to is all. But it . . . er . . . looks real nice on you, Amanda."

Buzz swiveled on his heels and then descended the steps. He halted abruptly and swung back around. "Oh, I almost forgot. Some guy came by to see you while you were gone. It was nobody I knew, though. I was measuring a cut on the plywood for the new windows when I saw the guy climb back in his car and drive off. I guess he didn't know I was in the barn."

Amanda frowned at the information. It was probably some traveling salesman, she decided. She certainly hadn't been expecting a visitor. And considering her new hairdo, she wasn't likely to have many in the future, either!

"Well, I'll see you in the morning, Amanda," Buzz said with a wave and a jagged smile.

Amanda closed the door and hurried off to rearrange the furniture in her guest bedroom to accommodate her grandfather. She still had Thatcher's income statement to put in order.

It was going to be a long, busy night.

Nick Thorn glanced at the four agents seated in his dining room and then tossed several Ziploc bags on the table in front of them. Four pairs of eyes widened in surprise.

"Damn, Nick," Richard Thorn croaked. "Where did you find all the rock?"

"Baled in hay, stashed in cattle feed sacks, and stored in Will Bloom's barn," Nick grimly reported. "I've spent the past several hours going over Bloom's house and barn with the forensics experts, gathering every possible piece of evidence and any clues I could get my hands on. I think I've stumbled onto a trafficking operation of immense proportion. The beauty of it is that the dealers and distributors involved are confident the police are none the wiser. If my hunch proves correct, an old friend of ours is overseeing this setup. The clever operation has his signature all over it."

Roger Proctor scooped up one of the sacks and stared at it. "And you think the little pissants involved are going to lay a trail all the way to the kingpin?"

Nick nodded. "If we can move fast and establish our base of operation, if we begin surveillance and plant agents at crucial locations in town, we can each take tours of duty watching Bloom Farm. The crack cocaine that has been muled into the barn will undoubtedly be picked up and distributed. If we can stash tracers in those bales, we could break this case wide open."

The tawny-headed Gibson Cooper glanced pensively at Nick. "You want to let the couriers walk to keep them ignorant of wiretaps and tails, I take it."

"That's exactly what I've got in mind," Nick confirmed. "But this operation has to be in place by tonight, and I need the MOs of every known criminal we tailed while I was on the undercover narc squad in the City. I couldn't pin Mr. Big down then—"

"And nobody else has been able to since you left, either," Nancy Shore broke in. "You have your private reasons for wanting to nail that sneaky son of a bitch's hide to a prison wall, and I have mine. You name the role you want me to play, Nick, and I'm yours for the duration."

"You can count me in, too," Roger Proctor seconded. "I've bagged up too many teenage bodies that OD'd on the streets because of that drug viper. If Mr. Big is spearheading the operation and you can find a way to put him behind bars—and keep him there—I'll be able to sleep more peacefully at night."

Nick smiled in triumph. "I was hoping all my big-city

friends would appreciate a change of scenery. I took the liberty of making the necessary arrangements for your temporary employment in Vamoose."

"I just hope this scheme of yours doesn't backfire like your last one," Rich Thorn muttered, staring pointedly at his younger brother. "You realize you'll have to clear a path and burn your bridges so innocent victims don't get mowed down—just in case things go badly. Any connection between you and that new girlfriend of yours could be extremely hazardous to her health. Mr. Big has a fetish for getting his revenge, somehow or another. The two of you had a personal feud going in the old days. I doubt he has forgotten it any better than you have."

Nick's smile vanished. "I'll be taking care of the matter of my girlfriend as soon as we have all our electronic surveillance equipment in place." He pulled a small paper bag from his pocket and sprinkled the contents on a saucer. "I found these cigar ashes at four different sites around Bloom's farm. Thanks to the morning dew, the evidence from a smoking cigar clung to chunks of damp gravel in the driveway, and to blades of weeds beside the barn. I found another trace beside the front porch step."

Rich glanced up. "Cigar ashes? World famous Havanas? You think Mr. Big might have imported a hit man to take Bloom out? Geez, Nick, all we've had in the past is circumstantial evidence and speculation. If we can link a hit man to Mr. Big, we could pin him down with drug trafficking, distribution, and a murder rap. I'd give my year's salary to get Mr. Big behind bars."

Rick frowned thoughtfully. "But I can't quite believe

a professional hit man would have been that careless with his job."

"Most of them don't leave their trademarks lying around in plain sight," Gibson Cooper put in.

Nick smiled slyly. "Most of them are accustomed to city streets, not rural areas. They may overlook little things like the moisture from dew preventing ashes from blowing in the wind and trampled weeds beside the barns leaving telltale signs of a struggle that concrete sidewalks and paved alleys don't give away.

"And of course, there is the possibility that this was an amateur at work. I had the forensics crew check the area in front of the corral gate. There was a partial bootheel indentation beside the smoothed area to indicate someone might have dragged the body. Forensics is also doing blood-spattering tests this afternoon," Nick added. "And the medical examiner is checking for hair follicles—at my request. If a hit man was involved, he may have been just far enough out of his element in Vamoose to give himself away."

Nancy Shore glanced at Nick. "Do you have any idea why the crime syndicate would want to dispose of Bloom? From your briefing, it sounds as though the perfect operation has been established here. The farm and its standard operating equipment provide a discreet cover for trafficking. Bloom was low profile and blended into the country environment so well that he has called very little attention to himself in the four years he's been here."

"If I were Mr. Big, I'd hate like hell to lose this convenient arrangement," Roger Proctor put in. "In unincorporated areas—like the regions around Vamoose—the drug mules have virtually gone undetected while they made their transports and distribution. Even you over-looked this obscure farmer, and you're a veteran from the City narc squad. Do you think the syndicate will try to plant someone like Bloom to keep the operation in existence?"

"I think," Nick said as he scooped up the Ziploc bags, "that Mr. Big has been silently scoffing at me since I quit the force and moved to Vamoose. I suspect he spun this intricately discreet web with spiteful satisfaction and plans to continue with it."

"The arrogant bastard," Rich scowled. "You put the squeeze on him a few years ago and he got you to back off by taking Diana down, all because there was a leak in our chain of communication, an informant. We didn't have sufficient evidence to trace the killing back to Mr. Big or to identify the mysterious hit man he used. This is probably his way of proving to himself, to you, to the DEA and the OSBI that we aren't clever enough to run him down."

"We all thought Mr. Big had taken his laundered drug money and had gone into legitimate business after that fiasco in the City," Gib Cooper commented.

"But he got greedy when crack cocaine became such a lucrative business," Nick speculated. "That was always his Achilles' heel. He worships money and the power it gives him. And this time," Nick added determinedly, "I'm going to hang him out to dry, if he *is* involved in this smuggling ring."

"We can't overlook the possibility that whoever bumped Will Bloom off may not have been involved with the syndicate operation," Rich spoke up. "Bloom may have had a conflict with someone outside the crime community. If that's true, Mr. Big may consider Bloom's death an inconvenience and he may want his own revenge on whoever threw a wrench into this division of his smuggling racket."

"I'm keeping that in mind," Nick replied. "But whether Bloom's death was a result of his dealings with the drug cartel or an unrelated act of violence, I damn well intend to break this ring wide open and pray like hell that we can link these submarine goods to Mr. Big."

"So how do you intend to handle this sting?" Nancy Shore questioned. "I'm anxious to know what disguise I'll need when I go undercover in Vamoose."

A wry smile quirked Nick's lips as he sank onto the vacant chair at the table. "Here's what I have in mind . . ."

Four

Bleary-eyed from working half the night on Thatcher's income statements, Amanda drove to the City. She veered into the driveway of her parents' well-manicured home, making note of the immaculate flower gardens and edged sidewalks. Mother saw to it that Daddy kept the lawn as neat and tidy as she kept the house. Nothing was out of place. . . .

Well, almost nothing, Amanda silently amended.

To Amanda's disbelief, she saw her grandfather sitting on the porch in a lawn chair. Cardboard boxes of unassembled furniture legs, tabletops, sanders, saws, and tool chests encircled him. A dingy felt hat sat atop his bald head. He was huddled inside an insulated vest and jacket to ward off the crisp morning chill.

It looked as if Mother had dumped Pops—and his most treasured possessions—on the front step and then locked the door.

Amanda stepped from her Toyota, noting the shocked expression that settled into her grandfather's wrinkled features.

"What the hell happened to your hair, Half Pint? It's almost as short as mine!" Pops croaked.

Self-consciously, Amanda combed her fingers through her Tinker Bell hairstyle. "Rookie beautician."

She marched up the front steps and halted in front of her grandfather. "How long have you been sitting out here?"

Pops checked the antique gold watch that was secured to his belt loop by a chain. "One hour and forty-seven minutes."

"Almost two hours?" Amanda crowed. "You could catch pneumonia."

"Your mother was anxious to be on her way to the sunny Caribbean," Pops snorted as he braced himself against his aluminum walker. His bones creaked as he hauled his aged body onto his unstable legs. "The old bat was afraid she'd miss her flight and would be stuck here with me." His false teeth gleamed in the bright sunlight. "I decided to sit out here to make her look bad in front of her neighbors. It worked. Two of them stopped by to invite me into the warmth of their homes, and they commented on your mother's lack of consideration for a man of my age."

Amanda grinned at Pops as she hoisted up a suitcase. "I swear, you get ornerier by the year."

"It's a direct result of being cooped up in the City, sharing my space with your mother."

Pops hobbled down the steps and then halted to size up Amanda's compact car. "You should've brought your pickup. We'll have a helluva time fitting all my stuff into that tin can you call an automobile."

"My rattletrap truck is only reliable on short runs around Vamoose," Amanda explained.

"This is gonna be a tight squeeze," Pops predicted as he maneuvered himself into the cramped car, knocking off his hat in the process. "There's some rope in one of the boxes. You'll have to tie my stuff in the trunk."

Fifteen minutes later, Amanda drove off. She and her

car looked like a scene that had leaped off the pages of *The Grapes of Wrath*. Pieces of furniture jutted from the windows and boxes bulged from the trunk.

"It'll be damned good to get back to the country." Pops pulled off his wire-rimmed glasses, cleaning them on the hem of his flannel shirt. "I was raised on a farm, you know. But fool kid that I was, I thought the big city was the place to be." He snickered. "I'd like to get your citified mother out on the farm. She probably couldn't function at all. That'd be too bad."

Amanda noted that Pops didn't sound very sorry. She suspected he would delight in taking Mother out of her element, leaving her to flounder. The thought held considerable appeal.

"I noticed in the obituaries that one of your fellow Vamoosians bit the dust yesterday. Was he a client of yours, Half Pint?"

Amanda nodded. "I don't think it was an accident," she confided. "But Officer Thorn—"

"The boyfriend?"

"That's the one," she affirmed. "He's chalking it up as an accident. In my opinion, Will Bloom was the victim of foul play." She stared deliberately at Pops. "But if you tell Mother I'm investigating the possibility, I'll poison your fruit-and-fiber cereal."

"*Me* tell your mother?" Pops chuckled as he replaced his glasses on the bridge of his nose. "Not me, Half Pint. I don't tell your mother anything I don't have to and only half the things I should—just to annoy her."

Amanda mashed on the accelerator and whizzed down I-40. "When you can spare the time, I was hoping you could repair the antique clock Will Bloom gave me."

"What's wrong with it?"

"It won't run, and that's all I know about clocks."

"I'll have a look-see after I piece the drop leaf table back together," he promised. "Your clock probably just needs cleaning. That usually proves to be the case."

By the time Amanda returned home to unload Pops's belongings it was nearly noon. Since Pops volunteered to throw some sandwiches together for lunch, Amanda hauled his tools and antique furniture parts to the new workshop. As promised, Buzz Sawyer had installed the windows and had even built shelves and a worktable from the odds and ends of leftover lumber.

Although Buzz was lax in paying his bills, he was one fine carpenter, Amanda noted. Pops had all the space he needed to hobble around on his walker while refurbishing and refinishing priceless antiques.

After lunch Amanda escorted Pops to the barn to show him the shop. He beamed like an antique lantern on a long wick and immediately began organizing his tools in alphabetical order on the shelves.

"While you're settling in, I'm going to run some errands," Amanda informed her grandfather.

"No need to worry about me." Pops scooped up an armload of C-clamps and arranged them on the shelf, according to size.

"I'll be back in time to fix your supper."

Pops grimaced. "I'll take care of that, Half Pint. I haven't had the chance to putter around in a kitchen since I was forced to move in with your folks. You know how your mother is about someone intruding in her private territory."

Yes, Amanda did, and she held Mother personally accountable for her own lack of culinary skill.

Leaving her grandfather to his afternoon project,

Amanda drove toward town. When she pulled into Thatcher's Oil and Gas, a new employee greeted her. Dressed in blue coveralls, a red rag dangling from his hip pocket, Gib Cooper sauntered over to prop himself against the hood of Amanda's car. He struck what she assumed to be a rakish pose, smiling around the toothpick clamped between his teeth.

"What can I do you for, sweetheart?" Gib crooned.

Amanda appraised Gib critically. Attractive though the new blond-haired employee could have been—if he spiffed himself up and dropped the good ole boy come-on—Amanda already had a boyfriend, and wasn't in the market for another.

"Where's Bubba Hix?" she asked, ignoring Gib as she glanced curiously toward the garage.

"Bubba is taking a week's vacation. Shall I fill 'er up, doll face?"

Amanda nodded and then opened the door, purposely catching Don Juan Cooper in the hip. As she walked away, she noted that Gib was monitoring her progress with all the finesse of a love-starved inmate. The man certainly didn't waste time, she thought as she surged into the service station to deliver the tax statements to Thaddeus Thatcher.

"What happened to your hair?" Thaddeus chirped.

Amanda was tempted to strangle the next person who asked her that question. "Here's your tax report," she announced, quickly changing the subject.

"Thanks, l'il girl," Thaddeus said, accepting the file. "Gertrude was getting worried about whether we were going to get the statement turned into the tax commission on time."

"Where did you find Bubba's replacement?" Amanda wanted to know.

"Who? Gib?" Thaddeus shifted awkwardly from one steel-toed boot to the other and stared at the Coca-Cola machine beside the door. "Oh, he's a friend of a friend. I offered to hire him temporarily, just until he can find a new job. Too bad about Will Bloom," he said, hiking up the britches that sagged beneath his spare tire waistline. "I guess the farm will be going up for sheriff's auction before long, since Will didn't have any family to inherit his property."

Amanda made a noncommittal remark and turned away. It struck her odd that Thaddeus wouldn't stare her squarely in the eye while discussing his new employee. Who the devil was Gib Cooper, some jailbird on parole? Knowing Thaddeus, he wouldn't want to alarm Vamoosians, but he would keep a close eye on his new help, of that Amanda was certain.

"Hey, l'il girl, did that land man ever catch up with you?"

Frowning, Amanda half turned. "Land man?"

"Yeah, you know, the business representative who contacts landowners about oil drilling sites and checks legal descriptions for mineral and surface rights. Some guy name of Jim Johnson from Petro Fuel came by the station to ask directions to your farm. He said something about wanting to lease some of your land to erect a gas and oil well.

"If he wants to draw up a contract with you, make sure you get what you've got coming," Thaddeus advised in a fatherly tone. "You're due surface damages for the well site, even if you don't own the minerals. Make 'em treat you fair now, ya hear?"

Amanda nodded and then strode off. She was more concerned about what excuse she could dream up to interrogate her first suspect—Georgina Green—than she was about dealing with Jim whoever-he-was. She didn't have time to worry about oil company drilling sites, not when she had a crime to solve in Vamoose.

When Gib Cooper waggled his eyebrows, smiled roguishly, and opened the car door for her, Amanda ignored him—again.

Gib squatted down, demanding her full intention. "How's about you and me grabbing a burger at Last Chance Cafe when I get off work," he said with a wink and a grin. "I've been waiting all my life to meet somebody like you, doll face."

Amanda suspected Gib used the same worn-out line on every woman he met. There was something about being propositioned by a grease monkey—with slicked-down hair and a toothpick stuck in his mouth—that turned her off. Rolling her eyes at Gib's lack of originality, Amanda revved her engine and put the Toyota into gear.

Her reply was the squeal of tires and the smell of exhaust fumes.

Wearing a fashionable, wide-brimmed hat to conceal her hair, Amanda rang Georgina Green's doorbell. A short medley of Elvis Presley melodies chimed back at her. A full minute later, Vamoose's former prom queen appeared, wringing her hands and glancing nervously first in one direction and then the other.

"Amanda Hazard, isn't it?" Georgina questioned.

Amanda decided Georgina—a drop-dead gorgeous

redhead—must be suffering from an anxiety attack. Either she'd done away with her former lover or Amanda's reputation for investigating the "accidental deaths" of her clients had put Georgina on edge. If Georgina had something to hide she wasn't doing it well. Her expression kept changing faster than weather fronts. The way she kept wringing her hands had Amanda wondering if the poor woman would twist off her bejeweled fingers.

Without awaiting an invitation, Amanda surged into the tiled entryway. "I stopped by to remind you of the Vamoose Annual Flea Market that's scheduled in two weeks. Beverly Hill thought you might want to know."

"What?" Georgina wrung her hands some more and stared blankly at Amanda. "Who?"

"You know Bev," Amanda prompted with a cheery smile. "She was a few years behind you in school. She's Velma Hertzog's niece—the beautician-in-training at Beauty Boutique."

"Well, I suppose I could round up a few things to bring to the park." Georgina glanced absently around her elegantly furnished—but noticeably cluttered—home. "A few clothes maybe."

Amanda cut to the chase, since Georgina was paying about as much attention as a two-year-old. What was with this woman anyway? "Too bad about Will Bloom, wasn't it? I guess you'll have to find somebody else to handle your grass."

Georgina's red head snapped up. Her hands jerked rigidly down to her sides and her fingers knotted into fists. "And what is *that* supposed to mean?"

Amanda blinked, startled by the woman's visible hostility. "It means exactly what you think it means." Whatever the hell *that* was! Amanda wasn't certain how she'd managed to hit an exposed nerve, but she had.

Georgina's penciled brows flattened over the slits of her aquamarine eyes. "I think you better leave right now."

"Why?" Amanda went for the jugular. "Just because you're extremely sensitive about the subject of Will Bloom? Gossip has it that you and he were on exceptionally friendly terms."

"Gossip," Georgina hissed through bared teeth, "isn't known for its accuracy."

"Depends on where you get the gossip," Amanda retorted as she glanced toward the staircase. She wondered how many times Will had been up and down those stairs while Daniel Green was at his city office, getting groomed for politics. "It has occurred to me that Will might have blackmailed you. I doubt you would want your husband to know about your relationship with Will. It must have been tempting to club Will over the head to keep him silent."

Georgina's eyes nearly popped from their mascara-rimmed sockets. "You think I killed Will Bloom?"

"It has occurred to me, yes."

Georgina burst out in a laugh that bordered on hysteria. Amanda watched Georgina grab her ribs and double over at the waist, cackling like an egg-laying hen.

No wonder Beverly Hill claimed Georgina never had her head on straight—because the woman had several screws loose. She was also edgy and easily provoked, and seemed to have the attention span of a termite.

"Trust me, killing Will was the last thing I wanted to do," Georgina said between spurts of giggles.

Amanda made it a point never to trust anyone who

insisted she trust them. Furthermore, the way the wacky redhead had worded the comment suggested she might have bumped Will off—unintentionally. Amanda decided to dig a little harder for the facts.

"If Will threatened to reveal your extracurricular activities to a husband who is contemplating running for public office, things could get complicated. You know how the press likes to put candidates and their families under a microscope and examine every facet of their lives. If word got out about you and Will, it would ruin Daniel's political aspirations, wouldn't it?"

Amanda knew she'd struck another nerve when Georgina's ivory complexion turned fire engine red.

"You have no right to barge into my home and accuse me of murder! I didn't do anything to Will!" she screeched.

Her shrill voice threatened to shatter Amanda's eardrums. Amanda automatically retreated a few steps.

"You don't know what the hell you're talking about," Georgina raged on. "And if you dare spread such nasty rumors around town, I'll sue you for . . . for . . ."

Amanda didn't volunteer to aid the floundering woman. She simply watched Georgina wring her hands a few dozen more times, while her wild-eyed gaze bounced off the walls. A real basket case, Amanda diagnosed.

"Get out of my—!"

Georgina's voice dried up when the door swung open and Daniel strutted inside, puffing on a cigar. Amanda sniffed the air, instantly reminded of the telltale odor she had noticed in Will's living room. Suspicion clouded her mind as she focused absolute concentration on the fashionably-dressed lawyer whose good looks matched those of his attractive but batty wife.

"Amanda Hazard," she introduced herself, extending her hand to Daniel.

Daniel blew another puff of smoke and then shook Amanda's hand. Amanda decided, there and then, that Daniel Green's political life was doomed. His limp fish handshake wouldn't win any votes. The country could do without a wimp in a position of power and authority. The USA needed somebody with a firm grip on the situation.

"I just filed as a senatorial candidate," Daniel announced, turning up the wattage of his smile. "I hope I can count on your vote, Amanda."

"Too bad Will Bloom won't be around to cast a ballot," Amanda said.

Daniel's cigar drooped at the corner of his mouth and his limp hand fell away. "Are you trying to suggest I might have had something to do with Bloom's death?" he asked.

"Why would you think I implied that? I only came by to remind your wife of the local garage sale."

Daniel's gaze leaped to his apprehensive wife and then zeroed in on Amanda. "What are you trying to do? Ruin my chances of winning the election? I will not have you slandering my good name, and I don't want you anywhere near me or my wife again. Whenever someone turns up dead in Vamoose and you start asking questions, the whole town runs scared, afraid we're all suspects. I don't want you flapping around here like the scarecrow of doom, engaging in ridiculous speculation that I was involved in our groundskeeper's death. It was an accident. Officer Thorn said so!"

Daniel whipped open the door to shoo Amanda out—run her out was more like it. She found herself shoveled onto the porch and heard the door slam decisively behind her.

My, my, the topic of Will Bloom is a touchy one at the Green residence. Now why is that, do you suppose, Amanda mused.

Amanda walked to her car, reasonably certain that both Georgina and Daniel Green had motive and ample opportunity. What a shame they didn't have the decency and consideration to confess to the crime, thereby saving Amanda time and effort.

Well, she thought as she drove away, nobody said investigation was easy. Daniel Green was right about one thing: When someone in Vamoose expired and Amanda began asking how and why, everybody got nervous and uptight. That was why she usually employed the tactful approach. But there was no way to be subtle with Georgina. The woman was a ditzoid.

Considering the defensive, hostile way the Greens had reacted, Amanda wondered if Will's "accident" might have been the result of combined efforts. Georgina was nervous enough to invite suspicion, but it was Daniel's cigar that sparked a memory Amanda definitely intended to pursue. She was quite certain cigar smoke was a clue that would eventually lead her to the person and or persons responsible. Somebody—the Greens perhaps?—had gotten careless while staging the not-so-accidental accident.

Glancing at her watch, Amanda zoomed off. She wanted to have another look around Will's house before she returned home for supper. If there were cigar butts lying around, Daniel Green was going to be more than a candidate for office, he was going to be a prime suspect for murder in the first degree!

* * *

"We've got a live one," Roger Proctor called to Nick Thorn.

Nick strode over to the monitor that was connected to the surveillance cameras Roger had installed at strategic points around Will Bloom's farm. From inside the cinder block shed—which had once served as a milk house—the agents could watch the goings-on without being detected.

Roger whistled wolfishly when the subject of surveillance stuck a well-proportioned leg from the opened car door. When the subject stood up, Roger panted, "Be still, my beating heart. Keeping tabs on this bombshell blonde will be my pleasure." He gave his carrot-colored head a marveling shake. "Will Bloom ran with one hot little number, didn't he? What we have here is USDA prime cut female. I wonder how she fits into this scheme?"

Nick scowled as he watched Roger drool all over himself, while the black-and-white monitor offered a detailed account of Hazard's every move. Her face shadowed by a trendy hat, Hazard snooped for clues.

When she squatted down beside the front porch, exposing her shapely bottom to the nearby camera, Roger made an off-color remark about the possibility of the broad being a good lay. Nick's protective instincts grabbed hold like hydraulic brakes.

"Watch your mouth, Roger," Nick snapped. "That happens to be my girlfriend you're slobbering over. I'd appreciate it if you would plug your eyes back in their sockets and reel in your panting tongue."

Roger jerked away from the screen that had fogged

with his heavy breathing. "No shit? *This* is your girl-friend?"

"No shit," Nick confirmed. Attentively, he watched Hazard run her well-manicured hand across the grass, in search of only God knew what.

"Damn, Nick, she's a real knockout. Too bad you have to cut her loose . . . What the hell is she doing out here anyway?"

"She thinks she missed her true calling," Nick explained. He appraised Hazard's alluring profile as she gracefully rose from a crouch to inspect the front porch in the same meticulous manner that she had surveyed the area around the sidewalk. "Hazard loves to play detective."

When Hazard produced a credit card from her purse and then slid it between the doorjamb and the lock, Roger's expression turned grim. "This gumshoe girlfriend of yours is going to complicate our investigation. Forensics didn't turn up any hair follicles or distinct footprints, but they found her fingerprints around here. If we let her come and go at will, there's no telling who she might scare off."

Nick was aware of that. "I told Hazard to butt out, but she obviously ignored me. If I keep nagging her about it, she'll become suspicious. I have to let her—and everybody else in Vamoose—think I consider Bloom's death accidental."

"And if you let Hazard tramp around the farm, she might encounter some pretty rough characters," Roger predicted.

Roger wasn't telling Nick anything he didn't know. "I plan to—"

Nick's voice evaporated when the door to the outdated

milk house creaked open and Rich Thorn ambled inside. Rich squatted down to pluck the stickers from his jeans. After his long hike through the weeds to reach the obscure shed, his clothes were snagged with dozens of goat-heads and sticktights.

"I'd like to mow a path up here," Rich grumbled, tossing another sticker aside. "But I suppose that would be as obvious as paving a yellow brick road. Working in the country does have its drawbacks."

"No kidding," Roger said as he switched on the camera inside Bloom's home. "In the city, we can park our surveillance van on the street and no one is the wiser. Out here, it would stick out like a sore thumb. So here we are, holed up in this shed with the spiders and mice."

"I'll call the office and request pickups for tailing possible suspects," Rich volunteered. He glanced curiously at the monitor that provided an arresting view of the woman who was strolling around Bloom's front room. "Who's the sex siren? Anybody identified her yet?"

Roger grinned as he hitched his thumb toward Nick. "Your brother has. This head-turner is his girlfriend."

Rich gave a quiet whistle. "Damn, little brother, I can see why you like to play cops and robbers and frisk—"

"Can it, Rich," Nick snapped. "I've already heard all the crude remarks from Roger that I care to hear."

Rich nodded his head in understanding. "I got a call from Gib Cooper awhile ago. He said he had the chance to meet Hazard at the service station, and that he is still drooling. I thought he was exaggerating about her good looks. Obviously he wasn't."

Irritably, Nick watched his soon-to-be ex-girlfriend snoop around Bloom's house. He frowned when Hazard sniffed the air like a bloodhound.

"What the hell is she doing?" Rich questioned, bemused.

"Your guess is as good as mine." Nick gestured toward the keyboard. "Switch on the next camera, Roger. Hazard is headed toward the kitchen."

The camera scanned the modern kitchen. All three men watched Hazard rummage through the cabinets and drawers. When Hazard had made her way upstairs to search Bloom's bedroom, Nick groaned in disbelief. This was the first time he'd had the opportunity to view Hazard in action. She proved to be highly efficient in her investigative procedures—something both Rich and Roger remarked upon.

Hazard went through every closet and chest of drawers with the same precision Nick practiced. Since she wasn't wearing gloves, she had stripped off her jacket and used the sleeves to cover her hands so she wouldn't leave more fingerprints.

To Nick's dismay, he was forced to watch Rich and Roger ogle Hazard's upper torso—accentuated as it was by the form-fitting, blue-and-white-striped, cotton-knit sweater that clung to her ample bustline.

"Oh, by the way," Rich rasped, between lusty pants of breath, "Gib said he hit Hazard up for a date before he knew who she was. After Thaddeus Thatcher told him whose gas tank he'd filled, Gib decided it might be a good idea if he kept company with Hazard—after you broke off with her, just in case she stumbled into trouble."

Nick snorted sardonically. "Gib may be one of the best special agents in the state, but I wouldn't trust him alone with Hazard for even five minutes. When it comes to pretty women, Gib is worse than a hormone-driven teenager. You tell Gib I said to keep his distance."

Both men smiled like barracudas. "That goes for the two of you as well," Nick added with a threatening glare. "I'll handle Hazard."

"You mean you haven't already?" Roger asked, grinning outrageously.

There had been a number of occasions in the past when Nick had enjoyed Roger's playful sense of humor. This, however, was not one of those times. Having other men fantasize about getting their hot little hands on Hazard played hell with Nick's overactive possessiveness.

"Nancy Shore went on duty this afternoon," Rich reported. "She has established her background information and put in a full day as cashier at Toot 'N Tell 'Em. With her skintight clothes and Dolly Parton blond wig, she has already incited gossip and speculation at the Last Chance Cafe. I stopped by the restaurant for a hamburger and heard her name being tossed around in several booths. If you have to employ phase two of this operation, Nancy will be a familiar name around Vamoose."

"So, when are you going to stage your breakup with Hazard?" Roger wanted to know.

"Soon," Nick replied as he watched one surveillance camera after another monitor Hazard's exit from Bloom's home. When she walked out the door, Nick felt a funny little twinge in his gut. He cursed Will Bloom and his shady ties to organized crime. The man had spoiled Nick's relationship with Hazard.

There was a strong possibility that Nick would never get back into Hazard's good graces when this covert operation was over. But Nick owed a long-standing debt to a tormenting memory, and he felt compelled to repay it, no matter what personal sacrifice he had to make.

The death of one girlfriend already weighed heavily on his conscience. He was damned if he was going to add another one to the list. He would do whatever necessary to ensure Hazard didn't become another casualty of the drug war!

Five

Amanda drove home, preoccupied by her conversation with the Greens, mulling over the clues she had discovered at Will Bloom's. As she suspected, there were clumps of ashes nestled in the grass beside Bloom's sidewalk and stale smoke still clung to the furniture and carpet in the living room. A thorough search of the house indicated that Bloom didn't smoke, because there wasn't an ashtray to be found anywhere.

Obviously his mysterious visitor did.

Amanda concluded that Daniel Green could have made a visit to Bloom's farm—with or without his nervous wife at his side. Considering Daniel's recent candidacy, the man had a strong motive for wanting the threat of scandal eliminated before it hit the headlines. If Georgina had been fooling around with Vamoose's handyman—and had been blackmailed by him—Daniel couldn't risk Bloom's going public. The media would have a field day with the young senatorial candidate.

"Don't jump to premature conclusions," Amanda cautioned herself. Bobbie Sue Hampton had yet to be questioned. Her name, among others, had also been linked to Bloom's.

There was a strong possibility that a woman could have cleverly used cigar ashes and smoke to throw an investigator off the track. The smoke and ashes could have been planted so that Amanda would think the prime suspect was a man.

This could be an ingenious "smoke" screen, Amanda reminded herself. She mustn't stereotype possible suspects. She had discovered during her first murder case—and each one thereafter—that things were not always what they seemed. The criminal mind could be very inventive when it came to covering tracks. She couldn't allow herself to forget that.

Georgina Green's comments and reaction had Amanda puzzled. Talk about things not being what they seemed! There was something about Georgina's nervous apprehension and Daniel's aggressive defensiveness that disturbed Amanda. Somewhere in her confrontation with the Greens was a vital clue. Amanda just hadn't had time to sit herself down and figure out what it was.

Pete, the three-legged dog, barked his head off, jostling Amanda from her thoughts. She parked in her driveway, noting that Hank the tomcat was clinging to the wooden supporting beam on the porch. From all indication, Pops had shooed Hank from the house, and Pete objected to the cat intruding on his territory.

Pops had never been a cat lover, Amanda reminded herself. He refused to share his space with those of the feline persuasion. Unfortunately, the neutered tomcat wasn't prepared to defend itself in the outside world, having spent the past few months as Amanda's pampered house companion. Hank's survival instincts were rusty.

"Pete!" Amanda yelled at the crippled dog that had treed the cat.

Pete whined in complaint when Amanda called him

off. Nonetheless, Pete hobbled away, plunking down beside the front door.

Amanda plucked up the frightened cat and strode into the house. Pops was seated at the kitchen table, his walker positioned an arm's length away. His bald head was bent over a slew of opened envelopes and stacks of entry forms. Steam billowed from the pots that boiled on the stove behind him.

"I'm home, Pops!" Amanda called to her grandfather.

Pops glanced at her over the rim of his thick glasses, and then he frowned at Hank. "I thought I put that damned cat outside. You don't have a trapdoor that he uses to come and go as he pleases, I hope. That fluffball will carry fleas and ticks in here to bed down with us."

Amanda inhaled a courageous breath and said, "Hank is a house cat, and I plan to keep him in here."

"I don't like cats," Pops said in no uncertain terms.

"You don't like Mother, either, but she stays in the house with Daddy."

Pops broke into a wicked smile. "Wanna trade my house pet for yours? I've suddenly developed a fond attachment for Hank."

"I've done my time with Mother, thank you." Amanda ambled to the table, staring over Pops's shoulder at his stack of mail. "What are you working on, Pops?"

Pops held up four envelopes, on which RUSH was stamped in bold red letters. Self-adhesive stickers were plastered beside his return address—or rather Amanda's address, as the case happened to be.

"I entered some sweepstakes contests, and I'm in the second stage. I've had all my mail forwarded to your address so I don't miss out on any of the bonus prize giveaways."

Amanda inwardly groaned. "Do you honestly believe you stand a chance of winning this one in a million opportunity?"

"One in two hundred thousand chance of a lifetime," Pops amended. "Of course, I will. I ordered the magazines and knickknacks from the catalogues included in the brochures."

Amanda stared at the order forms, on which Pops had scrawled item numbers and prices. "What are you going to do with five brass-plated handy hooks?" she croaked.

"It says here that the streamlined rod and hooks make use of minimal space behind doors. I can hang up my sweaters and vests so your mother won't fold them up and hide them every time I lay one down. I never can find a damned thing. She follows me around to make sure I don't clutter up that museum she refers to as her house." Pops gave a disgusted snort. "That woman is the pickiest housekeeper I've ever met. I'm surprised she doesn't keep your father on a hanger in the closet when she isn't using him."

"What about this twelve-inch stainless steel grill?" Amanda questioned. "I thought you said Mother didn't let you cook."

"She doesn't, but this grill is for cooking steaks and vegetables on the outdoor barbecuer. I'm planning to use it while I'm staying with you. I can cook for you and your boyfriend."

"But Pops, it will be weeks before you receive the items you've ordered. You aren't planning to stay that long . . . Are you?"

The smile that spread across Pops's wrinkled face indicated that he intended to stay longer than the duration of Mother's Caribbean cruise. Amanda had the inescapable feeling Pops wasn't the ordinary, garden-variety houseguest. He was setting up housekeeping on Amanda's rented farm. Mother, of course, would encourage that kind of thinking. Mother and Pops got along much better when they didn't see or speak to each other.

The bouncing lid of the boiling pot finally caught Pops's attention. He swiveled in his chair to see steam belching from the kettle of ham hock and beans. "Turn down the heat, will you, Half Pint. I have to finish pasting my prize-winning stickers on the rest of the entry cards."

Pops, she decided, didn't know what he was letting himself in for when he entered all the sweepstakes. He would be bombarded with piles of mail that instructed him to order numerous items and magazines that would entitle him to "Early Bird," "Hurry Up," "Good as Gold," and "Rapid Response" bonus prizes—if his name was selected. In addition to the grand claims and enticements, the entry forms stated that Pops had a chance to win a souped-up automobile, a dream home, a chance-of-a-lifetime vacation, and hundreds of thousands of dollars in cash.

Amanda hadn't realized that her grandfather was susceptible to advertising gimmicks! He could squander his retirement pension and social security checks on piles of useless gifts and magazines he would never read, believing he would increase his chances of nabbing the grand prize sweepstakes.

And pigs fly, thought Amanda. "Pops, I don't have much faith in this sweepstakes stuff," she said as she turned down the burner on the stove.

Pops puffed up like a helium balloon. "You'll have to eat your words when some hot-shot celebrity comes

knocking on the door with a cashier's check in hand."
Pops turned back to his entry forms and bonus stickers.
"Serve up the ham and beans, Half Pint. I'll put my
order forms in their designated envelopes and then clear
off the table for supper."

While Pops licked envelopes and filed information
packets from his sweepstakes, Amanda dipped up the
beans and sought a less sensitive topic of conversation.
"How are you coming along with your drop leaf table?"

"Fine," Pops muttered.

"Did you get the hand-carved legs bolted back into
place?"

"No, I'm still stripping off old paint and varnish."
Pops licked four more envelopes and set them aside.
"The tabletop is being glued back together and the C-
clamps are holding it in place until it's dry. I'll take the
clamps off tomorrow and sand the top before I reassem-
ble the table."

"I noticed my former client had an antique table in
his house," Amanda commented as she set the steaming
bowl of beans in front of Pops. "You might want to buy
it at the sheriff's auction." She stared pointedly at the
stack of sweepstakes envelopes. "That is, if you have
any money left after all these purchases."

Pop shook his spoon in Amanda's face. "Just you wait,
Half Pint. I may turn out to be the next millionaire in the
American Giveaway Sweepstakes. Then you'll be apolo-
gizing all over yourself for being a Doubting Thomas and
start kissing up to me, because I'm filthy rich. But when
I give away cash to my relatives, I'll give your share to
your mother."

Amanda wasn't going to hold her breath waiting for
Pops to become the newest member of the Millionaires'

Club. Pops may have been occupying his time with this sweepstakes business, but he was deluding himself with false hopes.

Halfway through dinner, Pops suggested that Amanda call Thorn and invite him over for the evening. While Pops fiddled with his malfunctioning hearing aids that had whistled during dinner, Amanda put in the call. When an unfamiliar male voice answered the phone, Amanda frowned.

"Is Nick there, please?"

"Who's calling?"

"Amanda Hazard."

"The girlfriend? I guess my little brother hasn't felt like checking in with you yet."

Alarm bells clanged in Amanda's head. "Is something wrong with him?"

"Yeah, I'm afraid so," Rich Thorn replied. "Nick had an accident this afternoon. The wheat auger got clogged up. He got in a hurry and tried to repair it without switching off the electric motor. The damned thing chewed up his arm pretty good. The doctor stitched him up, put his right arm in a sling, and told him to take it easy for a few weeks. Nick asked me to drive out from the City and help him plant his wheat crop, so I'm living with him for a while."

Well, Amanda thought, there went her chance of having any private moments with Thorn. Her grandfather was camped out at her house, and Nick's older brother was living in his. And worse, Thorn had practically ripped his arm off at the socket!

"Can I speak to Nick?" she requested.

"Sorry, but I doped him up with painkillers and sent him to bed. I'll bring him into the Last Chance Cafe tomorrow for lunch so you can see for yourself that he's still in one piece—sort of. How does high noon sound to you?"

"I'll be there," Amanda promised.

Amanda hung up the phone. With Thorn injured and out of commission during wheat planting, he was going to be in a foul mood. He was also going to be absolutely no help in tracking down the perpetrator who had disposed of Will Bloom. As usual, Amanda would have to conduct the investigation by herself.

"What's wrong with your boyfriend?" Pops asked.

"He had a farming accident."

"What kind?"

"He got tangled up with a grain auger—literally," Amanda reported.

"That's what happens when you mess with that newfangled equipment," Pops snorted. "If farmers would scoop grain from their trucks to their planters, those accidents wouldn't happen. He didn't lose his arm, did he?"

"No, but his right arm has been maimed. His older brother is going to help him plant his crop."

"I could drive the grain truck for them," Pops eagerly offered.

Amanda wouldn't have put her grandfather behind the wheel of any vehicle! The last time she had consented to ride with him, Pops had difficulty keeping his older model Ford between the curbs. Daddy had taken Pops's keys away from him immediately thereafter and had refused to give them back.

"I think Nick's brother has the situation in hand, but I'll be sure to tell them you volunteered to pitch in during wheat planting."

"When do I get to meet your boyfriend?" Pops levered onto his aluminum walker to carry the dirty dishes to the sink.

"Tomorrow at noon. We'll be dining at the Last Chance Cafe."

The moment the supper dishes were washed and dried, Pops removed his hearing aids and then propelled himself down the hall.

"You're turning in already?" she called after her grandfather.

Pops obviously couldn't hear without those auditory devices crammed in his ears, for he never missed a note of the tune he was singing. He maneuvered around the corner of the hall and then closed the spare bedroom door behind him.

Amanda glanced at her watch. It was eight o'clock. Pops would be up before the chickens. She could only hope her grandfather would allow her to sleep until six. He had always been an early riser, but this was ridiculous!

God didn't like to get up before the crack of dawn, and neither did Amanda.

If Pops was here to stay permanently, one of them was going to have to alter their daily routine.

On that grim thought, Amanda collapsed in her La-Z-Boy recliner to mull over the information she had gathered about this most recent murder case. Hank the tomcat took his customary position on her lap and promptly fell asleep, exhausted from his harrowing adventures in the out-of-doors.

For over two hours Amanda rehashed her conversations with Beverly Hill, Velma Hertzog, and the Greens. Something kept niggling at her, some clue she knew she had overlooked. She kept envisioning the indecipherable expression that washed over Georgina's face at the mention of her secret affair with Will Bloom.

Those guffaws of laughter weren't the reactions Amanda had anticipated, either. Georgina's nervous anxiety also had Amanda miffed. She kept recalling what Bev Hill said about Georgina not having her head on straight in high school. Apparently, Georgina's condition hadn't improved.

There had definitely been something going on between Vamoose's handyman and the flaky Georgina Green. What? Amanda wasn't certain, but she intended to find out.

"Any new developments?" Rich Thorn asked as his brother strode into the living room.

"One possible nibble," Nick replied. He sank down on the sofa beside his brother and then sighed tiredly. "Two males—one Caucasian, one Mexican—took a slow tour around the section where Bloom's farm is located. The subjects were driving a dented-up Lincoln. Roger Proctor traced the license plate to Manuel Pico."

"Is he employed?" Rich asked before sipping his beer.

Nick nodded his raven head. "Pico works at Uni-Comp Corporation in the City."

Rich frowned. "A supply house of some sort?"

"Computer software. It's a subdivision of a microchip distributor in Longhorn, Texas. Roger asked OSBI to run a check on the company to see if it's legitimate."

"Is it?"

"It seems to be."

Rich propped his stocking feet on the coffee table and

glanced at his brother. "Your girlfriend called earlier this evening. I told her about your supposed accident and explained why I'm here. I think she bought the story."

"Was she properly concerned about my injured condition?"

"She would have driven out here to check on you if I hadn't told her you were in bed, doped up with painkillers. I suggested we meet her at the café for lunch tomorrow."

Nick squirmed apprehensively and stared at the far wall. "Things were going good between us," he quietly confided.

"Just keep telling yourself that you're calling it quits for her safety and well-being," Rich advised. "If Bloom had the dangerous connections we suspect he had, you'll be sorry as hell if you don't split up with her now."

"Hazard will never get over this," Nick muttered. "She's already been through a divorce, and she carries a lot of emotional baggage because of it. She's going to be asking herself why she bothered taking a chance with me."

"Better that Hazard is alive to hate your guts than to be fitted for a pine box." Studying Nick's bleak expression, Rich leaned down to grab his boots. "Why don't you let me take the surveillance shift tonight. You and Roger need to get some sleep. I'll have Gib Cooper stand watch with me after he finishes setting up the bugs in the barn."

"Where's Nancy?" Nick questioned.

Rich grinned wryly. "She's establishing her notorious reputation in Vamoose with some local yokel who invited her to dinner at Last Chance."

"Oh yeah? What's the yokel's name?"

"Tommy Philpott."

Nick choked on his breath. "She'll have to fight him off with a stick."

"You know Nancy is a whiz at tae kwon do," Rich reminded him. "She can take care of herself. I've seen her do it a dozen times—and quite effectively."

When the door clicked shut behind Rich, Nick walked into the kitchen to get himself a beer. Tomorrow, he predicted as he sipped his brew, was going to be one of the worst days of his life. Nick could imagine the stricken look on Hazard's face when he broke off what had become a stable, rewarding relationship.

If not for the potential dangers in this particular case, Nick and Hazard could have remained on the closest of terms, but her connection to him could easily threaten her existence. Therefore, the good thing they had going had to be terminated without allowing Hazard to know why. Nick couldn't take her into his confidence, because Hazard would insist on helping with the case. If he gave her the go-ahead, there would be no controlling her. She would consider herself deputized to investigate—full steam ahead. Besides that, Hazard was terrible at taking orders. Her very nature demanded that she give them.

"Here's to you, Hazard," Nick murmured as he lifted his beer can in toast. "May you live long enough for me to crawl back to apologize for what I'm about to do to you—in hopes of keeping you safe from harm."

Amanda sloshed cold water on her face, trying to bring her brain to its normal state of alertness. Pops had been up for hours and had routed Amanda from bed when he banged pots and pans in the kitchen. Pops, of course, didn't realize he was making so much racket, since his hearing aids were still sitting on the table.

Amanda had stumbled down the hall, only to have Pops invite her outside to gather eggs from the henhouse. She was pleased to know Pops was happy about living on the farm, but she sincerely wished her grandfather would be more considerate of the working stiffs of the world.

After being served a hearty country breakfast and several cups of strong coffee, Amanda drove to her office on Main Street. When she had caught up on her paperwork and returned phone calls, she checked her watch. There was enough time to question Bobbie Sue Hampton before picking up Pops and meeting the Thorn brothers for lunch.

Shifting her mind into investigative gear, Amanda aimed her Toyota toward Hampton Horse Ranch, which overlooked the sandy banks of Whatsit River. Buddy Hampton was trying to make a name for himself among the elite horsey set. He spent an excessive amount of time—and money—at Oklahoma City's racetrack.

According to Velma and Bev, Buddy had been so intent in establishing his horse business that he had neglected his wife. Apparently Will Bloom had been around to console the horse widow and to make household repairs while Buddy was off to the races.

Amanda drove past the white cable fences that surrounded Buddy's brood barns and pastures. Although the Hamptons seemed to be affluent, Amanda knew the horse operation was still running in the red, because she kept the accounts and figured the taxes.

Bobby Sue Hampton kept up expensive appearances, as did Georgina Green, who could better afford it. Both women insisted on going first-class—and in grand style. Rumors of their illicit affairs with the local handyman would destroy the images they strove to maintain. Too bad neither woman had thought of that before getting mixed up with Will Bloom.

Bobbie Sue, it was said, was compelled to compete with her country music star sister, Amanda reminded herself. Billie Jean Baxter had set the standard of living to which Bobbie Sue now aspired. The two sisters, so it was said, liked to put on the dog.

Amanda knew Billie Jean could afford her expensive tastes, but Bobbie Sue couldn't. If Will Bloom had blackmailed Bobbie Sue to keep their affair quiet, it could have put the Hamptons' finances in a world of hurt.

Deciding to use Vamoose's annual garage sale as an excuse for a visit, Amanda hiked up the sidewalk to the grand house on the hill and knocked on the door. Bobbie Sue appeared, dressed in the latest Western fashion. Her jeans were so tight Amanda doubted the woman could bend over without splitting her seams. Like her celebrity sister, Bobbie also had a penchant for turquoise and silver jewelry.

Amanda didn't remove her sunglasses, for fear she would be blinded by glaring sunlight reflecting off the sterling silver.

"If you came by to remind Buddy that he has to show a profit on those blasted horses every seven years, he already knows this is the year," Bobbie blurted out, fiddling with her gaudy necklace. "He's probably down at the stables loading horses in the stock trailer or already on his way to that damned racetrack again. I'm thinking of packing his belongings and moving them into one of the stalls."

"Actually, I came by to see you."

Bobbie Sue looked stunned. "Me? Why?"

Amanda smiled cordially. "Would you mind if I came inside for a minute."

"I don't have much time. I have a hair appointment in twenty minutes."

"I guess I could have saved myself a trip then." Since Bobbie Sue wouldn't let her in the house, Amanda glanced discreetly inside the open door, making quick note of the ashtray on a narrow walnut table in the hall. She sniffed the air for telltale signs of smoke. Sure enough, she caught a whiff of tobacco—the familiar scent that permeated Will Bloom's home.

Amanda turned her full attention on Bobbie Sue, who was impatiently shifting from one freshly polished cowboy boot to the other. "Velma wanted me to remind everyone about the flea market. You might want to join in."

"I had planned to," Bobbie Sue said in a clipped tone. "If that's all you wanted, I need to be going."

"Well, there is one other thing," Amanda replied. "It's about Will Bloom."

Bobbie Sue stopped in the act of slinging her tooled leather purse strap over her shoulder. The color drained from beneath her meticulously applied coat of makeup. "What about him?"

The wary expression assured Amanda that Velma's assumptions were more than beauty shop gossip. "Have you found a replacement for Will yet?"

Bobbie Sue threw back her head, her eyes snapping. "A replacement for what?"

Amanda sighed theatrically. "Come on, Bobbie Sue,

let's not waste time since you claim to be so short of it. You and Will were on intimate terms and I know it."

"We were on speaking terms," Bobbie Sue insisted huffily. "Will repaired leaky faucets and built the deck on the back of the house, because Buddy has been too busy to even notice we had leaks in the kitchen and broken steps."

"Buddy was even too busy to remember he had a wife who needed more attention than he was giving her, wasn't he?" Amanda paused strategically, giving Bobbie Sue time to digest the question before firing another one. "Or does he know what I know about you and Will?"

"What the hell are you trying to say?" Bobbie Sue demanded through clenched teeth.

"That the two of you were having an affair," Amanda answered frankly. "Did Will try to blackmail you?"

Bobbie Sue staggered back against the doorjamb. Her mascara-lined lashes fluttered like a bird in a breeze. If the flaming color of her face was any indication, Bobbie was as guilty as original sin.

"How dare you!" Bobbie Sue yowled.

"Me? I'm not the married woman fooling around with the town handyman," Amanda calmly countered. "Question is: How far would you go to keep the affair quiet?"

"I did not kill Will Bloom!" Bobbie Sue shrieked.

Amanda wondered if Bobbie Sue was operating on the theory that the louder she protested, the better she would be believed.

The theory wasn't working.

"He and I—" Bobbie Sue's voice dried up and her wild gaze shot over Amanda's left shoulder.

Amanda saw the shadow fall across the porch and felt

the looming presence beside her. She had the uneasy feeling that Buddy Hampton had been at the stables behind the house and had hiked up the hill to see who had arrived. Judging by the snarling sound behind Amanda, she assumed Buddy had overheard enough of the incriminating conversation to be furious.

Although Buddy was fanatic about raising and racing horses, he was also reported to be crazy about his wife. Too bad he hadn't taken time to demonstrate his affection of late. Now Buddy knew the consequences of leaving a vital, restless woman to find affection and attention wherever she could get it.

As the breeze whirled around the side of the house, Amanda caught another whiff of smoke. Even before she pivoted to confront Buddy, she knew he would have a cigar clamped between his teeth.

Her prediction proved correct. The flared tip of Buddy's stogie was as red as his face.

"Damn it, Bobbie Sue, how could you!" Buddy roared, his fist clenched tightly around the lead rope he carried. "I've been busting my butt to get this ranch on the elite list of horse breeders. While I've been wearing myself out to keep this place afloat and trying to pay for those goddamn designer clothes you think you have to wear to compete with your sister, you've been screwing around with Bloom. God a-mighty, Bobbie Sue! Bloom wasn't fit to wipe his feet on our doormat."

Tears spurted from Bobbie Sue's eyes, taking the thick coat of mascara with them. She swiped at the tears, smearing her makeup. "Don't you dare blame me, Buddy. I got lonely sitting around here day after day, night after night. Will wasn't all that bad to look at, and he took a little time for me—something you haven't done in months."

"And this is how you repay me for trying to get ahead in this world? Thanks a helluva lot, Bobbie Sue."

"You care more about those horses than you do about me!

"I do not!" he blared at her.

"Do, too!"

Bobbie Sue burst into loud wails, followed by shuddering sobs. Amanda debated skulking off to let the couple resolve their differences. She knew what Buddy was feeling, having dealt with a cheating husband in her own first marriage. Buddy was getting well acquainted with anger and betrayal, Amanda predicted. As for Bobbie Sue, she was using every excuse in the book and trying to lay the blame for her infidelity at Buddy's booted feet.

Uncomfortable though the situation was, Amanda needed facts. She had to do what any competent investigator had to do—pose questions. "Where were you the morning Will Bloom was found dead, Bobbie Sue?"

"Are you kidding?" Buddy roared. "Are you suggesting that Bobbie Sue had something to do with Bloom's accident?"

"I'm not altogether sure it was an accident." Amanda studied Buddy, not quite convinced that his reactions fit this situation. Call her crazy, but something didn't quite ring true here. "Or could it be that you already knew what had been going on with Will and your wife. Did you decide to put a stop to it? Where were *you* the day Will Bloom was found dead in the dirt?"

"He was here with me," Bobbie Sue blubbered through her tears, to come to her husband's defense.

Amanda chose not to believe her. Bobbie Sue was trying to rack up brownie points with her husband after her shameful fall from grace. Amanda suspected Bobbie Sue was nobly rushing to Buddy's defense in an attempt to regain his respect.

And Buddy was falling into the trap. Amanda could see him doing it. He was staring at Bobbie Sue's smeared face, searching for the prodigal half of his soul. It was like something out of a fairy tale, but Amanda wasn't buying any of it. This scene was playing out just a little too sappy for her not to become suspicious.

Buddy looked much too forgiving for a man who had just now realized his wife had cheated on him. Furthermore, Amanda had seen too many criminals give convincing performances in an effort to save their guilty hides. Buddy could have bumped Bloom off and then put on this act to throw Amanda off the track.

Whether or not Buddy was actually going to take his two-timing wife back was his business. But if Buddy had disposed of Bloom in a jealous rage and pretended ignorance—until Amanda arrived to demand the truth—then it was her business.

Conniving and devious though Will Bloom had been, two wrongs didn't make a right, not in the gospel according to Amanda Hazard. If Buddy was playacting for her—and Bobbie Sue's—benefit, Amanda would hound his every step.

Likewise, if Bobbie Sue was trying to conceal her own guilt behind that flood of tears, Amanda would be waiting to wear her down.

"Were you home all day, Bobbie Sue?" Amanda questioned relentlessly.

"Of course, she was," Buddy said in her behalf. "We were together night and day."

"I do hope you can testify to that in a court of law without perjuring yourself."

Buddy's burning gaze threatened to fry Amanda to a crisp. "And you better believe I'm going to tell your boyfriend that you've been sticking your nose in places it doesn't belong."

"My boyfriend was involved in a farming accident and he can't handle the investigation himself," Amanda countered, undaunted. "I'm doing Thorn's legwork for him."

"Oh yeah? Well, I think I'll call Officer Thorn right this minute and see if he corroborates your story."

When Buddy stormed into the house, smoke rolling from his cigar—and his ears—Bobbie Sue rounded on Amanda. "You're going to be damned sorry for this," she vowed.

"Am I? Are you planning on keeping me quiet the same way you did Will?"

"You're really asking for it."

"How much was Will asking to keep quiet about your affair?" Amanda flung back.

"Do you think I'm the only one around here with something to hide?"

Amanda made note of the fact that Bobbie Sue had ignored the pointed question and had cast the spotlight of suspicion elsewhere. Interesting. Ineffective with Amanda, but still interesting.

"Why don't you give Jayme Black the third degree?" Bobbie Sue insisted. "She was always hanging around Will's home, showing up at unexpected moments."

"Does she smoke cigars, too?"

Bobbie Sue was momentarily taken aback by the un-expected question, but then she nodded her head vigorously. "I wouldn't put it past Jayme. There isn't much she wouldn't do."

Apparently Bobbie Sue had said all she intended to say on the subject of Will Bloom and Jayme Black. She whipped the door shut, but not before she made a wisecrack about Amanda's ultrashort hairdo.

"Go harass somebody else, *butch!*"

Wishing she had donned her concealing hat, Amanda wheeled around and stalked off. Her interrogation at Hampton Horse Ranch hadn't gone a damned bit better than the confrontation with the Greens. Furthermore, Buddy was probably ratting to Thorn, informing him that Amanda was conducting her own investigation of the case that did not officially exist. If Buddy did indeed tattle to Thorn, it would ruin what was left of his disposition—which had probably turned surly since he was recovering from his own accident.

Amanda wasn't altogether sure she wanted to keep her lunch date with Thorn. The conflict might become as volatile as the one between the Hamptons.

Despite this fiasco with the Hamptons, Amanda was convinced that Velma's gossip was accurate. Bobbie Sue *had* been fooling around with Will Bloom. That was a given. Whether Buddy had previous knowledge of the trysts, Amanda couldn't say. Buddy could have been bluffing—could have concealed his crime of passion from his wife and Amanda. He could have confronted Will Bloom and struck out in jealous fury. He could have covered the crime by staging what appeared to be an accident. And now that Amanda was suspicious, Buddy could be pretending outrage.

How many times, Amanda asked herself, had criminals accused of wrongdoing vehemently denied the accusations—and then later been indicted? These days, the guilty rarely confessed. Their defense lawyers wouldn't permit it. Heaven forbid that attorneys miss the golden opportunity to collect their enormous fees rather than saving taxpayers' money.

Amanda, having served jury duty, had several ideas as to how to correct the faulty judicial system. Furthermore, watching one day of senatorial hearings and the Simpson trial was incentive enough to make necessary changes!

Before Amanda got sidetracked by all the hypocrisy and injustice in the world, she focused her thoughts on the Hamptons. True, Buddy could have confronted Will and lashed out in a fit of temper. Also true, Bobbie Sue could have been so desperate to ensure Will's silence— when he became a threat to her lifestyle—that she did away with him. She could have left a trail of misleading clues behind her, just in case someone became suspicious.

The same motivation that might have prompted the Greens to take drastic actions against Bloom could have seized either of the Hamptons. At the moment Amanda couldn't decide which couple was the most likely to commit murder. But, since one clue seemed to open a whole new can of worms, Amanda vowed to reserve judgment until she had gleaned more facts.

She had another possible suspect to interrogate. Who Jayme Black was, and what connection she had with Bloom, Amanda didn't know—yet.

Amanda revved up her Toyota and buzzed off in a cloud of dust. She would have to wait until after lunch to dig up background information on Jayme Black. Amanda had fifteen minutes to drive home, load Pops and his walker in the car, and get back to town to meet the Thorn brothers at the café.

Amanda drove home with her fingers crossed, hoping Buddy Hampton had been unable to reach Thorn by phone. If Thorn discovered that she had been scaring up facts, against his orders, lunch was going to be anything but pleasant.

The Last Chance's greasy hamburgers weren't easy to digest, as it was. They were a conscientious cholesterol-counter's nightmare.

Amanda made a mental note to restock her supply of Rolaids before she arrived at the café—just in case Thorn had it in mind to chew on *her.*

Six

Nick Thorn wrapped the bandage around his right arm in angry jerks. Muttering an oath, he rammed his fist through the sling dangling around his neck. The call he had received from Buddy Hampton had him smoldering. Buddy had yelled into the phone in such a booming voice that Nick's ear was still ringing.

Damn it to hell, Nick fumed. He wished Hazard would do as she was told just once. But no, she had forged ahead with an investigation, leaping to ill-founded conclusions like a crazed jackrabbit, upsetting Buddy Hampton to no end.

From what Nick had been able to ascertain from Buddy's ranting and raving, Hazard had accused one or both Hamptons of murdering Will Bloom. Buddy also claimed Hazard had all but destroyed his marriage. For sure and certain, Hazard had put the Hamptons in extreme turmoil.

Although Nick was sure Bloom's death had not been accidental, he had focused his time and efforts on organizing a sting, hoping to break up the drug ring. Hazard, on the other hand, had plunged headfirst into a murder investigation. Knowing Hazard—and he had come to know her exceptionally well—she had made a beeline to Velma's Beauty Boutique to gather gossip that might provide a few *hair*-brained leads.

Nick didn't have the slightest idea what connection Buddy or Bobbie Sue might have with Will Bloom. He didn't have time to find out, either. He was committed to this covert operation. What he didn't need was Hazard stirring up Vamoosians and pointing accusing fingers at possible suspects. Nick wanted the drug cartel to think this sleepy little town was oblivious to the undercurrent of activity that involved Bloom. Nick desperately needed the element of surprise to ensure success. Hazard had botched up his plans—royally! She was forcing him to take drastic measures.

Richard Thorn poked his head around the bedroom door. "Are you ready, Nick?"

Nick gave a curt nod and spun around. "As a matter of fact, I'm in the perfect frame of mind to lay into Hazard."

Rich appraised the annoyed expression stamped on his brother's face. "Did something happen that I need to know about?"

"Hazard has been up to her old tricks," Nick grumbled as he brushed past his brother. "She has been questioning Buddy and Bobbie Sue Hampton. Buddy called and yelled at me over the phone for letting the human bulldozer conduct an investigation and accuse him of something he insists he didn't do."

Rich frowned pensively. "The Hamptons? Do I know them?"

Nick nodded affirmatively. "Bobbie Sue married Buddy Hampton, right out of high school," he prompted. "Her sister, Billie Jean, took off for Nashville to find fame and fortune—and did. But it was Bobbie Sue who had the better voice. I think Buddy secretly believes he held Bobbie Sue back. He's been running himself ragged for years, trying to compensate by building a horse empire. Even though he always claims Bobbie Sue tries to compete with her sister's social status, I think he wants Bobbie Sue to live in grand style so she won't have any regrets about marrying him instead of pursuing a professional singing career."

"What's all that got to do with Bloom's murder?" Rich inquired as they strode off the front porch.

"Damned if I know. But the Hamptons must have been mixed up with Bloom, or Hazard wouldn't have been poking around their ranch."

Rich steered Nick toward the passenger-side of the black pickup. "Better let me drive. You're supposed to be injured, you know." Rich slid onto the seat and then glanced somberly at his brother. "Hazard could be on the right track. The drug trafficking and Will's murder might not be related. It bothers the hell out of me that the body was dragged into the corral to stage an accident. It sounds like something someone who is familiar with farming practices would do, not a professional hit man. We have to keep in mind that, if Mr. Big is involved, he considers Bloom's demise an inconvenience."

"I'm as aware of that as you are, so you don't need to keep reminding me." Nick adjusted his sling and settled himself on the seat. "But I would have preferred to conduct this murder investigation after we deal with the drug cartel. Hazard is making waves we don't need right now."

"Have you devised a way to stop her?"

Nick watched the fence posts fly past the side window of the truck as Rich sped toward town. "You can't stop a runaway train, Rich. All you can do is derail her and put her in an emotional tailspin."

"I expect the scene at the Last Chance Cafe is going to get really ugly," Rich predicted. "Are you going to use Nancy Shore in this, too?"

Nick expelled an audible sigh. "I may have to go for the full effect if Hazard doesn't cooperate."

Rich turned onto the highway and headed toward the café. "Well, little brother, here goes nothing."

No, Nick thought as they cruised into Vamoose, *here goes* everything.

"Wait!" Pops erupted as Amanda backed out of the gravel driveway of her home. "I forgot my teeth!"

Amanda calmly shifted into drive and returned to the house. Pops was forever forgetting his teeth. It had become a common occurrence. "Where did you leave your dentures this time?"

Pops frowned. "I don't remember. I took them out after breakfast, before I went down to the workshop. They may be in the bedroom."

Five minutes later, Amanda plunked down into her compact car and then handed over the dentures, wrapped in a paper towel. Pops's teeth had not been in the bedroom. They had been left in a coffee cup beside the bathroom sink, soaking in Polident.

"Thanks, Half Pint," Pops smiled, toothless. "It's hell getting old. You can't see as well as you used to, you can't hear a damned thing and you can't remember anything."

"I doubt very seriously that you'll ever forget Mother," Amanda teased as she sped off.

"It still amazes me that you turned out as well as you did, what with your mother ruling the roost."

Pops removed his hat—which scraped against the low-slung headliner of the compact car—and glanced at Amanda. "So, tell me about this boyfriend of yours. The chief of police, right?"

Amanda nodded her head. "Nick Thorn looks like Tom Selleck with the mustache—"

"Who?"

"Never mind. And he acts like Andy of 'Mayberry, RFD.'"

That was something Pops could associate with.

"Countrified and laid-back, is he? Thorn sounds like my kind of man."

He was definitely Amanda's kind of man, except that he had shrugged off her suspicions of possible murder—again. Amanda had originally intended to draw Thorn aside during lunch and discuss the Bloom case. If Buddy Hampton had bent Thorn's ear, Amanda would just as soon not mention Bloom's name.

Thankfully, Pops and Rich would be on hand to serve as buffers.

If all went well, the foursome could enjoy lunch. Afterward, Amanda planned to question other individuals who could confirm or refute the Hamptons' and Greens' claims that they were nowhere near Bloom Farm at the time of the fatal incident. Amanda also intended to pursue the lead Bobbie Sue had tossed out. It could be, however, that Bobbie Sue had only served up Jayme Black's name to give herself some breathing space.

"Pull into this quick-stop shop, will you?" Pops requested, jolting Amanda from her pensive musings.

Amanda switched on her blinker and veered off the highway to Toot 'N' Tell 'Em.

"I spilled my bottle of glue this morning," Pops explained. "I need more so I can secure the carved legs to the tabletop I've been working on."

"The glue will cost double here," Amanda protested. "If you can wait until—"

Pops waved her off. "I need the glue this afternoon. Besides, I'll have money to burn after I win the American Giveaway Sweepstakes."

Amanda rolled her eyes as she climbed from the car to purchase the glue. Poor Pops needed a reality check, she thought, if he expected some famous celebrity would arrive on the doorstep to deliver a million bucks. He might as well be expecting a visit from the tooth fairy!

Nick's nerves were twitching, making him as jumpy as a cricket. Ensconced in his customary corner booth—beside his brother—Nick checked his watch at frequent intervals.

Hazard was five minutes late. Hazard was almost never late. She was the most punctual female he knew.

"Relax," Rich murmured as he watched Nick squirm on the padded vinyl seat. "This will be over soon, and you can give your complete attention to this assignment."

Nick opened his mouth to respond, but no words came out. He caught sight of Hazard sailing through the café door. Her hair was so damned short that she looked like a fairy! All that glorious blond hair that he loved to comb his fingers through was gone!

Nick silently seethed as he watched Hazard hold open

the door for her grandfather, who propelled himself
along on an aluminum walker. Nick wanted to bolt from
the booth and strangle Hazard on the spot—for what she
had done to her hair, for gleaning gossip at the beauty
shop and causing a domestic disturbance at Hampton
Ranch. She was causing problems Nick didn't need, not
when he was organizing the drug bust of the century.

As the twosome weaved around the tables of the
crowded cafe, Nick felt his blood pressure and temper
rising. He wouldn't have to pretend to be annoyed with
Hazard. Hell, he *was* annoyed, and he was going to give
her the full benefit of his temper!

Once and for all, Nick was going to break this particular amateur sleuth of investigating criminal cases that
were none of her business. Why couldn't she stick to
accounting and leave the detective work to the pros?

"I would like you to meet my grandfather, Floyd Hazard—better known as Pops," Amanda introduced as she
halted by the booth. "Pops, this is Nick Thorn."

"Pops," Nick said, hitching his thumb toward his
brother. "This is Richard."

Pops adjusted his spectacles and frowned disapprov-
ingly at Nick's scraggly appearance. "You're Vamoose's
chief of police? Don't you ever shave or clip your hair?
You look like a vagrant, not a cop."

"Pops!" Amanda gasped. "Thorn has been injured.
I'm sure he would have spiffed himself up if he had felt
up to it, wouldn't you, Thorn?"

"Why should I spruce up for a girlfriend who wears
a burr?" Nick snorted, eyeing her hair with blatant disgust. "You did it, didn't you, Hazard? You tramped off
to gather gossip at the beauty shop, after I specifically

told you not to get involved in what turned out to be a nonexistent case."

Hazard glowered at him. Nick glowered back.

"The price you paid for sticking your head in places it didn't belong was a scalping," Nick muttered sourly. "When the hell are you going to curb these investigative tendencies of yours?"

"Thorn," Amanda gritted out, "lower your voice."

"Why should I grant your requests when you ignore mine?" he tossed back at her. "Tell me, right here and now, that you will back off. And you better mean it, Hazard. I've already gotten one phone call from an irate citizen who voiced complaints about you. I don't want to receive more of them."

While Amanda stood there, staring at him as if he had gone insane—right before her very eyes—Nick did what he had to do. He rammed the knife a little deeper and made a spectacle of himself in front of the patrons of the café.

"Well, Hazard? Do I have your solemn promise that you're going to do exactly what I tell you, when I tell you to do it? I do not intend to become the laughing-stock of Vamoose, henpecked by a headstrong girlfriend. I want to know who is going to wear the pants in this relationship and I want to know now!"

People were starting to stare, just as Nick intended they would.

"Thorn, there are things about the incident in question that you don't know," Amanda tried to explain in a quiet voice.

"Yes or no, Hazard," Nick growled.

By that time, every head in the café had turned in synchronized rhythm to watch and listen to the argument that had broken out in the corner booth. Nick was aware that he had everybody's attention. That was the whole idea.

He also knew that Hazard was positively furious with him for lashing out at her in public. Nick inhaled a deep breath and forged ahead to ensure Hazard didn't wind up like Diana. He was willing to say and do anything to save Hazard's lovely hide.

"Yes or no, Hazard," he repeated gruffly. "Are you going to back off or are we through?"

Her blue eyes flared like propane torches. "No," she hissed like a disturbed cat.

"No, what?" he pressed her relentlessly. "No, you and I aren't going to become history or no, you aren't going to back off?"

"No, I'm not going to back off."

Nick scooted off the seat to stand toe-to-toe and eye-to-eye with Hazard. "Then it's over. We're finished. You can see who you want and I plan to do the same. This is it, Hazard. We're officially through, do you hear me?"

Who couldn't? His voice resounded around the suddenly quiet restaurant like a sonic boom. Nick glanced sideways, noting the shock and disbelief on every face. He looked like hell and he was behaving like an ass. Everybody thought he was as crazy as Hazard thought he was.

"You always considered yourself too high-class for the likes of me, haven't you?" he continued—loudly. "You don't have one shred of respect for my wishes or requests, if they don't coincide with yours. I'm not wasting any more of my time on you. It was a mistake from the beginning."

Nick wheeled away, because he couldn't bear to spend another second staring at Hazard's stricken expression and peaked face—surrounded by sheared hair. He had humiliated Hazard in front of an audience of friends and clients. He had treated her worse than her ex-husband had. She was fighting back the shiny tears that clouded her eyes, and Nick knew he had to make his grand exit before his firm resolve melted.

"I've got a wheat crop to plant with this maimed arm, and I have to take a leave of absence from the police beat until I mend. To make matters worse I have to deal with you. Thanks for nothing, Hazard. Good bye—*FOREVER!*"

Without daring to look back, Nick stormed toward the door. He continued to stare straight ahead, cradling his bandaged arm against his chest—one that felt as if it were about to cave in on him. "Come on, Rich, let's get back to work. I've lost my appetite."

I did what I had to do, Nick chanted as he stalked toward his pickup. *At least now Hazard has a good chance of survival. This is better than having her planted six feet under.*

Rich eased into the cab of the truck to crank the ignition. The engine growled to life, breaking the silence. "You okay, Nick?"

"Take me out to Bloom Farm," Nick scowled. "I'll relieve Roger from duty so he can get some rest."

"I don't think—"

"You don't have to think, damn it, just do what the hell I tell you. You're starting to remind me of Hazard, and that's the last thing I need right now."

Rich shifted gears and sped off, listening to Nick's muffled string of curses.

* * *

Amanda forced herself to breathe. She felt as if someone had rammed a doubled fist clear through her solar plexus. The mist of tears stinging her eyes made it impossible to see anything but the foggy blur of faces staring at her. When Pops's fingers folded around her forearm to steer her toward the door, she went without protest.

A chorus of voices offered consolation as she exited from the restaurant.

Amanda had never been so mortified in all her life. Thorn had done the inexcusable, curse his miserable, scraggly-looking hide. He had disgraced her in front of a café teeming with business clients and friends. The insensitive creep!

"The sorry son of a bitch," Pops muttered as he guided Amanda toward the passenger door of her car. "I don't know what the hell you saw in that scroungy-looking bastard in the first place. I hate to admit it, Half Pint, but your mother might be right. The man isn't good enough for you. You're better off without him."

That was the truth, Amanda thought as Pops crammed her into the Toyota. Not only had Thorn thrown his tantrum in front of dozens of Vamoosians who would carry the tale far and wide, but he had outraged her grandfather. Pops didn't know what to make of the shaggy, unshaven maniac he had met. Neither did Amanda.

The Thorn she had encountered was as easily provoked and emotionally unstable as Georgina Green. They both belonged in a loony bin.

When the car door whined shut, Amanda's dam of tears burst loose like flood waters. She bawled her head off, and there wasn't a Kleenex within reach.

"Give me the keys," Pops insisted.

Amanda handed over the keys without a second thought. She didn't realize her mistake until she heard the blaring horns beside—and in front of them—on the street.

"What's the matter with these people?" Pops scowled as he swerved sideways, slinging Amanda against the door. "Don't they know I need to get over to the outside lane?"

Amanda's only response was another outburst of tears.

"Here." Pops thrust his handkerchief at Amanda.

Another horn blared when the Toyota's right front tire hopped the curb.

"Switch on y-your"—hiccup, sob "—emergency b-blinkers." Sniffle, snort.

"Why?" Props questioned, taking his eyes off the road. Big mistake!

The car bounced over the curb—again. Pops jerked the wheel sideways and the Toyota thumped back onto the street where it belonged.

"The way you d-drive you'll k-kill somebody. P-put on the b-blinkers!"

While Amanda reduced herself to another round of tears, Pops fiddled with the buttons and knobs on the dashboard. The windshield wipers scraped and flapped and the headlights winked at oncoming motorists, but Pops couldn't locate the emergency lights.

"Damned newfangled cars . . . whoa!"

Amanda glanced up from her hankie to see that Pops had tried to adjust the seat to give himself more leg room. He had grabbed the wrong latch. The back of the seat had plunged downward, leaving Pops stretched out, staring up at the ceiling. Amanda lunged toward the steering wheel before the Toyota crashed into an oncoming vehicle. Horns blasted in protest.

A siren screamed as Amanda steered the car toward the grassy shoulder of the narrow pavement. She managed to get her foot on the brake before the car slammed into the sign that read: If you like it country style, then Vamoose.

Through blurred eyes Amanda saw Deputy Sykes—the temporary chief of Vamoose police department—hop from his squad car and dash toward her. Benny Sykes whipped off his mirrored sunglasses and gaped at Pops, who was still laid out on the collapsed seat.

"Amanda? What the devil is going on here? You were nearly involved in four wrecks before you reached the city limits."

"Pops accidentally adjusted the seat," Amanda explained through muffled sobs. "Help me get him into an upright position, Benny."

"Upright," Benny repeated automatically. He opened the door and levered Pops up where he belonged. When Benny tried to bring the back of the seat into proper driving position the headrest slapped Pops in the neck.

"Watch what you're doing!" Pops yelped. "I'm not as young and flexible as I used to be, you know."

"Right," Benny mumbled as he flicked off the windshield wipers. "Why don't you let me drive you and Amanda home in the squad car."

"I can drive just fine," Pops said indignantly.

"Just fine?" Benny repeated dubiously. "You were all over the road—"

The crackle of the two-way radio demanded Benny's attention. "Hold on, Pops, I'll be right back."

When Benny trotted off, Amanda slid from the seat

to remove Pops from his position beneath the steering wheel. He had proved to be a hazard to himself and all of Vamoose. Amanda decided that under no circumstances would she ever let Pops in the driver's seat again.

By the time Benny had taken the dispatcher's call, Amanda had shepherded Pops into the passenger seat and situated herself behind the wheel. Benny scuttled forward, looking sickeningly sympathetic. From all indication, news of Thorn's harsh rejection had spread through Vamoose like wildfire.

"I just heard the bad news, Amanda," Benny said as he propped his forearms against the side of the car. "I'm sure the chief didn't mean all the rotten things he said to you. And I don't think your hairdo is all that bad. A little short for my taste, maybe, but hey, it'll grow out."

All Amanda could manage was a nod of her clipped head. She couldn't risk speaking for fear she'd break into tears again.

"Thorn is just a little testy right now, is all," Benny defended his boss. "He cut up his arm, right smack dab in the middle of the busiest part of wheat planting season. He can't even handle patrol, you know. I'm sure he's just feeling angry, frustrated and helpless."

Well, join the club, Thorn, Amanda silently invited. *You ain't the only one!*

"When he has time to sit down and think it over," Benny continued, "I'm sure he'll be real sorry about the unfortunate scene at the Last Chance."

Amanda didn't think Thorn was sorry at all. She was never going to forgive him for what he'd done, even if he got down on his knees and begged and screamed and pleaded for her to take him back. They were finished— forever!

"Are you sure you don't want me to drive you home, Amanda?" Deputy Sykes persisted.

Amanda shook her head and shifted into drive, forcing Benny to back away.

"I'll give you a police escort, just in case," he called to her.

With lights flashing and sirens whining, Benny led the way to Amanda's rented farm. All the way home she cursed Nick Thorn up one side and down the other.

Just because he was having a bad day was no reason to take it out on her. The superficial, male chauvinistic louse, she thought bitterly. Thorn had hit the ceiling, all because of her horrible hairdo and her insistence on a murder investigation.

Amanda wouldn't have dumped Thorn just because he shaved *his* head. Thorn had no right whatsoever to bully her into promising to butt out of Bloom's case. *She* had only been doing what *he* should have been doing. Amanda had been on a noble search for truth and justice, and Thorn should have thanked her for it. Instead, he had raked her over hot, flaming coals—in front of everybody! She'd like to kill him.

Of course, bullheaded as Thorn was, he would probably claim his *own* death was an accident, Amanda silently fumed.

"I'll fix lunch," Pops volunteered as he and his aluminum walker clomped up the steps. "Go wash your face, Half Pint."

When the phone jingled, Amanda halted on her way down the hall and then reversed direction.

"Heartbreak hotel," she muttered in greeting.

"Amanda? I'm really sorry!" came the wobbly voice on the other end of the line. "Like, I never dreamed

Officer Thorn would go bonkers over your haircut. I didn't mean to ruin your life!"

Amanda found herself consoling the sobbing Beverly Hill. She also had to lie and say she loved her new do. "You haven't ruined my life, Bev. I love my hair, even if Thorn doesn't. I don't know what I saw in that jerk in the first place."

"Like, the whole town has gone crazy," Bev babbled. "Bobbie Sue Hampton was in here awhile ago, blubbering all over herself, because Buddy packed his clothes and moved into the stables.

"Like, I couldn't even cut Bobbie Sue's hair. She was worming and squirming in the chair, reaching for Kleenexes to mop up her tears. And now this thing with you and Thorn!"

Amanda felt a twinge of guilt—for all of five seconds. She reminded herself that one or both of the Hamptons could have been involved in a murder. If Bobbie Sue was crying buckets of tears, it probably served her right. The woman had cheated on her husband, after all.

"Deputy Sykes had to drive out to the ranch to disarm Buddy," Bev went on to say. "Buddy was shooting holes in the stables with his shotgun. His prize horses broke out of the stalls and scattered along Whatsit River. And then Georgina Green went berserk right before lunch."

"Georgina?" Amanda questioned.

"Yeah, like, one of her neighbors found her wandering down the street in her nightgown. Somebody said they thought she had been sniffing so much cooking spray that she didn't know who or where she was. Her neighbor found three cans of Pam on the kitchen counter—all empty."

High on Pam? Amanda frowned. She wondered if perhaps Georgina's guilty conscience had been eating her alive, making her wring her hands and shriek in near hysterics. Obviously Georgina had been under a lot of pressure, because of her secret fling with Will Bloom and the possibility of a scandal ruining Daniel's race for a senate seat.

If Georgina had clubbed Bloom over the head and dragged him through the dirt, before he could drag her name through the dirt, Georgina was carrying around a ton of guilt and it had gotten to her—big time. The crazy redhead must have decided to end it all.

Amanda wondered if Georgina realized that this incident would draw even more attention to her, rather than less. Probably not. The woman's brain cells were so coated with Pam that nothing—not even good sense—could stick to them.

"Like, I gotta go," Bev said. "I have another appointment in ten minutes and I have to redo my makeup. Aunt Velma says to tell you she's real sorry about what happened, too. Your next haircut will be on the house."

Amanda hung up the phone, thinking she wouldn't be needing a haircut for months to come. She wheeled toward the bathroom to wash her face and dry her tears, muttering one last curse at Thorn's name.

Thorn had made her ex-husband look like a crown prince in comparison. Right there and then, Amanda promised never to let Nick Thorn's tormenting memory intrude into her thoughts again. The good thing they once had going wasn't just history, it was a damned antique!

Seven

Determined to prove to Thorn—and everybody else—that the fiasco at the Last Chance Cafe hadn't fazed her, Amanda made a conscious effort to get on with her life. After playing phone tag for a few days, Jim Johnson, the land man from Petro Fuel Company, had finally contacted her at the office and invited her to lunch. As it turned out, Jim Johnson was no Thorn—and for that Amanda was grateful.

Amanda had taken off from work an hour early, intent on learning what the horse trainer at Hampton Ranch had to say about his employer. She drove slowly around Hampton Ranch, checking to see if Buddy and/or Bobbie Sue were home. Since the fancy crew cab truck and Caddy weren't in the driveway, Amanda headed for the stables.

She noted the new ventilation holes blasted in the tin and recalled what Bev Hill had said about Buddy going on a shooting spree with his shotgun. Buddy Hampton had an explosive temper. Amanda could easily imagine him—his weathered face aflame—having it out with Will Bloom. He had certainly let loose on Amanda with both barrels!

Dressed in the practical attire of Western clothes and boots, Amanda walked down the freshly cleaned aisle between stalls occupied by blooded horses. She noticed a pyramid of hay lined against the west wall, stacked in the same fashion as the bales in Bloom's barn. Glancing this way and that, Amanda searched for Haden LaFoe, but she found only horses of various sizes and colors.

"Haden! Are you here?" Amanda called to the barn at large.

"Outside!"

Amanda proceeded through the south end of the barn and approached the corrals. Haden, a wiry little man on the back side of forty, was putting an Appaloosa mare through a rigorous training program. A buckskin quarter horse had been saddled and left beside the gate. The animal stamped restlessly and crunched on its bit. Amanda gave the buckskin a wide berth, since the only kind of horse she had ridden were the ones on a carousel—with poles stuck through the middles of their fiberglass torsos.

"Haden, can I talk to you for a minute?" Amanda shouted over the pounding of hooves.

"Sure thing, Amanda. Take a seat on the buckskin and come join me. Since Buddy has been spending so much time at Pronto Bar and Grill, we're getting farther behind on exercising the livestock."

Amanda glanced warily at the buckskin and then focused on the skilled horseman who made the Appaloosa mare dance like a puppet at the end of the reins. *How hard can it be to ride?* she asked herself. *Since Haden made it look easy, it probably is.*

In determined strides, Amanda sallied forth to make the buckskin's acquaintance. The horse jerked up its head, its nostrils flaring at her unfamiliar scent.

"What? You don't like my perfume? Well, tough. I'm not too crazy about your fragrance, either."

The horse stamped a hind leg and tossed its head sideways, studying her with big brown eyes. Amanda marshaled her courage and grabbed the reins. Thinking hard and fast, she tried to remember which side of a horse John Wayne climbed onto in all his western movies.

The left, Amanda decided a moment later.

Wrapping her fist around the saddle horn, Amanda stuffed her boot in the stirrup. The buckskin sidled sideways when Amanda accidentally jabbed the horse in the flank.

"Whoa!" Amanda demanded in her most authoritative tone.

The buckskin did not whoa. Amanda hopped around on one leg, trying to maintain her balance.

The ornery horse all but laughed at her. The horse was beginning to remind her of Thorn—from the rear end.

Gritting her teeth, Amanda sprang upward, hauling herself into the saddle. The buckskin turned three tight circles while Amanda scrambled to seat herself in an upright position.

Immensely proud of herself, she reined toward the pasture where Haden LaFoe was putting the Appy through its paces.

"Kick him out and let him expend all that nervous energy," Haden instructed Amanda. "He'll settle down and behave himself after he's stretched his legs."

Amanda nodded and then dug her heels into the buckskin's ribs. The horse gathered itself and exploded forward. Amanda's head snapped backward when the horse shot off like a rocket. Her bottom smacked against the saddle, matching the thud of the pounding hooves beneath her.

For the space of a minute, she and the buckskin flew across the pasture with the rush of wind surging past them. Amanda held on for dear life, knowing she was about to be catapulted headlong onto the grass. Each time she bounced sideways on the saddle, the horse broke stride, making it even more difficult for Amanda to maintain her balance.

"Hey! I said to kick him out, not put him in a dead run . . . Watch out for that—"

THUNK . . .

"Tree limb," Haden finished a second too late.

Amanda never saw it coming. She had been focused on the horse beneath her. The low-hanging limb slapped her across the shoulder, tilting her farther off-balance. Amanda screamed bloody murder when she slid off the side of the galloping horse like a trick rider. In panic, Amanda threw one arm around the horse's neck and put a death grip on the reins.

The buckskin, tiring of its frantic pace, circled toward the Appaloosa and its trainer.

Haden eyed Amanda curiously as she bobbled in the saddle like a buoy. "Have you ridden very much?"

"No," Amanda croaked. "It's my first time."

"Well, why the hell didn't you say so," Haden hooted. "You could have gotten yourself hurt!"

"I wanted to ask you some questions," Amanda said, trying to emulate the ease with which Haden rode.

"You certainly got Buddy and Bobbie Sue stewed up the last time you came around asking questions," Haden said. "The two of them haven't been getting along very well lately, but now it's worse. Deputy Sykes told Buddy that he'd haul him to jail if there was another report of this place being shot all to hell."

"I need to know where Buddy and Bobbie Sue were the day Will Bloom died," Amanda requested.

"Is that what this is all about?" Haden questioned. "Well shoot, I wondered what was eating on Buddy. He's been so moody and distracted that everything I say goes in one ear and out the other."

"Is that so." Amanda murmured, trying to settle into a confident position that would leave the impression that she was in control.

The horse, she was sorry to report, did not seem that confident of her abilities. Amanda kept sliding around on the saddle, as if she had buttered buns, and the buckskin kept flinging its head and prancing sideways, making matters worse.

"Yep," Haden confirmed. "Buddy and I were exercising the horses a couple of weeks ago, when Bobbie Sue hopped in her car and drove off. Without a word of explanation, Buddy dismounted, jumped in his truck, and took off. It was as if he was planning to follow her, ya know?"

Amanda wondered where the trip had taken Buddy. To Bloom Farm perhaps?

"After that day, Buddy stamped and sulked around the stables. He hardly said a word to anybody, at least not any words I care to repeat. Then early one morning last week—"

"Which morning last week?" Amanda demanded.

Haden shrugged his thin-bladed shoulders. "Hell, I can't remember which one. Every day around here is pretty much like the next. We feed the horses, load some of them in the trailer, and drive to the racetrack. Then we come back to exercise the rest of the horses. I haven't had Sunday off since I can't remember when.

"Buddy has been driving off in his truck from time to time," Haden continued. "I don't know where he goes, but he comes back scowling and puffing on his cigar."

Amanda gave up trying to pin Haden down to a specific day. Clearly, he didn't remember the date of Bobbie Sue's disappearance and Buddy's stakeout.

"Anyhow," Haden continued, "Buddy wasn't gone very long the last time he followed Bobbie Sue. When he came back, it was as if he was relieved about something that had been bothering him, ya know?"

Amanda could guess why Buddy might have seemed relieved to have Will Bloom out of the way—permanently.

"Buddy was his old self for a few days . . . until you showed up." Haden shot her a dubious glance. "Now he's up to ten cigars a day and his disposition festers like a boil. He beds down in the stables with me, after he staggers in from a drunk. The man has gone all to hell. Sort of like Thorn."

Haden halted the big Appaloosa and then eyed Amanda speculatively. "You seem to have a strange effect on men. I'm not going to flip out after I'm through talking to you, am I?"

Amanda did something she hadn't done in years. She smiled with premeditated charm, blinding the veteran cowboy.

"You're perfectly safe, Haden. It's only the mental fruitcakes of this world who suffer strong, allergic reactions to me."

Haden grinned in response, displaying the gap between his front teeth. "Buddy has sure been acting like a fruitcake. It's as if somebody pulled the rug out from under him and he can't get his bearings. He's always been nuts over Bobbie Sue. Now that they've split up, he's lost all sense of direction, ya know?"

When Haden gouged his horse and trotted off, Amanda fought to control the buckskin. Left with no choice, she allowed the horse to chase after Haden. The two horses loped alongside one another for five minutes before Haden reined toward the corral.

While Haden held her horse, Amanda swung from the saddle. Her legs nearly folded up like lawn chairs when her feet touched solid ground.

"Steady, cowgirl," Haden said with a chuckle. "The next time you decide to go charging off on a horse, come see me first. You could use some riding lessons."

Amanda nodded mutely and then wobbled toward her car.

"Between you and me, I think Thorn made the biggest mistake of his life when he cut you loose," Haden called after her. "He and Buddy should both be committed."

Amanda appreciated Haden's support. She also wondered if Buddy Hampton might find himself commit-ted—to a penitentiary.

According to Haden, Buddy had come and gone from the ranch on several occasions, giving himself ample time to do Will Bloom in. The fact that Buddy had re-turned home "relieved" made Amanda highly suspicious. It sounded as though Buddy had found a way to resolve the turmoil in his life.

"We finally hit pay dirt."

Nick jerked himself from his pensive brooding to see

Roger Proctor hunkered over the monitor in the shed that served as surveillance headquarters. Nick bounded from his chair, staring at the monitor that glowed in the darkness.

Although Nick had insisted Roger return to the farm to rest, the agent refused to leave. Nick suspected his brother had filled Roger in on the fiasco at the Last Chance Cafe and requested the agent keep Nick company.

"Two subjects in a flatbed truck are pulling up to the barn," Roger reported.

"Switch on the audio devices in the barn," Nick requested.

The flick of a switch left the hum of a motor echoing around the cinder block shed. With his gaze focused intensely on the monitor, Nick plucked up the handheld CB to contact his brother.

"Robin Hood, come in."

"I read you, Jack-Be-Nimble. Over."

"Send your band of merry men an invitation for a late-night dinner."

"You want me to send them over to your palace?" Rich came back.

"No, just put them on guard duty," Nick requested.

"Do you already have company?"

"Nottingham's men have arrived," Nick confirmed. "All their protective armor will be stacked high in an hour. We'll escort our guests to their destination. It's the hospitable thing to do."

"I'll see to it that my band from Sherwood Forest spiffy up by taking a swim in the river, before they saddle up and ride."

"I'll keep in touch, Robin Hood."

When Rich signed off to place the call to the special agent forces, Nick turned his attention back to the monitor. The two subjects—one Caucasian and one Latino—pulled on their leather gloves and went to work. They spoke not a word, emitting only grunts and groans as they hoisted the hay bales onto the truck.

"Zoom in and print," Nick requested.

Typing the command, Roger keyed on both subjects and copied the picture. Seconds later, the printer spit out a fuzzy likeness of the two men in Bloom's barn. Nick snatched up the print and headed for the door.

"Where are you going?" Roger called after him.

"I'm going to tail the new arrivals, just in case they don't turn south toward Texas, as we predicted. Rich's agents will be waiting near the river, and I'm going to make double damned certain we don't lose them."

"Do you have a CB in your truck?"

"Yeah, I can contact Rich if I need to. You keep the handheld to contact both of us. Get as many prints of the truck load of hay and the subjects as you can."

"Don't worry, Nick, this report and the photos are going to look like a detailed diary by the time we get this drug ring to court. I'll have evidence galore."

Nick thrashed through the tall weeds and burrs to reach the truck he had parked in the row of cedars. Without switching on the headlights, he drove along the pasture fence and then waited for the hay truck to emerge from the barn. Forty-five minutes later the old model farm truck cruised toward town. When the subjects continued east rather than turning south toward the river, Nick contacted his brother to alert the agents to the alternate route.

When the special teams picked up the tail east of Vamoose, Nick sped back to his farm home to monitor the traffickers' activities. To his surprise, the truck was reported to have entered a darkened warehouse in the City—the same warehouse where Manuel Pico supposedly worked.

"Who would have thought Uni-Comp made computer supplies from straw," Richard Thorn smirked. "The company must not be as legitimate as its president and board of directors would like us to think."

Nick listened to the report on the activities taking place on the first and second floors of the warehouse. "I'd say this drug ring is one helluvan intricate operation. The submarine goods are obviously being trucked to Bloom Farm from the mill in Rawhide, Texas—under the direction of main operations in Longhorn. The drugs are hauled to the City warehouse, probably for final processing and distribution on the street."

"Did Roger track this Manuel Pico character down?" Rich asked. "Does he have a record of previous arrests?"

Nick shook his head. "Pico must be an illegal alien. The bureau has no information on him. Apparently he has been working with fake IDs."

Rich glanced grimly at Nick. "Either that or Pico moonlights as a hit man for the cartel and is flown in and out of the country using false identification to make him look as clean as new-fallen snow. Do you think Pico might be the one who took Bloom out?"

Nick shrugged a broad shoulder. "I don't have a clue where Manuel Pico fits in. He may be no more than a drug mule like Bloom. And then again, he may work cheap when the big boss needs a favor."

"Or maybe Hazard is on the right track," Rich said. "I'm still not convinced that one incident has anything to do with the other. Too bad you couldn't let your ex-girlfriend remain on her unauthorized investigation to pick up a few facts. We may need some leads when this operation is over."

The mention of Hazard's name put a grimace on Nick's stubbled face. It had been four days since he had staged the scene at the Last Chance Cafe, and his conscience was still eating him alive.

Deputy Sykes had dropped by the farm to jump down Nick's throat for humiliating Hazard in front of a crowd. Nick had heard the detailed account of Pops's driving adventures and near collisions in town—and on the state highway—not to mention Hazard's distressed condition when Sykes escorted her home.

According to the deputy, Hazard had cried enough tears to fill a pond. Also according to Benny Sykes, Nick had been voted the most unpopular personality in town. The majority of Vamoosians had sided with Hazard, convinced that Nick had gone off his rocker.

His scraggly appearance provided the special effect Nick had strived to project. All of Vamoose considered Nick to be a low-down, good-for-nothing bum whose farming injury had affected more than his arm.

The fact that Nick had paraded around town with the new cashier from Toot 'N Tell 'Em confirmed the local gossip about him going to the dogs. Nancy Shore had returned from work the previous evening to report that she had been snubbed and dressed down by several senior citizens who referred to her as Vamoose's Jezebel. Being seen with Nick hadn't won Nancy any friends in the close-knit rural community.

Nick's attempt to sever all ties with Hazard had proved one hundred percent effective. He and Nancy Shore had become the local outcasts and sympathy had been pouring in for Hazard from all sides.

Except for the Hamptons and the Greens, Nick amended. They were the only people who bothered to speak to him. Nick couldn't help but wonder why.

"Nick, pay attention." Rich gouged his brother in the ribs. "You're daydreaming again."

Nick pricked his ears and listened to the static-ridden, coded message from one of Rich's OSBI associates. The unmarked tails were reportedly following the hay truck south on I-35.

Without delay, Nick snatched up the phone to alert the Texas authorities to the convoy headed in their direction. He wanted to make certain the two subjects weren't apprehended. They were going to be allowed to walk all over Texas so the agents could track and confirm the route and destination.

"I'd bet the farm that the two subjects are headed for Rawhide mill, where Bloom purchased hay and cattle cubes," Nick mused aloud.

Rich lounged on the sofa, absently raking his hands through his tousled black hair. "I still can't believe this intricate drug ring has been operating in our own hometown."

"Nobody believed Oklahoma City could become the target of a tragic bombing, either," Nick said bleakly. "It only proves that the safest, most secure locales in this country are susceptible to crime, terrorism, and organized syndicates. We've become too damned naive and trusting, thinking we're living in our own private paradise."

"Damn, Nick, you've turned into a first-rate cynic the past week," Rich noted.

"It's been a bad week," Nick said, and scowled.

The unexpected rap at the front door sent Nick and Richard scrambling to collect the files and printouts scattered on the coffee table. On his way to the front door, Nick slipped his arm into the sling and glanced over his shoulder to survey the room. Assured that the files had been stashed out of sight, Nick answered the abrupt knock.

To his surprise, he found Pops propped on his walker, a plastic bag clenched in one bony fist.

"My granddaughter collected all the belongings you left at her house. I wanted to burn them rather than return them. I almost had Amanda convinced to build a bonfire and roast your effigy in the barnyard, but her *new boyfriend*," Pops added with spiteful delight, "showed up before I could locate the matches."

New boyfriend? Nick felt as if someone had slugged him in the gut. *What new boyfriend?* he wondered. It had better not be Gib Cooper. Gib was on a stakeout, not lining up hot dates.

Glaring pitchforks, Pops thrust the bag at Nick. "Here's your stuff, Thorn. I suggest you use the razor that's in this sack to make yourself more presentable. You look like the slob you are. While you're shaving, I hope your hand slips and you slit your damned throat!"

Nick stared at the contents of the sack, noting that his favorite toothbrush—the one that said: Brush with the fuzzy end—had been returned. He sighed heavily and then glanced at the old man. "Pops, I know you think—"

"It's Floyd to you, sonny boy," Pops cut in sharply. "What you did was unforgivable."

"Look, Floyd, I want you to know that I did what had to be done. I can't explain why and I can't take a chance with your granddaughter's life. It means more to me than my own life does."

Pops snorted derisively. "You know what I think, Thorn? I think you're full of shit. I drove myself out here to tell you so, too, even if Amanda forbade me to drive anywhere. Now that I've said what I've come to say, I've got nothing more to say to you! You can go straight to hell in a handbasket, for all I care!"

Before Pops could shuffle around on his walker and hobble off, Nick blocked his path. "I'm going to tell you something that is top secret." He stared intently at the irate old man. "If you say one damned thing about this to Hazard, I'll tear your brittle bones apart with my bare hands and swear to her that you were hallucinating in your old age."

Nick's black eyes flashed as he bore down on Pops. It was plain to see the old man was intimidated by Nick's wild appearance. The reflection that greeted Nick each morning in the mirror looked barely half-civilized—even to him. He suspected he looked worse now, because Pops shuffled back a step when Nick loomed over him.

"The fact is that I had to go undercover to work an important case," he confided to Pops. "The last girl-friend I had got caught in the crossfire and died, because of her connection to me. No matter what you think, I'm making damned certain Hazard is safe and sound. I would rather have her detest the sight of me for the rest of her life than attend her funeral."

Pop's jaw sagged to his chest.

"There can be no connection between the two of us, do you understand, Floyd? This has nothing to do with bad hairdos and male-versus-female egos. It's a matter of life and death, and you better not breathe a word about this conversation to Hazard."

Pops stared at Nick for a speculative moment. "Why should I believe a lunatic like you?" he said finally.

"You think I'd break off with a class act like your granddaughter if I didn't have to? Do you think I would announce to the whole damned town that we were through, invite ridicule and gossip, just for the hell of it?

"Everybody in town needs to think Hazard and I are finished, in case the wrong people come around asking questions."

"What about that Jezebel you've been running around town with?" Pops quizzed. "Is that part of this supposed act?"

"I've already said more than I should have," Nick muttered. "I would appreciate it if you would discourage Hazard from pursuing the Bloom case. This isn't a good time for her to be prowling around Vamoose, scaring up facts."

Pops's azure eyes widened behind his thick glasses. "Holy cow," he crowed. "Is that what this is all about, the Bloom case?"

"I'm not sure," Nick answered honestly.

Pops maneuvered down the front steps and then wobbled around to peer earnestly at Nick. "Are you on the level, boy? Because if you're not—"

"He's on the level, sir," Rich interrupted as he stepped beneath the porch light, flashing his badge. "This town is crawling with undercover agents, so you better not blow this case open. Innocent people could get hurt—your granddaughter in particular. I doubt you would want to be held accountable for that."

Pops's gaze bounced back and forth between the Thorn brothers. "My lips are sealed, boys. Just let me know if you need any assistance. Nobody would suspect a crippled-up bag of bones like me to be an informant. If I see anything suspicious I'll let you know."

When Pops toddled off, Rich sighed audibly. "I hope you know what the hell you're doing. Now that you've taken the old man into your confidence, he may screw up royally."

Nick pivoted toward the house. "And then again, letting Pops know that something big is going down may spare Hazard's life."

"Let's just hope nothing goes wrong," Rich murmured. He blinked in surprise when Nick exited through the door he'd just entered. "Where the hell are you going?"

"To make sure Floyd arrives home safely. According to Deputy Sykes, Pops is positively the worst driver in the county. I don't want him and the Toyota to get wrapped around a fence post."

When Jim Johnson strode into the accounting office Friday afternoon, Amanda greeted him with a smile. The streamlined man from Petro Fuel Company was courteous, polite, clean-cut and self-controlled—everything Thorn wasn't. Jim wasn't the least bit spontaneous or impulsive—like Thorn. For that, Amanda gave Jim Johnson high marks.

Jim had restored Amanda's faith in the male gender. He hadn't come on strong, like the toothpick-sucking grease monkey at Thatcher's Oil and Gas. Jim was every bit the gracious, dignified gentleman. A little dull perhaps, but Amanda wasn't looking for serious involvement. Never again!

After introducing himself to Amanda, Jim Johnson had explained that his company wanted to drill an oil and gas well on the property Amanda had inherited from Elmer Jolly. Although Elmer's will stated that his brothers would retain mineral rights, Amanda was due payment for surface damages for the site of production. Jim also offered to pay fifty dollars a day to pipe needed water from the nearby pond.

Amanda had checked around town to ensure the offer was competitive with prices offered by other oil companies. It was.

Amanda had studied the contract carefully, finding no loopholes. When Jim dropped by the office the previous day to invite Amanda to lunch, she wondered if she had accepted only because she had seen Thorn in town with the flirtatious cashier from Toot 'N Tell 'Em.

Probably another defensive reaction, she diagnosed.

Amanda had gotten a close look at the new employee the day she had stopped in to buy Pops a new supply of glue. She had taken one look at Nancy Shore and decided the floozy ran fast and loose. Nancy winked and batted her eyelashes at every male customer, and her skintight clothes had *willing* and *available* printed all over them.

Amanda had allowed herself to be seen with Jim on a few occasions. Although Thorn had crawled into the gutter to find himself a new girlfriend, Amanda had set her standards high and wanted all of Vamoose to know it. Even when Jim excused himself from their table at the Last Chance Cafe to speak with other landowners in the area, he never left Amanda alone for more than a few minutes. Consideration was another point in Jim's favor.

Maybe it was true that she was seeing Jim on the rebound, but he filled the empty void Thorn had left in Amanda's life. The big louse!

"I stopped in to see if we might be able to have dinner in the City," Jim said as he popped a breath mint into his mouth, while easing a hip on the edge of the desk. He smiled charmingly at her. "Do you have any plans for tonight, Amanda?"

"I'm afraid so."

"With another man?" Jim asked.

"A business acquaintance," Amanda qualified.

"A male business acquaintance?"

"Female."

Appeased, Jim rose to his feet. "Maybe we can spend Saturday night together."

"That will depend on what time I finish up at Vamoose's annual flea market."

"Well then, can I at least make arrangements to pick up the oil production contract before Monday? Or will you be able to squeeze me into your busy schedule?"

"I'll make my decision about the contract by Sunday evening," Amanda promised.

"If it works out, maybe we could catch a late movie in the City—after the flea market, of course." He smiled again as he handed Amanda his telephone number. "Call me if you get tied up late on Saturday, blue eyes."

When the door eased shut, Amanda turned her attention to the tax returns on her desk. Thank goodness Jenny Long was due back in the office on Monday to type forms and take phone messages so Amanda could spend all her time and energy sorting through her list of suspects.

Thus far, Amanda had been unable to contact Jayme Black, the elusive divorcée who lived on the outskirts of town. The woman never seemed to be home. That made Amanda suspicious. Since Will Bloom had been found dead in the dirt, Jayme had made herself scarce.

Amanda had decided to quit work early so she could have a look around the run-down farmhouse Jayme Black had rented from Ab Hendershot. After Amanda had put the finishing touches on the tax report for Cecil Watts and alphabetized his file, she grabbed her purse.

The card with Jim's phone number fluttered to the floor. Amanda plucked it up, thinking she might give Jim a call to invite him to dinner—with Pop's permission, of course. Amanda certainly didn't intend to do the cooking. It simply was not her forte.

"Thank you for that, Mother," Amanda grumbled as she breezed through the door. Thorn had criticized her culinary disasters quite often the past year. Amanda was not leaving herself open to ridicule again. Even though she had no intention of getting seriously involved with Jim Johnson, the very last thing he would discover was that she was a terrible cook!

Eight

Amanda glanced cautiously around Jayme Black's farm, noting the overabundance of weeds that turned the unmowed lawn into a forest. The house, which sat a half mile off the beaten path, was nestled in a clump of cottonwood trees. A dilapidated garage, badly in need of a coat of paint, stood empty.

Parking her Toyota beside the house, Amanda hiked off to inspect the garage. To her amazement, she found several blocks of broken hay bales stacked on warped wooden shelves. Blades of straw were strewn around the entrance of the garage.

According to the information Amanda had picked up at the Last Chance Cafe, Jayme worked in the city and had no interest in farming. So what were blocks of hay doing in her garage? Had the hay come from Hampton Horse Ranch or Bloom Farm?

Amanda stared at the screened-in back porch. Weaving around the maze of weeds, Amanda hiked off to inspect Jayme's house.

Since the screen door wasn't locked, Amanda surged inside. Her nose wrinkled in disgust when she saw the trash can heaping with discarded paper sacks from fast-food restaurants. She also noted a skimpy negligee—that had seen better days—among the garbage.

Amanda twisted the knob of the door leading into the kitchen and found it unlocked. She gasped in disbelief when she stepped into the kitchen to see stacks of moldy dishes piled in, and beside, the dingy sink.

Jayme Black's home looked worse than a pigsty. Filthy didn't aptly describe the condition of the rented home. In fascinated disgust, Amanda picked her way through the dining area and living room. The floor and furniture were littered with trash. It was the most repulsive sight Amanda had ever seen.

If Ab Hendershot knew his family homestead had been abused by this uncaring tenant, Jayme would have been ousted immediately. Amanda had never seen worse living conditions, except in big-city slums.

The stale scent of smoke permeated the trash-filled hallway. Amanda came to an abrupt halt at the bedroom door. Her eyes nearly popped from their sockets as she surveyed the room. An unmade king-size waterbed sat against the north wall, which was lined with posters of nude men and women. An ashtray on the scarred end table was filled to capacity with cigarette and cigar butts. A wide-ruled notebook and pen sat beside the ashtray.

Cigars again, Amanda thought suspiciously. If she knew nothing else, she was convinced that the wet ashes she had discovered beside Bloom's sidewalk and the scent of smoke hovering in Bloom's living room were important keys to this case.

Each and every suspect connected with Bloom had access to, or smoked, stogies. Either the murderer had deliberately strewn ashes and left lingering smoke in Bloom's home, or he/she was careless in leaving clues.

Curious, Amanda tiptoed over to open the notebook. To her disappointment, there wasn't a signed confession from the murderer or a single clue that could help Amanda solve this frustrating case.

Amanda turned to leave, but something caught her eye. It looked as if someone had spilled wet clumps of baking soda or powdered sugar onto the carpet near the headboard of the bed. Amanda hated to venture a guess as to what inventive role the substances played in Jayme's perverted sexual fantasies. For sure, Jayme Black was as close to white trash as anyone could get.

Amanda made a mental note to drill Velma Hertzog and Beverly Hill full of questions during the garage sale. She definitely needed to know the scoop on Jayme.

Checking the time, Amanda switched directions to exit the house. The sound of an approaching vehicle sent her scurrying through the screened porch before she got caught trespassing. Amanda had descended the rickety steps when a beat-up bucket of rust with bad muffler pipes sped down the driveway.

Amanda manufactured a smile when a tall, skinny brunette unfolded herself from the car. Her peace treaty smile, Amanda was sorry to say, wasn't effective. Jayme Black—tattoos of butterflies on both ankles, her noticeably thin body encased in a body-hugging knit dress that barely covered her thighs—glowered at her. When Jayme half turned to slam the car door, Amanda noticed the matching hickies on each side of her neck.

"What the hell are you doing here?" Jayme demanded hatefully.

Her smile intact, Amanda ambled toward Jayme. Between the cigarette dangling from the side of Jayme's mouth and the overwhelming scent of cheap perfume, Amanda could barely draw breath.

"I knocked on your door, but no one answered."

Jayme eyed her skeptically, squinting through the curl of smoke. "What do you want?"

Amanda discreetly appraised Jayme. The young woman looked to have as many rough miles on her as the pile of metal she called a car. "I was Will Bloom's accountant and I would like to ask you a few questions about your relationship with him."

Jayme's head snapped up, overexposing her hickies. "I don't know anything about anybody named Bloom."

"Not according to the information I've received," Amanda countered.

"Oh yeah? Who the hell told you I knew Bloom?"

Jayme's defensive hostility sent Amanda's suspicions into a full-scale riot. "I'm sorry, but I am not allowed to divulge my sources. It's unethical." She wondered if Jayme Black knew the definition of the word.

"Well, you better divulge your sources, sugar," Jayme sneered as she snatched a snub-nosed pistol from her purse. "I don't take kindly to people spreading gossip about me or tramping around my place without permission."

Amanda stood perfectly still when the speaking end of the weapon targeted her chest. Jayme Black was either paranoid or crazy—maybe both.

"I only wanted to ask you a few questions," Amanda assured her.

"I don't feel like giving answers," Jayme snapped. "Get your prissy ass off my property before I call the cops."

"I just wanted to know where you were when Will Bloom died."

"I was working in the City, just like I do every day,"

Jayme replied. "Now you know what you came to find out, so take a hike."

Amanda strode toward her car, noting that the barrel of the pistol monitored every step of her retreat. The weapon remained trained on Amanda as she cautiously backed around Jayme's transportation.

When Jayme swaggered up to tap her pistol against the car window, Amanda was very much afraid the woman had decided to blow a new part in Amanda's short tuft of hair.

Hesitantly, Amanda rolled down the side window.

"Instead of snooping around here, you should be pestering Georgina Green and that big brawny cowboy," she said with a smirk.

"Big brawny cowboy?" Amanda repeated.

"That Hampton character," she clarified. "I saw him cruising past Bloom Farm a couple of times."

"I thought you said you didn't know Will Bloom."

Jayme smiled cattily around her flaming cigarette. "I just remembered who he was. Ask the cowboy what he was doing in his fancy crew cab truck, with its dual exhausts and chrome bumpers, circling Bloom's house."

"Did you see Georgina Green at Bloom's house, too?" Amanda quizzed the suddenly talkative brunette.

"Maybe." Jayme's makeup-caked face cracked in a cocky grin. "Maybe not. Go ask *her* about Bloom."

"I already did. She didn't have all that much to say."

Jayme tossed the cigarette into the grass and snubbed it out. "Maybe you just didn't ask her the right questions."

Before Amanda could press Jayme for an explanation, she whirled around to saunter toward the screened porch. Amanda decided not to push her luck, for fear any answer she received would be accompanied by a speeding bullet. Jayme Black was a little on the flaky side, not to mention frightening.

Taking a steadying breath, Amanda drove home. Jayme's references to Georgina and Buddy had left a dozen troubling questions buzzing through her mind. She felt as if she were spinning in circles, getting nowhere fast.

What secret was Bobbie Sue Hampton harboring about Jayme Black? What did Jayme really know about Buddy? And what, Amanda wondered, were the right questions to ask Georgina Green?

Jayme lit another cigarette and then stuffed her pistol in her purse. She watched Amanda's red Toyota disappear around the corner before turning toward the house. "Damned snoop," she muttered.

Once inside, Jayme snatched up the phone and dialed. Her nail-bitten fingers drummed against the wall while she counted four rings on the other end of the line.

"Hello?"

"It's me, Jayme. That Hazard lady has been here."

There was a moment of silence. "Are you sure it was her?"

"Of course, I'm sure. I saw her picture in the *Vamoose Gazette* after she solved a murder case. Even if she chopped off her hair, I would recognize her anywhere. She wanted to know what I knew about Bloom."

"Damn."

"My sentiments exactly. You better watch your step."

"Sound advice. You better watch yours, too."

Jayme replaced the receiver and glanced around the

cluttered dining room. She snatched up the envelope that she had left on the table and then stuffed it in her purse. Damned good thing Hazard hadn't gotten her hands on *that!*

Amanda yielded to the impulse to turn back onto the highway rather than head directly home. She had promised Pops she would be home early that afternoon to spend some time with him, but this case took precedence.

The past few days had been hectic. Even during the evening hours Amanda couldn't make herself sit still. She paced the house, burning nervous energy by cleaning house—until the night Pops accused Amanda of becoming as fanatic as Mother.

The humiliating spectacle with Thorn at the Last Chance Cafe kept playing over in her mind, tormenting Amanda to no end. She still hated Thorn, of course, but damn it, he was a hard man to forget.

Willfully, Amanda discarded her betraying thoughts of Thorn. She hoped he was immensely happy with his blond bimbo from Toot 'N' Tell 'Em. And *that,* Amanda thought, had been the killing blow. She would never—ever—take Thorn back after he had stooped so disgustingly low. He could crawl on his belly like the snake he was, beg forgiveness until his face turned blue, and she still wouldn't speak to him!

Concentrating solely on her conversation with Jayme Black, Amanda aimed her car toward Bloom Farm. The strewn hay in Jayme's garage reminded Amanda of the scattered straw in Bloom's barn and Hampton horse stables. Jayme's cocky grins and cryptic comments kept taunting Amanda, leaving her searching for possible connections between the victim and the prime suspects. Her mind was awhirl with facts that refused to settle into logical order.

Ms. Black with a gun in the yard. Stale smoke and a murderer in Bloom's living room. Stainless steel, state-of-the-art kitchen appliances. Georgina Green going bonkers in the street. Buddy Hampton, chewing on a cigar and carrying a rope, casing Bloom's farm . . .

Amanda felt as if she were playing a mental game of Clue! A dozen disjointed thoughts continued to tumble around in her mind. Maybe there was no connection whatsoever, but a niggling little voice alerted Amanda that every suspect she had questioned had offered information that could lead her to the killer.

Bloom's case was worse than gathering scattered pieces of a jigsaw puzzle. Nothing fit easily into place. She just had to be diligent and patient.

Amanda veered onto the dirt path leading to Bloom's barn. She didn't have the faintest idea what she was looking for, and wouldn't until she found it. Yet, instinct had brought her back to the scene of the crime.

Briskly, she walked around to the side door of the barn, snagging her pantyhose on a clump of stickers in the process. The thorns dug into her ankles, making her favor her left leg. Amanda hobbled inside and eased her hip onto the stack of hay. She needed to remove her hose before the stickers permanently embedded themselves in her skin.

She had ruined countless ensembles of professional wear during her search-and-find missions. Her expensive pantyhose had become yet another casualty. She could see why private detectives might wear cheap trench coats and wash-and-wear clothing. It cut down on expenses.

"Wow! This stakeout is more fun that the ones I usually get stuck with," Gib Cooper chuckled, leaning closer to the monitor in surveillance headquarters. "Your ex-girlfriend has arrived. Damn, Nick, is it getting hot in here or is it just her—?"

When Nick's arm shot past Gib's shoulder, and he switched off the surveillance camera, Gib erupted in protest. "Hey, what are you doing?"

"I'll be damned if I'm going to stand here and watch you zoom in on Hazard's hiked skirt," Nick growled at the agent.

"Touchy, aren't you?" Gib teased wickedly. "Your brother said you had it bad for Hazard, but who would have thought you would be so protective of an ex-girl-friend."

"Lay off, Gib, you're ruining my good disposition," Nick snapped.

"I didn't know you had a good disposition, at least not since I arrived in Vamoose." He glanced wryly at Nick's stubbled face and unkempt hair. "You aren't still mad at me because I tried to pick Hazard up before I knew who she was, are you?"

Nick's reply was a disgruntled snort. He reached around Gib to flick on the camera, thankful Hazard had removed her pantyhose by the time the surveillance camera again focused on her.

"I don't think your distraction technique worked on Hazard," Gib remarked. "She keeps coming back here, like a boomerang. I wonder what she's looking for now?"

Nick muttered a curse on Hazard's name. He had hoped she would sulk and mope around for at least a week after he had called it quits in such an unmerciful manner. But Hazard had proved to be relentless and unshakable in the face of an investigation.

Hell, if I'd keeled over and died, she probably wouldn't have spared more than a day mourning my passing before striking off on this latest crusade, Nick thought angrily.

According to Pops, Hazard had already lined up a replacement boyfriend. Not that it was a big surprise, thought Nick. With Hazard's Las Vegas legs and knock-'em-dead figure, men trampled over each other to ask her out on dates.

Nick's resentful thoughts scattered like dandelion seeds as he watched Hazard poke around the hay bales that had been left behind by Manuel Pico and his unidentified companion.

"Well, shit," Nick scowled.

Frustrated, he watched Hazard break open a block of straw and shake it. He held his breath, hoping one of Bloom's cleverly concealed sacks of coke didn't plop to the floor.

Thank God, one didn't.

Tensely, Nick watched Hazard pace around the crumpled sacks of cattle feed, pausing at regular intervals to shake the contents on the ground. Good fortune smiled on Nick when Hazard's search through the discarded paper sacks—from which he had removed the stashes of cocaine—turned up nothing. If she decided to slit open one of the sacks in the north corner of the barn, Nick would be sweating it.

"That was close," Gib murmured as his gaze followed Hazard toward the barn door. "Too bad we can't cordon off the farm without inviting questions." He glanced sideways at Nick. "Do you think Hazard suspects drugs?"

"I don't know," Nick replied, "but if Hazard doesn't quit showing up here, she might meet up with trouble before we can rescue her."

"I could entertain her," Gib volunteered. "I have nothing against gorgeous females with Tinker Bell hairdos."

"You have nothing against anything in skirts," Nick muttered.

"It was a joke, Nick," Gib insisted. "Damn, you've lost your sense of humor. You were a helluva lot more fun in the old days, when we worked on the Narc squad in the City."

Nick breathed a sigh of relief when Hazard exited the barn with her damaged pantyhose in hand. Whatever Hazard had been looking for, she obviously hadn't found—he hoped. If that daring female didn't back off, she would encounter the kind of hard-core criminals who wouldn't bat an eyelash at killing her.

What was with Hazard anyway? Wasn't a thriving accounting business enough to satisfy her? Why was she hounded by this driving need to resolve the mystery surrounding the death of one of her clients?

The woman obviously had more curiosity than she knew what to do with. If things didn't add up the way she thought they should, her analytical mind searched for a satisfying explanation.

There was something to be said for a woman with

fewer brains than Hazard possessed, Nick mused. Too bad he had progressed through that phase in his life when getting laid was his primary motivation. Now that he had matured, he discovered that he appreciated a woman's brains as well as her body.

"Come in, Jack-Be-Nimble."

The blaring, handheld CB demanded Nick's attention. He snatched it up, absently watching the camera that filmed Hazard's departure from the farm. "Jack here."

"We've got solid confirmation," Rich reported. "Little Boy Blue wasn't fast asleep when the sheep were in the meadow and the cows were in the corn. But Blue did blow his horn."

Nick deciphered his brother's coded message for Gib. "The tails who followed Manuel Pico—and friend—to the City warehouse made a midnight drive to Rawhide, Texas. The truck left town with a pile of straw, probably to be recycled into bales that conceal more submarine goods."

"Little Miss Muffet isn't on her tuffet, eating her curds and whey," Rich came back.

"The two suspects are en route with another load of goods," Nick translated.

"Jack be nimble, Jack be quick—or you'll burn your ass on a candlestick. Over."

"I didn't realize the Thorn brothers were so fond of nursery rhymes," Gib smirked as he flicked off the monitor and grabbed his baseball cap.

Nick stuck the CB in his shirt pocket and headed for the door. "I'd like to hang around to photograph the subjects when they return from Texas, but if they see my truck parked in the trees, it might blow the stakeout wide open."

Nick tossed Gib the keys to the four-wheel drive

truck. "Make an appearance in town while folks are setting up for the garage sale."

Gib blinked, baffled. "What? Why?"

"Because you're new in town and you need to mix and mingle," Nick replied as he cut his way through the weeds. "Besides, Hazard will probably be there to scare up a few more facts. Keep an eye on her—from a distance. I want a full report on who she talks to and what she has for sale."

"Oh, goody," Gib grumbled sarcastically. "This is my dream assignment come true."

"This is a rural community," Nick reminded his complaining companion. "You do as the country folks do or they notice."

"And where will you be while I'm sorting through everybody's junk?"

"Wallowing in the weeds with the ticks and fleas to monitor what's going down," Nick informed Gib. "As long as my pickup isn't around for the subjects to spot, I can keep my eye on them."

"Be careful," Gib cautioned. "You'll be on your own for the next few hours. Nobody will be able to get to you in time if you blow your cover."

Nick found himself a thick clump of weeds that provided a clear view of the road that led to Bloom Farm and then parked himself on the ground. His stomach growled in objection to skipping supper, but he ignored the pangs. He was used to surviving on Hazard's cooking catastrophes. At the moment, he would have gladly wolfed down a plate full of that disgusting creamed tuna on toast she usually served to him.

* * *

While Thorn was chewing on his fingernails to stave off starvation, Amanda was savoring Pops's homemade chicken and noodles. She had bitten into a few bones that Pops's failing eyesight had overlooked, but she had no complaints. Pops had fended for himself for so many years that he had become an excellent cook. Too bad Amanda couldn't say the same.

"I got the drop leaf table pieced together this afternoon," Pops announced between bites. "It's been sanded and stained and looks pretty good, even if I say so myself."

"You're coming right along with your project. I wish I had been as successful." Amanda reached for the creamed peas. Pops liked to cream every food group.

Pops's shiny bald head bobbed up and down in agreement. "I decided to have a look at that antique clock of yours while I was waiting for the wood stain to dry. There was a plastic bag stuck inside the workings of the clock that prevented it from keeping time. I've got the workings soaking in kerosene. By later tonight, I should have the clock cleaned, polished and ready for operation."

Amanda took a bite of peas and sighed happily. She hadn't eaten this well in years.

"That's one expensive clock you've got, Half Pint. You could sell it for a thousand dollars at any antique shop."

"You should see the rest of Will Bloom's antiques. He's got an heirloom walnut poster bed that would have you drooling."

"Maybe I can afford to buy some of those treasures at auction, after I win my sweepstakes."

Amanda allowed the topic to die a graceful death. She was certain her grandfather's chance of winning a sweepstakes were one in a zillion.

Pops propped his elbows on the table and stared thoughtfully at Amanda. "I hope you aren't pursuing that Bloom case. I'd hate to see you get yourself into trouble. You're my favorite granddaughter, you know."

"I'm your *only* granddaughter," she corrected.

"My point exactly. If I lose you, I've got nothing."

Pops was beginning to sound like Thorn. Amanda needed no reminders of the man who had ripped her heart out by the taproot—and in front of an attentive audience.

"I'm taking a load of salable items into town for tomorrow's flea market," Amanda said as she cleared the table. "Would you like to come along and view the goods?"

"It sounds more interesting than staying here and putting up with that lazy damned cat of yours. And speaking of pests," Pops added, "that three-legged dog—"

"His name is Pete."

"Whatever. He hobbled into my workshop this afternoon, sniffed around, and then peed on the trash can. I would have lugged the barrel outside to clean it out and wash it off, but I couldn't balance the damned thing with my walker. The whole place smells like an outhouse."

"I'll clean the workshop tomorrow after the garage sale," Amanda promised as she scrubbed the plates.

While Amanda tidied up the kitchen, Pops sat down to peel and stick the labels for the collection of audiotapes and CDs in the most recent phase of the sweepstakes. The man didn't even own a CD player, for crying out loud! Amanda shook her head in dismay, wishing she could convince him that he was wasting his time and money.

While Amanda dried and replaced the dishes in order

in the cabinets, Pops braced on his walker and then wobbled down the hall to soak his dentures.

"I'll be ready to leave in fifteen minutes," Amanda called after him. "Can you be ready—?"

Her voice trailed off when she noticed that Pops had laid his hearing aids on the table—again. She had wasted her breath. He hadn't heard a word she'd said.

Precisely fifteen minutes later, Amanda had loaded the items for the flea market in her jalopy truck. The two gawd-awful lamps Mother had given her for Christmas, an evening gown she no longer had occasion to wear, a partial set of china she had received as wedding gifts and various sundry items that had been cluttering cabinet and closet shelves were among the junk she was anxious to haul off. Not to be forgotten were the two gifts Thorn had given Amanda.

Amanda had decided the garage sale was a godsend—the symbolic break from her past. Once she carted off memorabilia that reminded her of her ex-husband—the jerk—and her ex-boyfriend—the louse—she would be in better spirits. Tomorrow was going to be the first day of the rest of he life. She was never going to become emotionally involved with a man again. Twice was too many, and both relationships had gone sour. From time to time she would accept dates with men like Jim Johnson, but nothing serious was going to develop.

Thorn had cured Amanda—for good.

And speaking of Thorn, Amanda fully intended to rub her investigation in his face when she tracked down Bloom's killer. It would be the only time she spoke to him this century.

With sacks and boxes stacked in the back of the truck, Amanda and Pops rumbled toward town. The highway was more congested than Oklahoma City's rush hour traffic.

"Damn," Pops grumbled, "I've never seen so many overloaded pickup trucks in one place at the same time. You would think this was Vamoose's social event of the season."

Amanda tended to agree. The traffic was as heavy as it had been during the Vamoose country fair. Anticipation sizzled through Amanda's veins. If she couldn't dig up information tonight, then she was losing her investigative touch.

She had learned one important lesson when interrogating prime suspects of a crime. The direct approach didn't work worth a damn. She was going to revert to her previous tactic of subtle interviews. All she had accomplished with the Greens, the Hamptons, and Jayme Black was to invite hostility.

"Yoo-hoo, Amanda! Over here!"

Amanda stared across the parking lot to see Velma Hertzog waving her thick arms like propellers. Beverly Hill stood beside her aunt. Amanda could see her thick coat of grape-colored, half-moon eye shadow from thirty yards away.

"Who's that?" Pops questioned, squinting through his glasses.

"The beautician and her niece—the rookie."

"The one who sheared your head? Maybe you'll get lucky and she'll sell her scissors at the flea market," Pops popped off.

Amanda helped Pops down from the cab of the truck and then unfolded his walker. She asked him to make his way through the crowd to hold a place beside Velma and Bev. After Amanda toted two card tables and a makeshift clothes rack into position, she made a dozen trips to and from the parking lot, gathering her junk—or treasures—depending on one's perspective. Whatever the case, Amanda was anxious to participate in her first-ever flea market.

Nine

Before Amanda could hang her high-fashion garments—relics from her days working at the corporate accounting office in the City—on the makeshift rack, a half dozen women were sorting through her clothes, demanding to know what price she was going to place on them.

"The navy blue dress will probably sell for two dollars."

"Two dollars?" Velma howled from behind her. "You better let me mark the prices for you, hon. This must be your first garage sale."

"As a matter of fact, it is. How'd you know?"

Velma snapped her gum and rolled her fake-lashed eyes. "You're practically giving this stuff away, that's how I know. You have to make people pay the big bucks for these designer clothes." Velma pulled an adhesive label from her Pepto-Bismol-colored smock and placed a five-dollar tag on the dress.

Five dollars was big bucks? Not in Amanda's book.

"Now, hon, price the rest of these dresses accordingly," Velma instructed. "And these dishes! My God!" Snap, pop. "This china looks brand-new! You can't sell it for fifty cents apiece!"

Velma's buglelike voice attracted several professional

garage sale shoppers. They swarmed Amanda like killer bees.

"Save this one for me," one of the women called out. "I'll be back first thing in the morning to pick it up."

"I'll take the orange dress. And my Lord, look at these matching lamps! Aren't they the most incredible things you've ever seen?"

Amanda stared at the gaudy gold lamps with their tasseled shades. Incredible? The only thing incredible to Amanda was that someone actually wanted the hideous things.

There was no accounting for some people's tastes.

"That's Georgina Green's mother," Bev Hill pointed out to Amanda. "She's been bouncing around here like a pogo stick for thirty minutes."

"Can you blame her?" Velma questioned with a pop of her gum. "She had to haul Georgina to the hospital's psychiatric ward, you know. I guess that cooking spray she was sniffing really fogged her brain. Naturally, her mother is upset about it. Who wouldn't be? As you might expect"—crack, chomp—"Daniel is trying to keep it hush-hush to avoid the news media."

"Like, Georgina was acting strange when she came in for her weekly appointment," Bev put in. "When Aunt Velma was doing her hair, Georgina couldn't sit still to save her soul. I went: What's up with you, Georgie? And she went: 'Nothing! Who said something was wrong? And don't call me Georgie!'

"Geez, like, she nearly bit my head off for no reason."

Warning bells clanged in Amanda's brain. She could hear Jayme Black's smirking voice ringing in her ears. *You must not have asked the right questions . . .*

"According to Georgina's mother, Daniel posted a No

Visitors sign on his wife's hospital door. He won't let anybody near her," Velma confided. "The poor woman must have cracked up—big time."

Now why, Amanda asked herself, had Georgina suddenly started sniffing Pam and getting so high she could have passed herself off as a NASA rocket? Overwhelming guilt, maybe?

"Here comes Bobbie Sue Hampton," Velma murmured aside. "She can probably use every cent she can get from the garage sale. Since Buddy told her to get out of his house, Bobbie Sue is practically penniless."

"When did that happen?" Amanda questioned.

"Last night. According to Haden LaFoe, Buddy came home rip-roaring drunk, yelled at Bobbie Sue, and then passed out on the floor. Bobbie Sue hauled her stuff to her mother's soon afterward."

"They were living too high on the hog as it was," Velma said. "Now it will be worse, because they're both accustomed to spending more money than they could make. Financing two households will be difficult."

Amanda surveyed the haggard-looking woman who was hauling a wheelbarrow full of Western clothes and cowboy boots to her booth. Amanda wondered if Buddy knew his wardrobe was about to go on sale.

The instant Bobbie Sue caught sight of Amanda, she glared daggers.

"Wow!" Bev chirped. "Was that lethal glare aimed at me? I only clipped like a quarter inch off her hair when she came sobbing into the beauty shop. She's not mad at me, too, is she?"

"Now don't you fret, sugar." Crackle, pop. "You're coming along just fine, even if that rascal Thorn made that nasty remark about Amanda's haircut." Velma draped her beefy arm around her niece's drooping shoulders. "I think Amanda's new do is cute."

Velma's smile turned sympathetic when she glanced at Amanda. "I'm really sorry about what happened. I think Nick Thorn has gone as crazy as Georgina. Every time I see Nicky with that floozy from Toot 'N Tell 'Em I want to wring his neck. He looks awful with that prickly beard lining his jaws, that coal black hair falling into his eyes and hanging over his collar. He's turned into a deadbeat bum or something, hasn't he? And to think he used to be a well-respected pillar of this community. It's disgraceful!"

Amanda refrained from interjecting a comment. The only adjectives she could conjure up to describe Thorn were four-letter words.

While Amanda priced her items, she posed several casual questions to Beverly Hill. Subtly, she worked her way around to the topic of Jayme Black. But Velma, who had rabbit ears, leaped into the conversation, giving Amanda the lowdown on Jayme.

"Talk about worthless," Velma said with a shake of her head. "You would never know that girl was raised in a well-to-do family."

"Like, she's the only child of an only child," Bev added. "She's my sister's age, but Jayme looks ten years older."

"That makeup she wears is drying out her skin," Velma declared as she stuck price tags on her oversupply of bamboo tree shampoo. "I tried to tell Jayme so, and she told me where I could go and what I could do with myself when I got there." Snap, crackle. "I swear, that girl needs her mouth washed out with soap."

"She never had friends her age," Bev commented.

"My sister said nobody liked her much, because she was spoiled rotten and unbearably self-centered. She was always a troublemaker, trying to pit one best friend against the other. It's no wonder she ended up divorcing that slug she married. Like, he is as worthless as she is. Now Jayme hangs out with the high school kids when she's in town—which isn't often, thank goodness."

"Last I heard, Blake Black had been released from jail," Velma inserted. "What a loser that boy is."

"I saw him drive through town the other day," Bev said with a dismal shake of her head. "Like, the world would be a better place if Blake was stuck in jail."

"Violet Barnstall said she saw him at Thatcher Oil and Gas. Still dressed like a hoodlum, she said." Snap, pop.

"What happened to Jayme's parents?" Amanda questioned curiously.

"Like, nothing happened to them. They just got fed up and wrote Jayme off as a lost cause. They cut off her money supply before she drained them dry."

Velma glanced discreetly around and then leaned close to relay a juicy piece of gossip. "I think she's turning tricks for some of those high school boys who want to experiment with . . . S . . . E . . . X," she quietly spelled out.

Amanda wasn't surprised. That slum of a bedroom she had seen—with its obscene posters—had looked like something decorated in Early Bordello. Maybe Amanda should ask the males of the senior class what erotic benefits they derived from lumpy powdered sugar and baking soda.

While Amanda was organizing the cooking utensils she never used on the card table, someone latched onto her arm and spun her around. To her surprise, Daniel Green was looming over her, an angry expression puckering his face.

"I want to speak with you—in private," he hissed.

Before Amanda could accept or decline, Daniel propelled her toward the playground equipment beside the fairgrounds.

"Sorry to hear about your wife," Amanda said, in hopes of diffusing Daniel's irritation. It didn't work.

"I'll just bet you are." Daniel thrust his hand into his coat pocket and then brandished a crumpled paper in Amanda's face. "What are you up to now, Hazard? You may think this childlike scrawl threw me off track, but I know damned well this note is from you. I happen to be a lawyer, in case you've forgotten."

Amanda didn't have the foggiest idea what Daniel implied. "What has that got to do with anything?"

"I can have you arrested for this," he seethed. "I sure as hell don't intend to pay it, either!"

Amanda snatched the paper that Daniel was waving beneath her nose. She read the blackmail note, written in sloppy adolescent penmanship.

Deer Danny boy,
Unles you want everbody to no about yore wifes bad habits. Leave $10,000 in Blooms barn Saturday nite.

Amanda's stunned gaze leaped from the letter to Daniel's face. "I did not write this note."

"You're lying," he growled. "I received it the day after you came to see my wife. Georgina got hold of it first and freaked out. I hope you're happy, Hazard. It's your fault my wife went nuts!"

"Don't try to foist Georgina's mental instability off on me. She was loony long before I started asking questions, and you know it."

"If the media gets hold of this, you better believe I'm going to hold you personally and *publicly* responsible," he said. "By the time I'm through, voters will be begging to have me elected, and I'll see you indicted on criminal charges. No jury in this state will find you innocent, Hazard."

Amanda deflected his smoldering glare. "Did you fling the same threats at Bloom?" she wanted to know. "Did he counter your threat with one of his own, making you lose your temper?"

Daniel's long fingers curled like a choker necklace—the exact size of Amanda's throat. "Don't mess with me, Hazard. I carry a lot of clout."

"Is it heavy?" she smarted off.

Daniel bared his white teeth and hissed, "I'll be damned if I let some two-bit accountant spoil my senatorial aspirations. I'll find a way to ruin you, don't think I won't!"

Amanda suspected Daniel Green wouldn't have let a man like Will Bloom stand in his way, either. Daniel was suffering from delusions of greatness. Until now, Amanda hadn't realized how obsessed he was with winning the election.

"Be warned, Hazard, you'll be extremely sorry if you don't back off and leave me alone."

Amanda watched Daniel stamp off. She was curious as to why all her lines of questioning kept bringing her back to the Greens and the Hamptons. Could both families have been involved in some sort of conspiracy?

This murder case was more complicated than Amanda had anticipated. Somebody obviously knew something incriminating about the Greens and had tried to make a profit when Daniel declared his candidacy. But who? Could one of the Hamptons be involved in extortion to cover their staggering expenses?

"Good question," Amanda muttered as she ambled back to the fairgrounds. "I wish I knew where to find a good answer."

Nick's chin thudded on a clump of burrs and his eyes popped open. He had lain in the weeds for hours, trying to make himself stay awake. Resting on stickers kept him from dozing off for an extended period of time. Spending days without sufficient sleep was beginning to take its toll. Hard as he tried to remain alert, he kept nodding off. But no matter what, Nick was determined to be on hand when Manuel Pico and company returned from Texas with the hay truck.

With a muffled groan, Nick hauled himself upright and then sat down cross-legged on the ground. His muscles were as stiff as a starched shirt. He glanced impatiently toward the gravel road that was barely visible in the darkness. Where the hell was that damned truck? The submarine goods should have arrived by now.

The hum of an approaching aircraft caught Nick's attention. At first he thought the low-flying plane was the usual variety that sprayed pastures and hay meadows for weeds and pests. He shifted his groggy brain into high gear when it occurred to him that the twin-engine plane might be trying to make an emergency landing.

On hands and knees, Nick crawled through the weeds to gain a better vantage point. When the lights of the plane angled downward during the approach, Nick bounded to his feet and dashed toward the line of cedar trees. To his relief, he didn't hear the anticipated crash. Instead, he heard the bump and creak of the aircraft making a successful landing.

Fishing the compact binoculars from his jacket, Nick scanned the obscure section of Bloom's pasture. "Well, I'll be a son of a bitch," he muttered.

There, partially concealed from view by a windrow of trees, was a dirt landing strip. To the average observer, it looked as though Bloom had been doing dirt work to level the field for drainage. Obviously not. The pilot of the plane had known precisely where to touch down.

The door swung open, and the interior lights from the plane revealed the silhouette of a man. Recognition flashed through Nick's mind, resurrecting haunting memories. Although Nick couldn't see the man's face clearly—didn't need to—he recognized the arrogant, self-assured stance, the stocky physique that was wrapped in the finest clothes money could buy.

Mr. Big had arrived on the scene.

Nick itched to call in reinforcements and land the drug cartel's big fish, but he wanted to tear this complex operation apart at the seams and haul in the upper echelon, as well as every pusher and trafficker involved. Much as Nick hated to do it, he had to let Mr. Big walk.

Dust billowed around the headlights of the vehicle that approached from the south, via gravel roads. Nick scowled.

"Damn it to hell, Hazard. That better not be you or I'll wring your gorgeous neck, unless Mr. Big gets to you first!"

Nick expected to see a compact Toyota or jalopy truck appear from the fog of dust. Instead, a rusted Chevy with bad muffler pipes veered across the cattle guard leading to the pasture. Nick watched the vehicle bounce across the rough terrain and halt near the aircraft.

When Mr. Big strutted down the steps and approached the car, Nick tried to zoom in to identify the driver. When the car door creaked open, no lights illuminated the interior. Nick couldn't tell who had arrived to confer with Mr. Big.

The conversation lasted no more than three minutes. Nick didn't have time to call his brother to put a tail on the vehicle before it whizzed off in a cloud of dust. Luckily, Nick got a description of the plane that taxied down the dirt runway. Of course, he wasn't going to be the least bit surprised if the aircraft's ID number changed often, making it difficult for the authorities to trace Mr. Big. The man was a stickler for seeing to minute details that might lead back to him.

The plane, with spotlights flashing, circled the farm—twice. Like clockwork, the now-familiar hay truck rumbled toward the barn from the opposite direction.

Nick picked up his CB and sent a coded message to Rich, announcing the truck's arrival, requesting that a new tail be placed on it to avoid suspicion. And then Nick waited while more hay bales were loaded up and hauled away from Bloom's barn.

An hour later, the truck sped away, followed at an inconspicuous distance by Thorn's black Ford pickup.

According to Rich's nursery rhyme message, Roger Proctor was in pursuit of the drug traffickers.

Nick had expected the drug ring to move swiftly after Bloom's death. Since Bloom had no next of kin, his property and belongings would be placed on the auction block. The drug ring had to make their pickups and drops before the sheriff of Vamoose County started kicking around the farm.

Nick intended to let the mules run their circuit twice before sending in the agents. He wanted to gather enough evidence to convict everyone involved in this specialized operation.

Nick had waited years to pin down Mr. Big. He sure wasn't going to jump the gun before he reeled in the king fish and served him up to the courts on a silver platter.

When the coast was clear Nick hiked toward the barn. As expected, another stack of hay and paper sacks had disappeared. Mr. Big was clearing out the evidence to protect himself and his operation.

Even though Nick had forgone supper and sleep, it had been a rewarding evening. He had confirmed the fact that this was indeed Mr. Big's illegal drug circuit. Somehow or other, Nick vowed, he was going to see that vicious mastermind behind bars. The son of a bitch could do his strutting in an eight-by-eight cell.

Amanda bolted straight up in bed. She had lain awake for hours, trying to figure out what had been nagging at her. And suddenly, like a bolt from the blue, she realized what had seemed different about Bloom's barn.

It had been larger than she remembered!

When Amanda had hopped onto the haystack to remove her ruined pantyhose, she thought something had been out of place. She had become too preoccupied with searching the hay bales and the discarded feed sacks—in hopes of making a connection between Jayme Black and her straw-filled garage. In the process, Amanda had overlooked the obvious.

Somebody had loaded up part of Will Bloom's hay and carried it off. There had definitely been more bales in the barn the day she had poked her head inside to locate Will Bloom.

Amanda flung the quilts aside and then bounded from bed. She strode down the hall to retrieve Bloom's accounting ledger. If he had sold more than six hundred dollars' worth of hay, there should be a notation or a canceled check in his bank statements and ledger.

Could Buddy Hampton have purchased hay for his high-powered horses?

Amanda scooped up the ledger and switched on the light. With practiced efficiency she scanned the accounts. To her disappointment she found no indication that Bloom had sold his hay to Buddy Hampton or anybody else.

Just what she needed—a new wrinkle in an already-perplexing case. It was obvious someone was stealing hay from a dead man's barn. Some people had no scruples whatsoever.

Will Bloom hadn't been gone more than two weeks and theft had already occurred. If someone decided to raid his home, they wouldn't believe their good fortune. Thieves could haul off expensive furnishings by the pickup loads and no one would be the least bit suspicious, because all of Vamoose considered Will Bloom to be borderline poor.

Amanda's thoughts trailed off when she noticed the phone number that had been written upside down—in blue ink—on the bottom of page four in the ledger. Spinning the book on her lap, she studied the number. Although the area code indicated an Oklahoma number, the prefix wasn't a Vamoose listing.

Amanda glanced up at the antique clock Pops had reassembled after they returned from setting up the booth at the community garage sale. It was half past midnight. She reached for the phone. She might scare the living daylights out of whoever answered her call, but she would dearly like to know whose number Will Bloom had jotted upside down—in blue.

The phone rang once, clicked with static, crackled, and then the line went dead. There was no busy signal, no nothing when she tried the number again. Odd, she thought, replacing the receiver.

Yawning, Amanda set the ledger aside. She was too tired to pore over Will's accounts, searching for that illusive clue. Today had been another hectic day, and Saturday was guaranteed to be a flurry of activity.

Amanda was about to experience her first garage sale. Even if she couldn't dig up valuable information to solve this case, at least she could dispose of the unwanted memorabilia and gifts Thorn had given her. The gold locket and sapphire-studded bracelet that Thorn claimed matched the color of her eyes exactly were going cheap. No way was Amanda going to cart that jewelry home. She would give it away first, even if Velma objected.

The expensive trinkets were worthless to Amanda. And so, by damn, was Thorn!

* * *

Amanda found herself swamped by prospective buyers the moment the gates to the fairgrounds swung open. Professional shoppers, skilled in the art of talking down prices, bombarded her. But Velma Hertzog was close at hand, refusing to let Amanda hand over skirts, blouses, dresses, cooking utensils, and seasonal decorations for nothing.

To Amanda's surprise, Gib Cooper took time from his duties at Thatcher's Oil and Gas to rummage through Amanda's junk. He bickered with her over the fifty-cent price tag she had placed on a sterling silver cake server before he purchased it. What the man wanted with a silver cake server, Amanda had no idea.

Gib hung around her booth for another few minutes before he returned to work at the service station.

By noon, most of Amanda's items had been picked over. Her clothes rack hung empty. The two card tables held only a few articles—except for the two pieces of jewelry Thorn had given her. For some unexplained reason, no one in Vamoose would touch the locket and bracelet that Amanda had once worn with pride and satisfaction. Maybe the jewelry was jinxed.

Velma and Beverly still had piles of extra-large T-shirts, well-used hair rollers, a stack of magazines—with the coupons snipped out of them—and several pieces of lopsided pottery that Velma had made in her community college class.

As for Pops, he was in hog heaven. He had rummaged through everyone's goods to find several antique treasures. He was a master at wringing the cheapest prices from the participants of the garage sale, Amanda noticed.

"Did you hear the news, hon?" Velma leaned away from her chair to convey the latest gossip. "Millicent Price told Ruby Allen who told Ramona Slimp who just told me that Bobbie Sue Hampton is headed for stardom in Nashville."

Amanda glanced toward the buxom brunette who was sitting behind a distant card table, arguing prices with a prospective buyer. "Is that a fact," she said, wondering if the truth might be that the guilty party wanted to skip town—fast.

"When Billie Jean heard that her sister and brother-in-law were splitting the sheets, Billie Jean pulled some strings in the country music capital."

Amanda tried to look properly impressed. She still thought Billie Jean Baxter's gonglike voice was highly overrated, but if the onetime Vamoosian had made it big in Nashville, who was she to argue with Billie Jean's astonishing success?

"Like, Billie Jean bought Bobbie Sue a plane ticket to Nashville," Bev Hill inserted. "They're going to cut a duet demo, sorta like the Judds. Bobbie Sue claims she can't wait to shake off the dust from this one-horse town and kick up her bootheels."

Now why, Amanda mused, *would the ex-lover of a murder victim be in such a rush to do that?*

"Jayme Black was heard to say the same thing," Velma put in. "But look how she ended up. I knew she was headed for trouble. Sure enough, she found it." Pop, crackle.

Bev shook her head sadly, her Shirley Temple curls bouncing around her plump face like corkscrews. "I was afraid something like this would happen, too. Kinda makes you wonder if her ex-husband's release from the pen had anything to do with it."

A frown beetled Amanda's brows. "Anything to do with what?"

Velma blinked her fake eyelashes. "Didn't you hear that Jayme was found dead inside her car in the City's slum district this morning?"

Amanda felt the air leave her lungs in a whoosh. Her mouth opened and shut like a damper on a chimney. "WHAT!" she yelped.

Several heads turned in her direction. Amanda struggled for hard-won composure.

Velma nodded affirmatively. "That's what Deputy Sykes said when he came into the Last Chance Cafe to grab a quick cup of coffee. Jayme went out of this world with a broken neck . . . Oh, my gawd . . . !"

When Velma's voice transformed into a howl, and she stared at the entrance of the fairgrounds, Amanda swiveled in her chair to see what had captured the beautician's attention. Amanda felt as if she had taken a bullet in the chest when she saw Nancy Shore casting sheep's eyes and hanging all over Nick Thorn like laundry on a clothesline. It was mortifying, disgusting! And worse, everyone turned around to see how Amanda was reacting to the new arrivals. Amanda felt like a specimen under a microscope.

"The nerve of that man," Velma muttered between cracks and pops of her chewing gum. "I swear, Nicky has gone all to hell the past two weeks. And would you take a gander at that sleazy cashier from Toot 'N Tell 'Em. She must have the morals of a tramp."

Velma surged to her feet, her thick neck bowed. "I'm

going to tell Nicky exactly what I think about the new leaf he turned over—"

Velma's broad bottom smacked against her metal folding chair when Amanda jerked her down. "If you plan to read Thorn the riot act for my benefit, don't bother," Amanda insisted as convincingly as she knew how. "I don't care what he does or whom he does it with. We're finished—kaput."

Velma scrutinized Amanda for a long, pensive moment. "Are you sure, hon? I thought the two of you were the perfect match—the Prince Charles and Princess Di of Vamoose."

"Yeah, well, we all know how that fairy-tale romance turned out, don't we?" Amanda smirked.

"Are you certain you don't want me to have a few words with Nicky?" Velma persisted.

"I'm absolutely positive," Amanda said with great conviction. "I'm seeing Jim Johnson and glad of it."

Velma retracted her acrylic, hot pink claws and glared at Thorn for good measure. "Nicky, the stupid fool, spoiled the best thing he had going. That nice Jim Johnson should thank Nicky for turning you loose. Everybody says Jim is the most polite and courteous man they've ever met. He's spoken to several property owners around town to find out how many of them haven't already leased their land to competitive oil companies for drilling sites. And Jim always dresses neat as a pin." Her disapproving gaze leaped to Nick Thorn. "Unlike some thugs I could name."

To Amanda's thorough disgust, Thorn—his uninjured arm draped around the shoulder of Nancy's leopardskin jacket—strode forward. Without a word of greeting, he thrust his good hand into the pocket of his grimy blue jeans and tossed a ten-dollar bill in Amanda's direction.

"I'll take those two items of jewelry," he announced, staring at the air over Amanda's head.

Amanda silently congratulated herself when she managed to hand over the items without throwing them in his unshaven face. "You can have them for nothing," she insisted, returning the money. "Ironically, that's what they are worth to me."

When Thorn presented the secondhand gifts to his bimbo girlfriend, Nancy flung her arms around his neck and then gave him a peck on the cheek, leaving her fire engine red lipstick print for all the world to see.

Amanda wanted to throw up.

"For me, Nicky?" Nancy cooed in a grating, nasal voice. She sidled closer, clinging like English ivy as Nick turned around and walked away.

Amanda wanted to grab the unsold skillet on the card table and pound on Thorn's injured arm.

"What a bummer," Beverly Hill muttered as the chummy couple sauntered away. "Like, somebody ought to have Nick shot."

Amanda wondered if Jayme Black's ex-husband had toyed with the same vindictive retaliation—and then followed through with it.

A fleeting thought shot through Amanda's brain like an arrow, pinning down an elusive clue that had—until that very moment—escaped her. "Holy hell!"

Bev's and Velma's accordion-like jowls dropped open when Amanda bounded to her feet. "What's wrong?" they chorused.

"Velma, will you bring Pops home? I just remembered something I forgot."

"Well sure, hon." Smack, crackle. "But what—?"

Amanda didn't have time to answer Velma's question. She grabbed her purse and zigzagged through the milling crowd to reach her jalopy. An alarming vision was forming in her mind, and disjointed clues swirled—a few of them attaching to one another as they settled into place. Amanda quickly reviewed the facts.

Scattered hay in Jayme's garage, matching the variety scattered on the floor of Bloom's barn. Missing hay bales. Clumps of a powdery white substance beside Jayme's bed. A hidden fortune concealed from the world. Georgina Green's jittery reactions and suicide attempt. . . . Only it wasn't attempted suicide at all, was it? It was a bad habit . . . from drug consumption and years of abuse.

Amanda sped off in her truck, exceeding the speed limit, hoping Deputy Sykes hadn't set up one of his infamous traps. Her destination was Jayme Black's rented farmhouse. Amanda had the unshakable feeling that Jayme Black had been pushing drugs—distributing them to the high school students she was reportedly hanging around with.

If Amanda wasn't mistaken—and she rarely was—Georgina Green's cooking spray incident was an attempt to manufacture her own highs when her drug supply went dry—or dead, as it had in Bloom's case.

Amanda suddenly remembered her conversations with Georgina and her own innocent comment about getting someone else to tend Georgina's grass after Bloom died. Georgina had taken offense at a seemingly harmless remark. Then she had burst out laughing when Amanda accused her of having an affair with Bloom.

Obviously, Velma's assumption that Vamoose's handyman had been hitting on various women in the community for sexual reasons, wasn't entirely correct. Will Bloom had been dealing drugs! Amanda was certain that was why Georgina had sniffed Pam—because she couldn't get hold of her usual supply. And that, Amanda also reminded herself, was what Jayme Black implied when she had told Amanda that she hadn't asked Georgina the *right* questions.

Someone else in Vamoose must have known about Georgina's secret highs, Amanda reasoned. That was why Daniel Green had been blackmailed and Jayme had turned up dead. That was why money was expected to be delivered to Will Bloom's barn—where several bales of hay had gone missing!

Suspicion loomed on Amanda's mental horizon. Was it Daniel who had penned the note and then accused Amanda, in hopes of throwing her off the track? And how had Bobbie Sue known about Bloom's connection with Jayme Black if she hadn't been messing with drugs herself?

Amanda took the country corner on two wheels and caromed down Jayme's driveway. She leaped from her pickup in a single bound, making a beeline for the screened porch.

The house looked exactly as Amanda had left it—a filthy disaster. Amanda strode through the trash-littered living room and then hurried down the hall. Her gaze landed on the white substance embedded in the carpet. She was pretty sure it wasn't baking soda or powdered sugar—as she had so naively thought.

Squatting on her haunches, Amanda reached inside her purse for a piece of paper. She came up with the business card that held Jim Johnson's phone number.

"Sorry, Jim, but crime-solving takes precedence here,"

she said to herself. Using the card as a makeshift dust-pan, Amanda scooped up the substance. Glancing around, she saw a sandwich-sized Ziploc bag crumpled beside the end table.

After she had tipped the substance into the bag, Amanda tucked it in her purse.

Instinct urged Amanda to search the straw-filled ga-rage once again. She had to ascertain whether the hay had come from Bloom's or Hampton's barn.

"Thorn, you're going to have to take me seriously, even if I have to pry you loose from that bimbo with a crowbar," Amanda said aloud, as she plucked up a hand-ful of hay. "We've got big trouble in Vamoose."

Amanda wheeled toward her truck. She needed to track Bobbie Sue down before she hopped a plane to make her getaway. But Amanda was prepared to bet her life that Bobbie Sue wasn't scheduled to leave for Nash-ville until the following morning, not if she planned to pick up the extortion money she hoped would be in Bloom's barn.

It was beginning to look as if the other half of the new singing sister duo might have to do her crooning behind bars.

Ten

By the time Amanda returned to the fairgrounds, Vamoosians were departing the annual flea market with their treasures. Bobbie Sue Hampton had plopped behind the steering wheel of her shiny Caddy. Quick as a wink, Amanda scuttled toward her.

"We have to talk," Amanda insisted.

"I have nothing more to say to you," Bobbie Sue snapped. "I have places to go and things to do."

Not surprising, thought Amanda. *When a sleuth has a few probing questions to ask, murderers are always busier than bumblebees in buckets of tar.* Amanda had learned that during the first year of "Magnum, P.I." reruns. Tom Selleck always had to chase suspects down to get them to talk.

Of course, Tom always got the job done, because he wasn't too preoccupied with blond bimbos to realize crimes had been committed—the way Thorn was.

"When was the last time you saw Jayme Black alive?" Amanda blurted out.

Bobbie Sue's eyes popped. "Now hold on, Hazard. You've already tried to pin Will Bloom's death on me. Now it's Jayme's, too?"

"How did you know Jayme bit the dust?" Amanda quizzed suspiciously.

"Same way everybody else does, I expect. Velma and her sidekick niece have motor mouths that have been running all day."

A likely story, thought Amanda. "Did you drive out to Bloom's farm very often, Bobbie Sue? And you better come clean—here and now," Amanda warned in a no-nonsense tone. "At the moment, you're my number one suspect, and you better convince me you weren't involved or I'll have you hauled in for official questioning so fast it'll make your head spin."

Bobbie Sue looked the other way, heaved an audible sigh, and then nodded reluctantly. "I only drove out to Bloom's farm twice. And for your information, I was only with him once."

"Intimately?" Amanda pressed, digging for precise details.

"Yes," Bobbie Sue gritted out. "I don't even know how or why it happened. Will had completed the back deck and I was all enthused about it, hoping Buddy and I could kick back and spend some time together—just the two of us. I had visions of mixing drinks and enjoying the view of rolling pastures beside the river."

Amanda felt like Dear Abby while she listened to the lovelorn's sad tale. "Go on," she encouraged.

"Buddy didn't have time to sit down and enjoy the view. He said he didn't know why we needed that stupid deck. It was a waste of wood and money."

"He took the wind out of your sails," Amanda observed.

Bobbie Sue blinked back a mist of tears and nodded affirmatively. "I decided to mix a few drinks and enjoy the view—without Buddy. Will was sympathetic to my frustration. I offered him a drink—or three. And some-how or other he and I ended up in . . ."

Amanda got the picture, even if Bobbie Sue couldn't bring herself to elaborate.

Bobbie Sue inhaled deeply and plunged on. "The weekend before Will died, I received a note from him through the mail."

"In sloppy handwriting and misspelled sentences?" Amanda questioned.

Bobbie Sue glanced up, bemused. "No, it was neatly printed. Why?"

"Never mind. You were saying?"

"Now that you mention it, there was something about the note that disturbed me. It had been taped shut. I guess I forgot all about that after I read it."

Taped shut? Amanda mused, but she kept her mouth closed so Bobbie Sue wouldn't lose her train of thought.

"Will demanded money to keep silent about our one-time tryst. I had gotten drunk to drown my disappoint-ment in Buddy, made a careless mistake, and Will was exploiting it. I wanted to shoot him!"

"Or club him over the head and drag him through the dirt?"

Bobbie Sue glared at Amanda. "Absolutely not!" she stated emphatically. "When Buddy went down to the sta-bles to exercise the horses, I drove off to see Bloom, hoping to reason with him."

"Obviously he wasn't receptive," Amanda concluded.

"No, he wasn't. I told Will I couldn't afford ten thou-sand dollars in hush money, because we were in debt up to our eyeballs. I guess he'd looked at the size of our ranch and assumed we were rolling in dough. He laughed at my excuse, so I told him he could ask you to verify the fact that we were operating in the red, if he didn't believe me."

"And Will said . . . ?" Amanda prompted, impatiently waiting for Bobbie Sue to fill in the blank.

"He said he wasn't letting me off the hook, because he needed the cash so he could vamoose from Vamoose."

Amanda's brows puckered thoughtfully. Now why would a man who was dealing dope and living high—behind a modest facade—need to beat a hasty retreat?

Will had definitely gotten desperate, Amanda reminded herself. She had sensed that during their phone conversation. But why was he desperate for cash?

"I was beside myself," Bobbie Sue confided. "Will suddenly became like Dr. Jekyll and Mr. Hyde. He had been nice to me before, and that day he turned ruthless. I didn't know where I was going to get the money. I couldn't bring myself to tell Buddy what I'd done. Even though he ignores me and spends all his time with those damned horses, and Haden LaFoe is a closer friend to him now than I am . . . I still love that big lug . . ."

Amanda watched Bobbie Sue burst into tears. She knew exactly how Bobbie Sue felt. Big lugs were difficult to forget, even when they did a woman wrong.

"Was that the same day you realized Will was associating with Jayme Black?"

Bobbie Sue bobbed her head and swiped the back of her hand over her flushed cheeks, rerouting the streams of tears. "When I got in my car to leave. I saw Jayme coming around the corner of the barn. Her car must have been parked down there, because it wasn't in the driveway by the house. Knowing Jayme's wild reputation, I got worried about the one-time fling I'd had with Will, while I was drowning my sorrows in whiskey. I was afraid I . . . I didn't want to even consider the possibility of . . ."

Amanda suspected Bobbie Sue didn't approve of the company Will Bloom was keeping. There was no telling what nasty little diseases Jayme might have been transmitting—that Bobbie Sue might have contracted.

Bobbie Sue flexed her hands on the steering wheel, an indication that Amanda's line of questioning was making her apprehensive. "I was afraid to tell Buddy the truth and afraid not to. You know how Buddy is. When he loses his temper, he—" She clamped her lips shut and switched on the ignition. "I have to pack for my trip."

"One more question," Amanda insisted hastily. "Did you see Will the morning he died?"

Bobbie Sue swallowed hard. Her gaze bounced around, as if her eyeballs were stuck in a pinball machine. Her apprehensive reaction assured Amanda that Bobbie Sue had been there.

"Will was already dead beside the barn when I went back to tell him I couldn't raise the money," she said in a rush. "But I didn't kill him, and I gotta go!"

"Well, damn," Amanda muttered as Bobbie Sue made tracks. Was it Buddy who opened the blackmail note and discovered his wife's involvement with a drug dealer who posed as Vamoose's down-on-his-luck farmer and handyman? Had Buddy silenced Will and then decided to apply the same technique to squeeze money from Daniel Green, in hopes of collecting funds to pay his debts?

Buddy could have seen Georgina at Bloom Farm while he was casing the place, checking on his wife. He could have been in such a murderous, jealous rage that he sought the full measure of revenge against Will

Bloom and became desperate to keep his head above financial waters.

Buddy certainly had opportunity, Amanda reminded herself. Haden LaFoe reported that Buddy had left the farm—destination unknown—on several occasions.

Ah yes, thought Amanda. *Buddy Hampton definitely knows more about this case than he's letting on.* He had also lied to her. Jayme claimed she had seen Buddy's fancy truck cruising around the section where Bloom's farm was located. That, added to Haden LaFoe's testimony, made Buddy a prime suspect.

And now Jayme Black, who had seen Bobbie Sue and Buddy and Georgina with Will Bloom, had also ended up dead. The killer, whoever he—or she—was, had silenced those who knew too much.

This case was giving Amanda a queen-size headache. Before she leaped to ill-founded conclusions, she had to determine if the clump of hay she had taken from Jayme Black's garage was the exact-same variety as the kind found in Buddy Hampton's stables or the type in Bloom's barn—if there was any left by now.

This time, when Amanda entered Will's barn, she was going to break open a few bales rather than sift through the broken blocks. She was reasonably certain those bales concealed the drugs that Bloom had sold to Jayme Black for distribution to high school students.

Thorn was going to hear about that, too, Amanda decided. There was an intricate drug ring working in this naive little rural community. Bloom's death had caused a domino effect that sent Georgina Green to the funny farm, caused domestic conflicts between the Hamptons, and taken Jayme Black's life.

Amanda shuddered to guess who would be next on

the list. Georgina Green had become a near victim, because of her abusive habit. Daniel Green must have known about his wife's fixes and tried to keep it quiet. Someone had discovered Georgina's addiction and planned to profit from it. Who? Was it Buddy Hampton, who was in this case up to his neck? Or was Daniel Green so desperate to avoid scandal and dodge Amanda's questions that he had staged his own blackmail note? Either man could have written the note in barely legible penmanship for his own devious purpose.

With undue haste, Amanda whizzed off, serenaded by the rattle of her old truck. Her destination was Bloom's barn, and then on to Hampton stables if the hay variety didn't match.

"Damn." Amanda slammed the heel of her hand against the steering wheel. She had done it again—forgotten to ask the right questions. She needed to know if Bobbie Sue had ever been in Bloom's home, if she knew about the elegant furnishings that were concealed behind his modest living room.

Amanda also needed to know if Bobbie Sue had done drugs and had prior knowledge of Georgina's addiction. Bobbie Sue probably knew a whole lot more than she had said and she could have spoken in half-truths to get Amanda off her back. The prospective country star wanted to keep quiet, hoping to avoid scandal—just like the aspiring senatorial candidate.

As Amanda sped over the gravel road toward Bloom Farm, she spied the cattle standing in the corral. It looked as if someone had been feeding the livestock and had kept the water tank full. Whoever had assumed the farming duties must have stumbled onto the drugs.

Great, she thought in exasperation. *Now whose name*

will have to be added to the list of prime suspects? She had collected another name this afternoon—Jayme Black's ex-con of an ex-husband. For sure, Blake Black was around here somewhere, and Amanda hated to venture a guess as to what the hoodlum had been doing with all the spare time he had on his hands these days.

"Well hell," Nick scowled as he studied the monitor from his concealed location in Bloom's shed.

Roger Proctor added his own curse. "What is Hazard doing back here again? That woman is too smart for her own good. She's got the investigative instincts of a trained detective."

Nick had discovered that for himself—three times already. He did not need to hear Hazard's praises sung by a veteran drug enforcement agent.

Nick had hoped to send Hazard reeling when he showed up at the flea market to buy back the jewelry he had given her. Apparently his arrival hadn't fazed Hazard in the least. Her one-track mind was focused on this investigation and—like a pit bull, with its jaws clamped shut—wouldn't turn loose.

Gib Cooper had contacted Nick the minute he saw the necklace and bracelet on sale at the flea market for five dollars apiece. Nick had paid a helluva lot for those gifts, and he refused to let someone pick them up for nothing. Call him sentimental, but those expensive gifts meant something to him, even if Hazard had decided to toss them out with the other unwanted junk.

"Son of a bitch," Nick grumbled when he saw Hazard clip open a hay bale with a pair of pliers. Blocks of hay tumbled to the barn floor, revealing the stash of drugs.

To Nick's disbelief, he saw Hazard fish into her purse to compare an identical plastic bag containing a granulated, white substance. *Where the hell did she get that?*

"Where the hell did she get that?" Roger voiced Nick's astounded thought.

"I don't know," Nick muttered.

"You better brief Hazard on what's going down," Roger advised. "She knows enough to get herself in the worst of all possible trouble."

"If I brief her, she'll be in here trying to tell you how to do your job. She's told me how to do mine often enough."

"This ain't no crackpot gumshoe at work," Roger insisted as he watched Hazard aim herself toward the stack of feed sacks. "She may be going at this investigation from an unconventional angle, Nick, but I can't criticize her methods when she's getting accurate results."

Nick gaped at Roger.

"Okay, so I don't have to worry about my male ego being bruised by a beautiful, brainy ex-girlfriend whose skills of analysis and observation compete with mine. But geez, Nick, you can't argue with her success. The fact remains that Hazard may have gleaned information that might be vital to our case. We're running out of time. We can't keep stalling the sheriff about organizing an auction for this farm. He's going to start wondering why you keep putting him off."

"I want the entire circuit of this drug operation on videotape, so we can arrest every member of the higher echelon and every peon involved," Nick insisted. "You know as well as I do that we need to have evidence aplenty if we hope to convict Mr. Big and his little rascals."

Roger nodded reluctantly. He watched Hazard tear

into the brown paper feed sack to retrieve another bag of submarine goods.

"Little Jack Horner sat in a corner, eating his Christmas pie," Roger recited, his astute gaze fixed on Hazard. "He stuck in his thumb and pulled out a plum and said, 'What a brave boy am I.'"

Roger glanced meaningfully at Nick, who wore a thunderous scowl. "Hazard pulled out a plum—or rather a stash of coke, as this case happens to be. Brave girl that she is, she is going to get herself in a world of hurt, even if you don't want Mr. Big to know you still have a fond attachment to Hazard.

"Do I need to remind you that the vehicle we tracked down last night belonged to one Jayme Black?" Roger asked grimly. "She got mixed up in this mess and now she's down at the morgue, taking up space. Do you want Hazard to end up like that?"

Nick muttered a curse as the surveillance cameras tracked Hazard's hasty departure. "All right, Rog, I'll compare notes with Hazard first chance I get."

"You better make it quick. She may not have more than one chance and very little time left," Roger said. "If Mr. Big's informant knows Hazard is wise to his scheme, he'll take her out. You may have to put Hazard under protective surveillance until this bust goes down. Pull Nancy Cooper off her stakeout at Toot 'N Tell 'Em and let her shadow Hazard."

Nick nodded his shaggy head. If he hadn't known it already, he was reminded that Hazard had the homing instincts of a Patriot missile. She wouldn't back away from trouble even if a bomb exploded in her face—as it actually did during her last unauthorized investigation.

Nick clutched the CB and radioed his brother. Speak-

ing in scrambled code, Nick ordered Rich to terminate
Special Agent Cooper's employment at the quick-stop
and have her tail Hazard.

"I feel better, even if you don't," Roger murmured
when Nick completed the call. "You and Hazard would
make quite a team, if you ever decide to return to special
investigations."

"What makes you think Hazard will ever speak to me
again?"

Roger smiled faintly. "That could be a problem, communication being as vital as it is in this line of work."

Nick wasn't as concerned about communication as he
was about keeping Hazard alive for the duration of the
case. He was going to have to do something—quick. But
Nick, unlike Roger, had considered the possible reper-
cussions of making contact with Hazard at this stage of
the game.

Someone in Vamoose was feeding information to
Mr. Big. That was obvious. Jayme Black had turned
up dead. Nick suspected there was a connection. If there
was, Hazard could become next in line for execution.

So how was he going to contact Hazard without alerting Mr. Big's spies that there was something going on
between him and Hazard?

Nick checked his watch. As soon as it was dark, he
was going to crawl to Hazard's farmhouse and make
contact. It would have to be tonight. At the rate this
daring amateur sleuth was digging for facts, she might
not survive until tomorrow.

Amanda grumbled when she glanced down at the fuel
indicator. Her gas-guzzling truck was operating on noth-

ing but fumes. She would have to make an unplanned detour to the service station in town.

When Gib Cooper swaggered toward her, Amanda rolled her eyes. She predicted Romeo Cooper would come on like gangbusters again. The man was permanently on the make.

Gib leaned his hip against the side of the truck and flashed a knock-'em-dead smile around his toothpick. His greasy blond hair and stubbled jaws ruined the seductive effect he sought.

Only Nick Thorn could look like an unkempt renegade and still appeal to the feminine senses. It brought out Thorn's Native American heritage in a wild, exciting sort of way that Amanda couldn't explain. It just did, even if she still hated Thorn for being an insensitive, male chauvinist louse.

"Hey, pretty lady, how about me and you painting this little town red tonight," Gib propositioned.

"Sorry, I'm fresh out of paint and brushes."

Gib chuckled, as if Amanda were the wittiest creature in Rocky Mountain jeans and Justin Roper boots. "I love a woman with a sense of humor. Wanna try to charm the pants off me?"

That, Amanda imagined would require little effort. "Sorry," Amanda said, her tone not the least bit apologetic. "I promised to help my grandfather polish his dentures tonight."

Gib leaned his folded arms against the door of the truck, his expression serious. "You got something against good ole boys like me, sugar?"

"Just fill up the truck," Amanda snapped, tiring of the seduction game, which only Gib was playing.

Amanda didn't have the time or inclination for Gib's

crude courting ritual. Her mind was spinning like a whirlpool, clues churning in her thoughts, seeking to attach themselves to facts. Amanda desperately needed to sit down and organize her information so she could proceed to the next phase of her investigation in a practical manner.

Suspicions about the Hamptons, the Greens, and Jayme Black fairly screamed at her. Discovering the stash of drugs in Bloom's hay and feed sacks indicated that organized crime was operating in Vamoose.

The alarming realization put Amanda on edge. This was her haven from the hectic fast-lane life of the big city that she had walked away from. This was her countrified sanctuary, her home. How dare some crime syndicate set up housekeeping in down-home, small-town America!

"Okay, honey, this is your last chance," Gib said as he handed her the fuel ticket. "You don't know what a great time you're missing."

Amanda thrust a twenty-dollar bill at the grease monkey, wondering if he was smart enough to make correct change. She drummed her fingers on the dashboard while Gib swaggered toward the cash register. She wanted to go home and collect all her information in a neat, organized pile—now. Every second she delayed made her cranky and restless.

"Amanda! You're just the person I need to see!" Gertrude Thatcher hailed her from the service station door, waving a computer printout like a flag of surrender. "Could you come into the office for a minute? I need your help."

Amanda climbed down from her truck and followed Gertrude down the hall into the back office.

"According to this official-looking notice, we didn't

pay our taxes for the diesel we sold," Gertrude said worriedly. "I mailed the check with the tax report you filled out for the tax commission. I know I did."

Amanda accepted the notice thrust at her and studied it carefully. "This notice was mailed the same day your check should have arrived." She handed the paper back to Gertrude. "I suggest you call the office and ask them to confirm the arrival of your check so Uncle Sam doesn't slap a penalty on you."

"On Saturday?" Gertrude asked dubiously.

"Maybe you'll get lucky and get an answering machine. You can leave your message and the secretary can clear up this mistake before you follow up with a call on Monday."

Gertrude plunked down in her chair and reached for the phone. She glanced at the number listed on the notice and quickly punched the buttons.

"Well, that's weird. It sounds like I've got a bad connection . . . Oops," Gertrude smiled sheepishly. "I dialed the fax number instead of the phone number. No wonder I didn't get an answer."

Amanda impatiently waited for Gertrude to make the call. When some grouchy overbearing male answered and lit into Gertrude in a thundering voice, Amanda snatched the receiver from Gertrude Thatcher's shaky hand.

"Now, look, buster," she cut him off at the pass. "You may be having a bad day—"

The barking voice came at her again. "Well, it isn't my fault you can't get all your work done on weekdays and have to come into the office today. My client mailed her tax report and payment on time. Your office sent her a warning notice that she will be penalized if she doesn't pay up. Why don't you check your mail before you send threatening letters to the honest, hardworking citizens of this state?

"Get off your lazy butt and pull up the Thatcher Oil and Gas account on the computer. My poor client is about to have a coronary, thinking she's going to be hauled to jail for tax evasion. There are murderers running around loose, committing crimes far more serious than making the mistake of relying on the government's sluggish postal system to deliver their bills and payments promptly!"

Gertrude patted Amanda's tense arm and frowned in concern. "Do you think it's a good idea to rip the employee to shreds? He might come down here and close our doors or suspend your license. I don't know how or when it happened, but the IRS has become as powerful as the president, maybe even more so. We shouldn't ruffle their feathers."

Amanda's emotions were in chaos. She had entirely too much on her mind—Thorn's shocking breakup, two murders, and the adjustment to having Pops underfoot. Turmoil had suddenly become Amanda's middle name, and she did not function well when her life was out of whack.

That was Thorn's fault, too, Amanda thought bitterly. Their relationship had become the unwavering constant that she could depend on in life. Now she was drifting through chaos like a rudderless ship, like a tumbleweed in the wind, like a windblown kite . . .

Get a grip, Hazard! You'll be as wacky as Georgina Green if you don't watch out, came that rational voice from deep inside.

Amanda gave herself a mental slap and brought herself under control.

Three minutes and twenty seconds later—according

to Amanda's wristwatch—the booming voice came down the pipes.

"We made a mistake," the tax agent growled. "Ignore the notice."

When he slammed down the phone, Amanda winced at the harsh sound. "Well, that's that. You can tear up the notice, Gertrude. Your account is paid in full."

Mission accomplished, Amanda returned to her truck to find Gib Cooper cleaning her windshield and polishing the chrome on her side mirrors.

"This is your last chance to enjoy the best night of your life," Gib insisted, flashing his best smile.

"I thought I had my last chance ten minutes ago," she reminded him.

"For you, doll face, I've decided to be generous. So, how about it?"

"No thanks."

Amanda climbed into her truck, exceedingly proud of herself for her restraint. She could have sliced that grease monkey to shreds with her switchblade tongue—if she had wanted to. If Amanda hadn't been so anxious to get home, she might have. Gib didn't know how lucky he was that Amanda hadn't cut his male ego into bite-sized pieces.

Ah, it's going to be sheer relief to return home, Amanda thought to herself. She needed to push back in her recliner, relax, and gather her thoughts.

But how could she keep Pops from distracting her? At least she had a few miles to go before she had to come up with the solution to that problem.

"Hey, honeybunch, you forgot your change!" Gib called out as Amanda shifted her jalopy into gear and prepared to sail off.

Amanda accepted the dollar bill and two quarters he thrust at her. Before she could drive away from the gas pumps, a four-wheel drive truck—with all the fancy chrome trimmings—pulled in. Amanda stared at the heavily tinted window, waiting for the driver to roll down the window and identify himself.

She already had a pretty good idea who it was.

When Gib strolled over to wait on the customer Amanda studied the sun-bronzed face and glassy red eyes that came into view when the electronically operated window rolled down. A black felt Stetson sat at a cockeyed angle on Buddy Hampton's head. A half-smoked cigar dangled from the corner of his turned-down mouth. When Gib asked Buddy to extinguish the cigar—before he blew up the gas tanks—the drunken cowboy shot Gib a scoffing glance.

"Look, pal, maybe you don't care if you blow yourself to smithereens," Gib grumbled, "but there's a world of beautiful women I haven't made love to yet. So gimme a break and let me keep my vital male parts intact, will ya?"

Eventually, Buddy did as requested.

There were a few questions Amanda was dying to ask Buddy Hampton. Well, not exactly dying, Amanda cautiously amended. According to Bobbie Sue, Buddy was hell in boots when he lost his temper. Amanda wondered how well behaved Buddy was when he was drunk.

Pulling away, Amanda drove to the nearest side street and waited to see what direction he took. Within a few minutes the souped-up truck peeled out and sped down the highway—weaving noticeably. Amanda mashed on the accelerator to catch up. As anticipated, the truck veered west at the country intersection that led to Hampton Horse Ranch.

Well, so much for going home. Amanda had a suspect to pursue.

"Subject detoured west off the highway, rather than heading in the expected direction," Nancy Shore reported. "Subject looks to be making contact with a rough-looking cowboy."

Nick Thorn came back with orders to remain within seeing distance of the subject of surveillance, until she returned home and a replacement arrived—him. Nick intended to make contact with Hazard before the nagging feeling that hounded him got worse.

Under the cover of darkness, he was going to sneak up to Hazard's house. It might take him hours to get her to listen to him, but the situation was becoming dangerous. The special agents in the city were frantically working to identify and locate the plane Mr. Big used for fast transportation.

Mr. Big was a man accustomed to ditching tails, and at present, his whereabouts were unknown. That made Nick nervous.

Until the man was located, Nick was going to tie Hazard to a tree in the middle of nowhere. Under no circumstances was he going to let her get caught in the cross fire when the long-awaited drug bust went down!

veered west at the country intersection that led to Haughton Horse Ranch.

Well, so much for going home. Amanda had a suspect to pursue.

Buddy became the prime suspect, rather than Dauntry in the Bentley murder case. Nancy Shore requested Sheriff Jones to be making contact with a

Eleven

When Amanda arrived at the horse ranch, Buddy—who looked to be four sheets to the wind—was staggering toward the house. Amanda pulled in beside Buddy's truck. He flung himself around, glaring at her through bloodshot eyes.

"Now what the hell do you want?" he slurred in question. "Haven't you ruined my life already? Aren't you ever satisfied?"

Amanda strode boldly up the sidewalk and hooked her arm around Buddy's elbow. "You need a cup of coffee, pardner."

"Nope, I need another drink. The last one I had is wearing off."

Amanda nearly keeled over when Buddy breathed on her. What were they serving at Pronto Bar and Grill? Kerosene? She made a mental note not to strike a match anywhere near Buddy. He was flammable.

When he fumbled with the door key, Amanda snatched it away and opened the lock. To her dismay she saw the shambled results of Buddy's temper. The once-tidy house looked like a war zone. Broken lamps lay on the living room floor, strewn about like casualties of battle. Empty beer cans were stacked in pyramids, like hay bales, beside ashtrays heaped with cigar butts.

The room reminded Amanda of Jayme Black's pit of a home. Amanda's overactive sense of cleanliness and alphabetic order was offended.

"Look at this place!" she scolded the drunken cowboy. "Bobbie Sue kept this house looking like a palace. You've had it to yourself for only a few days and wham!"

Buddy scowled darkly as he braced himself against the nearest wall for support. "Don't start with me, Hazard. I'm as pissed at you as any man can get."

"No, you aren't," she argued. "Thorn already holds that title." One well-manicured index finger shot toward the sofa. "Park your carcass, Buddy-boy. I'm going to fix you a cup of coffee."

To her surprise—and relief—Buddy obeyed the order. He dragged off his cockeyed hat, exposing the matted hair known to the cowboy world as "hat-head."

"The damned sonuvabitch . . ." Buddy muttered as he half collapsed on the couch.

"Hold that thought and we'll discuss it in depth when I get back."

Amanda dashed toward the kitchen to brew coffee. In her effort to hurry the coffeemaker along and provide Buddy with a strong dose of caffeine, she dumped four times the usual amount of coffee into the container. While the appliance belched, gurgled, and hissed, Amanda scurried back to the living room to check on Buddy. He was sprawled out, raking his beefy fingers through tufts of disheveled hair and swearing inventively.

Five minutes later Amanda reappeared with a steaming cup of tar-colored coffee guaranteed to peel the lining off Buddy's liquor-polluted digestive tract and unpickle his brain.

"Drink," Amanda demanded.

Through blurred eyes, Buddy glared at her even as he accepted the cup. "No wonder Thorn dumped you," he said sluggishly. "You're worse than a marine drill sergeant."

"Shut up and drink," Amanda commanded.

When Buddy took a taste and then made an awful face, Amanda pushed the cup back to his lips so he couldn't set it down.

"Now," she said, staring intently into eyes that looked worse than fifty miles of Commissioner Brown's bad roads, "tell me where you went when you skipped out on exercising your horses."

Buddy's head came up and his gaze narrowed. "Who said I went anywhere?"

"The good fairy told me," Amanda said smartly. "Now cut the crap and answer my questions. From where I sit, you're guilty of murder, and maybe even extortion."

"Did she accuse me of killing lover-boy Bloom?" Buddy muttered, reaching for a cigar.

Amanda snatched up the stogie, broke it in half, and tossed it aside. She meant business here and she wasn't putting up with any nonsense or distractions.

"*I*'m accusing you," she corrected. "You are going to have to do some powerful convincing to change my mind. Given your flashes of temper and possessiveness where Bobbie Sue is concerned, you are my prime suspect." *For the moment,* Amanda silently stipulated. She was going for effect. It had worked splendidly with Bobbie Sue.

"I need more coffee," Buddy mumbled, massaging his aching head.

Amanda debated about leaving the room, wondering if Buddy might follow her and attack her while her back was turned. Or could he be planning to make a run for it?

"Will you be here when I get back, Buddy?"

He stared her squarely in the eye, his expression bleak. "Do you think I can make a fast getaway in the condition I'm in?"

"It has occurred to me that you might try, yes."

Buddy slumped against the sofa. "I'm not going AWOL, sarge. Get me some more of that motor oil you call coffee."

Amanda strode off, monitoring Buddy's every move—until she veered around the corner. She poured a quick cup and scuttled back, relieved that Buddy was where she had left him.

Buddy took a cautious sip and then propped his throbbing head in his hands. "I did it," he confessed. "I just couldn't tolerate the thought of Bloom messing around with my wife and living to brag about it."

Amanda blinked. "You did?"

He nodded. "I clubbed the sorry SOB over the head and dragged him into the corral. I shook the cattle cubes from an open feed sack in the barn and made it look like an accident."

"Did you notice anything strange about the feed sack?"

"Strange? What do you mean strange?"

"Never mind."

Amanda had been wishing and hoping the perpetrator would confess and make her job easier. But she would have preferred that the *real* guilty party identify him- or herself. Amanda knew Buddy was confessing to protect someone else.

"Go ahead and call Thorn. Let's get this over with."

The only thing more exasperating than a criminal who wouldn't confess to his guilt was an innocent party—

driven by misguided affection and a sense of duty—who did confess to something he didn't do.

"You can drop your martyr routine," Amanda snapped. "I know you're trying to protect your wife. For heaven's sake, Buddy, if you are so crazy in love with Bobbie Sue, why did you kick her out? I could have sworn you were prepared to forgive her—for anything and everything—the day I was here."

Buddy glared at Amanda. "How the hell did you get so damned smart, Hazard?"

"I was born a woman," she said flippantly. "Now quit trying to distract me and let's get down to brass *facts*. Three weeks ago you inadvertently opened your wife's letter that turned out to be a blackmail note from Will Bloom. Then you taped it shut, didn't you? You didn't know what to do about what you had learned, but you were compelled to follow Bobbie Sue to Bloom's farm, afraid she was going to do something drastic. Then you cased the place, still trying to decide how to handle the situation with Bloom. Two weeks ago, you followed Bobbie Sue back to the farm again. Unfortunately, you didn't arrive in time to actually see her kill Will, but you knew she had, because you found the body crumpled beside the barn. In order to protect Bobbie Sue, you dragged Will into the corral and strung out the cattle feed to make the scene look like an accident."

"I thought I was supposed to be doing the talking," Buddy muttered.

"You've had entirely too much to drink, and you keep getting sidetracked. Just correct me if I make a wrong assumption." Amanda glanced at him curiously. "How am I doing so far?"

"You haven't missed a lick," he mumbled, sipping his coffee.

"Since you had been casing Bloom Farm, maintaining surveillance, Jayme Black saw you. I expect you saw her a time or two, too. She was a regular at Bloom's farm, wasn't she?"

Buddy nodded in confirmation.

"When I showed up to find Bloom dead, you didn't want Bobbie Sue implicated, so you kept your mouth shut and pretended to know nothing about the situation. And by the way, you put on a splendid performance for my benefit," she added. "But then guilt started eating away at you."

"Damn, Hazard, you *are* good!"

"Thank you. And then you started hitting the bottle—hard and fast—telling yourself that you had driven Bobbie Sue into another man's arms because you weren't home when she needed you. If you had driven her to infidelity and murder, you knew you had to get her away from town before I dug too deep. You threw Bobbie Sue out of the house, knowing she'd call her sister. Since you believed you had held Bobbie Sue back from a successful singing career, you made the noble sacrifice and set her free. You're so crazy about that woman that you even confessed to murder to protect her."

Buddy gaped at Amanda for a full minute. "God almighty, does anything ever get past you?"

Amanda nodded glumly. "The real murderer has eluded me. Your wife says she didn't do it and I believe her. All you did was move the body, hoping to make the crime look accidental so you could take the heat off her.

"Now that I've had time to sit myself down to analyze you and your actions I just talked myself out of calling the authorities to have you arrested. You were my best guess. Now my theories don't hold water."

Buddy braced himself on a hip and reached for the wallet in his back pocket. "See what this does to your theories. Maybe you can figure this out," he said, handing Amanda the envelope.

Amanda unfolded the letter, noting the familiar scrawling and misspelled words. The extortion note demanded ten thousand dollars be delivered to Bloom's barn Saturday night—or else the world would know Bobbie Sue had been unfaithful. Furthermore, Buddy would become the laughingstock of the racetrack, outdistanced by another stud—or words to that effect.

"When did you receive this?" Amanda questioned.

"It came in today's mail."

"So naturally you hightailed it to the Pronto Bar and Grill to drink yourself half-blind, hoping Bobbie Sue had already caught a plane to Nashville before this whole mess blew up in your face."

"I hope she's flying off into the wild blue yonder by now," Buddy said.

"She isn't," Amanda reported.

"Well damn . . ."

Amanda sifted through the information stored in her brain, trying to figure out who had sent the extortion notes to Daniel Green and Buddy Hampton. One suspect came quickly to mind, but if Amanda's speculations proved correct, another player had entered this game of murder and extortion.

Unfortunately, resolving this complex case would have to wait. Amanda's tender-hearted tendencies—ones honed and nourished after months of living in this tightly knit, rural community—were nagging her to death.

"Go take a shower, Buddy," she ordered abruptly.

"What? Why?"

"Because I said so."

Obediently, Buddy staggered to his feet and stumbled toward the bathroom. Amanda found herself cleaning up the house while Buddy made himself presentable. She had all of Buddy's *Western Horseman* magazines and *Quarter Horse Journals* stacked in chronological order by the time he reappeared.

"If you think I'm going to supply the muscle for you to solve this case, think again, Hazard," Buddy mumbled as Amanda steered him out the door. "Even after two cups of your coffee I can't see straight. I won't be worth a damn in a fight."

Amanda swooped down to grab a handful of pansies that waved their colorful heads in the garden by the sidewalk. She thrust the bouquet at Buddy.

"All you have to do is tell Bobbie Sue what you told me—"

"I didn't tell you anything. You were reading my mind." Buddy dug in his heels, refusing to stir another step. "Hold your horses, Hazard. I'm not going to see Bobbie Sue and that's that. She's better off without me. I've held her back too long. She can outsing her sister and she should have been doing it for years, instead of playing house with a worthless cowboy like me. All I did was drag her into debt, trying to build up a name she could be proud of."

Amanda grabbed Buddy by the hair on his ultrasensitive head and towed him to her truck. "When I decide to play Cupid, then you're going to cooperate. All you have to do is stand there, with your fist full of pansies, and smile your best smile. I'll do the talking."

Despite Buddy's reluctance, Amanda drove off, determined to patch up the marriage she had unintentionally broken up.

"Subject has left with the drunken cowboy in the rattletrap truck," Nancy Shore checked in. "Companion appeared to resist, but the subject grabbed him by the hair and hauled him away."

"What?" Nick came back.

"You copied correctly. I like the subject's assertive style."

Nick thought he detected an undertone of amusement. "You would," he smirked.

"The twosome is headed north to town," Nancy added.

"Keep me posted."

"Gladly. This is more interesting than a soap opera. Over and out."

Nick set the radio microphone aside, wondering who on earth Hazard was dragging around by the hair and what this incident had to do—if anything—with Hazard's private investigation. He wished she would go home so he could sneak up and ask her what in the hell she had been doing!

Amanda parked in front of Buddy's mother-in-law's home. The trunk of Bobbie Sue's Caddy stood open like a giant, yawning crocodile. Two suitcases had been loaded, Amanda noted.

By the time Amanda convinced Buddy to climb down from the truck, Bobbie Sue had sailed out the door, a cosmetic travel bag in her hand. Bobbie Sue halted in her tracks when she saw Buddy.

Buddy did exactly as he had been told. He smiled and stood like a soldier at inspection—a clump of pansies in his fist.

"Buddy doesn't want you to leave, but he won't stand in your way if Nashville is your heart's desire," Amanda said without preamble. "He thought he was protecting you, after the incident with Bloom. By pretending ignorance he was going to let the situation ride. But after I started raising doubts about Bloom's death, he kicked you out of the house to set you free. He's been feeling guilty about preventing you from making your own name in the country music industry. The big lug is as crazy about you as you are about him. He even cares enough to let you go if that makes you happy."

"Buddy?" Bobbie Sue said tentatively.

Buddy glanced at Amanda for guidance. *Men!* she thought. *They never know when to take their cues.* Once you got them under control—and it was a time-consuming task—they hesitated to function. All that business about men being more attentive and sensitive played hell with the masculine psyche.

"Am I going to have to do *all* the talking for you?" Amanda questioned.

Still Buddy hesitated, and Bobbie Sue wasn't helping matters one bit. She stood there, spilling sentimental tears, staring expectantly at Buddy.

"Oh, for crying out loud," Amanda muttered impatiently. "Buddy, Bobbie Sue is still nuts about you, too. I think Will Bloom took advantage of her at a weak moment, in hopes of collecting the money he needed to skip town. Just because the two of you drifted apart doesn't mean it has to be over forever. But one of you better find the nerve to make the first move. None of us is getting any younger."

In supreme satisfaction, Amanda watched the Hamptons take steps in the right direction. Her heart gave a sentimental tug when they flung themselves into each other's arms in a mutual attempt to squeeze the stuffings out of each other.

Wheeling toward her truck, Amanda realized that playing fairy godmother and Cupid was distracting her. She had to get home and think this investigation through, now that it had taken a new twist. Having lost two probable suspects should narrow the field. She should be able to crack the case by a process of elimination.

Now that Blake Black was reported to be in the vicinity—probably up to his usual no good—Amanda would have to contemplate how he fit into this scheme of things.

Considering the demise of his ex-wife, Blake could have been involved in several capacities, hoping to make a fast buck, after his "extended vacation" in the pen.

Convenient, wasn't it, that Jayme had turned up dead so soon after Blake had been set free? His job opportunities in the drug world were looking better by the day.

Amanda drove home, wishing she'd had the foresight to quiz Velma and Bev about the charges that sent Blake Black to prison. Ten to one they were drug related.

"Subject left companion who is now doing a tonsillectomy on a brunette," Nancy Shore briefed Nick.

Nick frowned at the message, but he didn't comment.

"I'll follow Cupid home. Mary Quite Contrary is over and out."

Nick sincerely hoped that the Oklahoma tornado would blow home soon. If Hazard made another detour, he might never get the chance to alert her to the trouble brewing around her.

"Damn it, Hazard, go home!" Nick muttered as he paced the floorboards, impatiently waiting for Special Agent Shore—alias Mary Contrary—to report in again.

"Did we clear much money at the garage sale?" Amanda asked as she breezed into the house.

"Three hundred forty-two dollars," Pops reported. "And you should see my great finds. Some folks don't know what expensive treasures they gave away for practically nothing." He directed her attention to his feet. "I got these house shoes for fifty cents."

Amanda stared at the long-eared puppy faces stitched to the toes of Pop's shoes. He looked ridiculous—but satisfied.

"I also picked up an antique chair for two dollars. A little glue and sanding and it will sell for fifty dollars at the shop where I take my items for consignment."

Before Amanda could sit down and prop up her feet, Pops hitched his thumb toward the back door. "You forgot to clean out the wastebasket in my workshop," he reminded her. "I took the antique chair down to the barn when I got home. The foul scent nearly knocked me over. The workshop smells like a diaper pail."

Amanda had intended to sanitize the trash can that her dog had lifted his leg on. Surely Pete wasn't jealous of Pops. She had heard of pets punishing their owners by leaving smelly deposits when unwanted guests over-stayed their welcome, but Amanda hadn't thought Pete was the temperamental type of canine that pulled such disgusting stunts. Obviously she had misjudged him.

"I'll take care of it right now, but I have some work to do later, Pops. I need to be able to concentrate. I'd appreciate it if you could keep the volume turned down on the TV while I sort my thoughts."

"Sort your thoughts about what?"

"The Bloom case."

"I think you should leave this case up to the proper authorities," Pops advised.

Amanda frowned. "You're starting to sound like Mother—and Thorn."

Amanda knew she had offended Pops. He jerked up-right, as if he'd been slapped in the face. His head held high, he hobbled over to park himself in her favorite chair. Grabbing the remote control, he turned up the volume so loud that Pete howled on the front porch and Hank the tomcat ran for cover.

Amanda headed to the barn—with sponge and disin-fectant in hand—to sanitize the trash can. From the workshop she could still hear the roar of the television.

Richard Thorn ambled into Nick's bedroom and ex-tended the fax message he had received. "The Vamoose County sheriff's office just sent out an APB to pick up Jayme Black's ex-husband for questioning. Thus far, he hasn't been located."

Nick shrugged into a clean shirt and then glanced at the paper Rich held up to him. "When was the suspect released from the penitentiary?"

"Two weeks ago," Rich reported. "You think Blake Black followed Jayme to Bloom's farm and took the man out?"

Nick shrugged noncommittally. "I've been too busy trying to set a snare for Mr. Big to determine if Bloom's murder was a direct result of his drug transaction or a simple case of jealous fury."

"Blake Black may not have made contact with his wife at all," Rich mused aloud.

"Right," Nick said. "That's why Blake stopped at Thatcher's Oil and Gas on his way through town to fuel up. Vamoose was just an incidental pit stop. According to Gib Cooper, the bad boy of Vamoose has been seen driving around town in his fender-bent car several times. I wish the hell I knew where he is now. I've got that itchy feeling that something is about to happen."

"Me, too," Rich said as he handed Nick the two-way radio. "I'm going to stand watch at Bloom Farm with Roger. Not being able to locate Mr. Big makes me nervous. Something is up, or we both wouldn't be sensing it."

"I'll send Nancy Shore back to the house to handle communications when I relieve her from surveillance duty. Gib should be coming in for backup, after he makes a quick check of Jayme Black's farm house. The authorities plan to cordon the place off when Gib completes his search."

Nick grabbed his boots and then sank down on the edge of the bed to pull them on. Rich was silent for a moment.

"Make double damn sure you don't get careless, bro," Rich cautioned. "If Mr. Big's mysterious informant sees Hazard as a threat—because she's been snooping around—sighting you around her place will tip off the kingpin. I don't want this to turn into a hostage situation for you or Hazard."

Neither did Nick. Hazard had been seen in too many places, asking too many questions, putting too many people on edge. People who stepped on the wrong toes invited elimination. Hazard didn't have a clue how sensitive Mr. Big's toes were.

Nick did.

"I suggest you belly-crawl to Hazard's house, as if you were crossing a battle zone," Rich called after his brother.

"I had planned to. And don't try to contact me, Rich. I'll check in with you when the coast is clear—"

"If you're up to your ass in trouble, then you damned well better call me," Rich said in an emphatic tone.

Nick hoped it wouldn't come to that. If it did, it would mean that Hazard had already found herself in circumstances reaching catastrophic proportions.

"Good grief, Pete," Amanda choked out when the pungent smell met her at the workshop door. "We are going to have to do something about your personal hygiene habits!"

Armed with stout disinfectant, Amanda forged through the converted granary to snatch up the offensive trash can. From the smell of things, Pete had marked his territory more than once. The place reeked!

Amanda carried the plastic trash dispenser across the corral to the fifty gallon garbage barrel that sat beside the water hydrant. She hosed down the trash can, and then sprayed a double dose of disinfectant. When she dumped the trash into the large barrel, chunks of plywood, empty glue dispensers, and cans of wood stain and varnish clanked against the metal barrel.

In shock, Amanda watched a plastic sack—containing an all-too-familiar white substance—slide from the trash can. Amanda reached through the rubbish to retrieve the sack.

Pete, who made a habit of following Amanda around the barnyard, barked his head off. Amanda gaped at the three-legged dog. Pete was a drug-sniffing hound? Obviously he had tried to alert her and Pops as best he could. Pete's methods of hiking a leg on the trash can, leaving an unpleasant smell behind, had finally claimed Amanda's attention.

Amanda studied the contents of the Ziploc bag. So this was the sack that had been stashed in the workings of the antique clock Bloom had given her. Will had been trying to send Amanda a message. He had known trouble was brewing.

Where was this bag of drugs supposed to lead her? Thus far, Amanda had been going around in circles, frantically trying to connect all the suspects to the crime.

With fiendish haste, Amanda scrubbed the inside of the trash can and replaced it in the workshop. She had the unnerving feeling Will Bloom had also left clues in the accounting ledger he had asked her to pick up from his farm that fateful day. That upside-down phone number, written in blue, must have some connection. She couldn't wait to get her hands on the ledger to see what other messages Bloom had left for her.

With Pete hopping at her heels, Amanda trotted back to the house. She paused at the back door, sucked in several breaths, and tried to appear calm. She couldn't alert Pops to her bubbling anticipation of solving another case. He was becoming overprotective, trying to discourage Amanda from her natural inclinations of investigation.

Striving for a casual, relaxed air, Amanda strolled into the living room, "The workshop has been sanitized," she hollered over the loud volume of the TV.

"Good. I hope that dumb dog leaves that trash can alone. He's already clogged up my nasal passages."

"I'm sure Pete will be on his best behavior." Amanda scooped up the ledger on the bookcase. "I'll be working in my bedroom."

Without so much as a glance in Amanda's direction, Pops nodded his bald head. Apparently he was still pissed off about being compared to Mother.

Amanda practically ran down the hall in her haste to scan the ledger. Sitting cross-legged on her bed, she thumbed through the accounting book with practiced efficiency. Her gaze landed on the string of numbers penciled at the bottom of page eight.

A bank account number? Amanda wondered. She flipped back to page four to study the phone number printed in blue.

Amanda picked up the phone to place the call. Again, she heard a click, buzz and hum.

Her thoughts skidded to a halt, remembering what had happened when Gertrude Thatcher had accidentally dialed the tax commission's fax number rather than phone number.

Bingo!

Following the theory that Bloom had left clues every fourth page, Amanda flipped to page sixteen. Another phone number—or fax number—with Vamoose's prefix appeared. On a hunch, Amanda grabbed the phone book. As she suspected, the phone number belonged to the late Jayme Black, who had made her drug pickups—concealed in straw—from Bloom's barn.

A memory flashed in Amanda's mind. She distinctly remembered seeing the wide-ruled theme notebook lying on the end table in Jayme's bedroom. When Daniel Green had brandished the extortion note in her face the previous evening, Amanda had been too distracted to notice the familiarity of the paper. The same held true of the note Buddy had received today.

Now that Amanda had time to think about it, she remembered the notes Daniel and Buddy had received had been written on wide-ruled paper with perforated edges—just like the ones in Jayme's notebook.

A coincidence? Amanda didn't think so.

"Holy shit," Amanda chirped as the clue slipped into place. Jayme Black knew which questions to ask, because she was aware of Georgina's addiction. Jayme must have decided that Daniel's senatorial candidacy and Bobbie Sue's fling were prime opportunities to make extra money.

But who had bumped Jayme off? Did Jayme know too much? Did she know who killed Bloom?

Amanda would have dearly loved to know if anyone else in Vamoose had received an extortion note from Jayme Black before the troublemaking prostitute had been found dead. Too bad Jayme had gotten greedy and had paid the supreme price. Jayme Black had probably known a lot more than she had been allowed to say.

Amanda knew the domino theory of cause, effect, and chain of events applied to this case. Will Bloom's illegal activities were like a spiderweb that branched out in several directions. Although Will had kept a low profile and appeared to be harmless, he was a wealth of information and collector of expensive items that no one knew he had in his possession.

The accounting ledger was probably full of valuable clues—if only Amanda could piece them all together. But for sure, she was going to be on hand at Bloom's barn after dark, to see if anyone showed up to collect the extortion money that Daniel refused to pay and Buddy couldn't afford to pay.

Scanning page twenty, Amanda discovered another phone or fax number that had been penciled between the debits and credits. It was a long-distance number. Amanda had no idea who it might belong to.

The doorbell chimed, breaking her concentration. Muttering, Amanda set the ledger aside and padded down the hall. Pops hadn't realized they had a visitor. He had removed his hearing aids and was staring at the television screen—sulking. Amanda ignored his cold shoulder treatment and answered the door.

"Amanda?"

Jim Johnson, looking as clean-cut and freshly scrubbed as ever, stood on the porch. Amanda silently groaned. She had forgotten about making a date with Jim. She had been too involved in picking clues and questioning suspects. Jim popped a breath mint while he appraised her oversize flannel shirt and faded blue jeans. "Does this mean tonight's date is off?"

"I'm afraid so," Amanda apologized. "Something has come up. Business. I have to go out later. I'm sorry you drove all the way out here from the City for nothing."

Jim smiled in amusement. "May I ask you something, Amanda?"

"Shoot."

"Are you always so difficult to date or did I catch you at a bad time in your life?"

"Bad timing, I'm afraid. One of my clients—" Amanda shrugged evasively. "I have some loose ends to wrap up."

Jim nodded and then performed an about-face. "I'll try you again next week, if that's all right."

Amanda watched him walk away, wondering if she shouldn't call him back to make a clean break, here and now. The humiliating truth was that nothing permanent would ever come of this relationship. She was still stuck on Thorn—the infuriating louse.

She really was a glutton for punishment, wasn't she? Since she couldn't have Thorn—and she would never take him back after the awful way he had treated her— she wanted no one else.

Opportunity lost, Amanda thought as Jim drove away. Men could come and go from her doorstep, but she was doomed to pine for that dark-eyed Prince Charming who had turned into a toad and was fooling around with the bimbo from Toot 'N' Tell 'Em.

"So what does that make you, Hazard?" she asked herself.

An idiot.

Amanda closed the door and then veered around the La-Z-Boy recliner where Pops sat, making a spectacular display of ignoring her.

Nick switched off the headlights of his truck and drove a half mile, following the steel fence post reflectors that glistened in moonlight. He turned into the open field gate where Nancy Shore sat in her car, keeping surveillance on Hazard's house.

"Any activity?" Nick questioned as Nancy—minus her long blond wig—stepped out to meet him.

"Not much. Hazard dumped the trash in the barn and returned to the house. A late model car pulled up, stayed for only five minutes, and then drove away."

"Anybody we know?"

Nancy dodged Nick's intense gaze. "Yeah, the new boyfriend. My view was blocked by the barn. I couldn't tell whether Hazard drove off with him or not. I tried to contact you, but you had already left your house."

Nick hoped Hazard had gone out with her boyfriend. He wanted her as far away from trouble as she could get. And there was going to be trouble. Nick could smell it, feel it in his bones.

Years on the City's police force had finely tuned his senses. When Mr. Big suddenly went underground, he usually turned up somewhere else. And somewhere, somehow, hell always broke loose shortly thereafter. Of course, Mr. Big made certain his name was never linked, even if it was *his* bejeweled finger that pushed buttons that gave orders passed through his intricate chain of command.

"I told Gib you would be back at my house in a few minutes to handle the contacts with the team of agents on standby," Nick said as he ushered Nancy back to her car. "If we give the signal, the agents are going to strike simultaneously at the Uni-Comp warehouse and Texas mill. Now, if only Mr. Big will show his face so we can nab him, I'll be one happy cop."

"Are you still going to attempt to contact Hazard?" Nancy asked. "She may not be there, you know."

"If I can't reach Hazard tonight, I'll warn her grandfather. Hopefully, Pops can dream up an excuse to keep her at home for the next couple of days."

"Have Pops fake illness," Nancy suggested as she started her car. "At his age, that won't draw Hazard's suspicion."

Nick decided that was an excellent idea. If he couldn't warn Hazard away and swap information with her, he would settle for keeping her occupied for the next forty-eight hours.

Employing his marine and police training, Nick crouched in the grass and made his way from one tall weed to the next. He moved, undetected, toward Hazard's farmhouse, knowing he would be as welcome as the plague.

Well tough. He would tie Hazard down, tape her mouth shut, and make her listen to his explanation. When she calmed down—say in a couple of hours—he would demand that she share the information she had gathered on this case. Between the two of them, perhaps they could fuse several missing links together for a solid lead, bust the drug ring wide open, and then solve Bloom's murder. They might even get lucky and locate Jayme Black's murderer while they were at it, Nick thought to himself.

If Hazard—the super sleuth of Vamoose—was as efficient as usual, she had already dug up facts about Jayme. It never ceased to amaze Nick that Hazard's sources—ones that were taboo and unacceptable in the detective manual—always worked for Hazard. How she put two and two together still fascinated Nick.

It must be her mathematical, alphabetically organized mind, he decided. He sincerely hoped Hazard survived this latest case to teach him a few of her unorthodox techniques.

Amanda grabbed a Diet Coke and aimed herself toward her bedroom. She halted in mid-step when another thought flew at her like a lightning bolt. She had played the recording of Jayme's voice over and over in her mind—despite the loud blare of the TV. The pistol-packing prostitute, who spoke through the smoke of the cigarette clamped between her lips, was accustomed to taking risks. She had taken one too many.

Jayme talked tough because she was tough. Amanda wondered if Jayme's ex-husband had been the one who led her astray, or if she had gone down the wrong road all by herself. Amanda also wondered if Blake Black smoked cigars or cigarettes. She would like to track him down and ask him.

Amanda sighed as she sank down in the middle of her bed. The cigar thing again. This investigation always came back to those damned cigars, to the telltale scent of smoke and discarded ashes.

Amanda flipped to page twenty-four in the ledger to find another mysterious phone—or fax—number. These days she never knew which. Those ingenious devices were playing hell with her investigation.

Amanda forgot to breathe. She simply stared at the ledger, her mind whirling like the spin cycle of a washing machine. The phone number—written in red—that she found on the last page of the ledger had a hauntingly familiar look to it. Amanda grabbed the phone book once again to check the number. She was certain she wasn't going to like what she found.

Bull's-eye!

She leaped off the bed, clutching the ledger to her chest. She had to locate Thorn—now. This was no time to let personal conflict interfere in seeing justice served. She was onto something big here, really big! The final phone entry in Bloom's ledger—a hastily scrawled clue on the last page—was his way of alerting her to who had knocked at his door that fateful day.

Bloom's murderer must have been interrupted by Bobbie Sue and then Buddy's appearance. Amanda arrived on the scene shortly thereafter, making it impossible for the killer to check to ensure all the tracks were covered. When Amanda started posing questions, the killer got nervous.

Grabbing her keys, Amanda all but ran down the hall. Pops glanced up, startled. "Where are you going at this time of night, Half Pint?"

"To see Thorn," Amanda announced.

"You're going to make up with him?"

"Sort of," Amanda hedged. She didn't want to worry Pops. He was fast becoming the male version of Mother.

With a hasty wave of farewell, Amanda burst through the front door. When one intended to fly over gravel roads at unreasonable and imprudent speeds, one needed to drive a truck. Amanda was taking no chances of hitting high center in her compact car. She needed to speak to Thorn—immediately. If he was entertaining that bimbo at his home, Amanda would—

Amanda yanked open the door to her jalopy truck, promising herself that she wouldn't lose her temper— much. She needed Thorn's expertise as a cop, now. Later, she would strangle him if he was doing the horizontal hootchie-cootchie with the tacky cashier from the quick-stop!

Twelve

Nick muttered a curse into the weeds when he saw the headlights of Hazard's old truck flick on and heard the growl of the engine. He had crawled halfway across the pasture and had no chance to flag Hazard down. The truck roared off in a cloud of dust.

Balancing on his knees, Nick grabbed the CB to call Gib Cooper. "It's Jack-Be-Nimble. I wasn't quick enough. Over."

Static broke through the chirps of crickets and birds. "Copy, Jack." Gib responded. "Where's Mary Contrary?"

Gib's coded question indicated that Nancy Shore had yet to reach Nick's farm. "I want Mary Contrary to reverse direction. I'm losing H—" Nick caught himself before he broadcast Hazard's name over the air waves. "I need tail—quick!"

"Don't we all," Gib chuckled.

The sound of an approaching aircraft caused Nick's nerves of steel to vibrate like harp strings. The uneasy sensation at the base of his neck and the middle of his gut became more pronounced. The same bad vibes that assailed him when he discovered Bloom's stash of drugs in the barn now hounded him. Nick felt a sense of panic, not knowing where Hazard was headed, while a suspicious plane loomed overhead.

Nick gave the emergency signal that requested all special agent teams remain on a state of red alert. Then he took off toward Hazard's house at a dead run. He had to track Hazard down—fast. Nick prayed that Pops knew where Hazard had gone—or that Pops was with her.

The barking dog and squawking chickens announced Nick's arrival. He didn't waste time trying to sneak up to the house. It was too late for stealth and silence.

The blaring television indicated Pops was still at home. Nick leaped onto the porch and pounded on the door. There was no answer.

Nick glanced apprehensively at the barn and outbuildings, wondering if a sniper was lying in wait. He couldn't afford to get himself gunned down before he located Hazard and put her under protective custody.

Wasting no time, Nick slammed his shoulder against the locked door. Hinges creaked and wood splintered as Nick barreled into the living room to see Pops propped in Hazard's favorite chair. The old man shrank away in alarm, very nearly catapulting himself from the recliner.

"Hell and damnation, Thorn," Pops gasped, clutching at his chest. "You nearly gave me a heart attack! What are you doing here?" His bug-eyed gaze dropped to Nick's right arm. "I thought you were seriously injured."

"I suddenly got better. Where's Hazard?" Nick demanded to know that very instant.

Pops blinked owlishly, still gaping at the looming figure dressed in black. "Amanda already left."

"I know that," Nick muttered impatiently. "Where'd she go?"

"She was on her way to see you. Didn't you cross paths?"

"No, I'm on foot," Nick scowled as he stalked through the room. "I need to use the phone."

While Pops levered himself from the chair and grabbed his walker, Nick made his call. When Gib answered, Nick blurted out, "Jack here. You-know-who is supposed to be on her way to my farm."

"What am I supposed to do when she shows up and she wonders what I'm doing at your place? Turn invisible . . . ? And where the hell is Mary Contrary?"

"Damned if I know, but call me the minute what's-her-name shows up." Nick hurriedly rattled off Hazard's phone number. "There's a plane headed in our direction. Tell Robin Hood to get his transport off the premises before it's spotted by the incoming aircraft. Radio for backups. We need our men ready to move at a moment's notice."

"Got it."

Nick hung up the phone and then wheeled around to see Pops studying him astutely. There was something about Pops that reminded Nick of Hazard. The thought stood his nerves on end again.

"She's in trouble, isn't she?" Pops questioned anxiously. "What's going on, Thorn?"

Nick avoided the direct question by locking every window and the back door—just in case. He must have glanced at the phone a hundred times, willing it to ring, wanting the reassurance that Hazard had arrived safely.

The phone didn't ring.

Nick checked his watch for the umpteenth time. Several minutes had passed. Considering the speed at which

Hazard had been driving when she soared off, she should have reached his house by now.

Or had she piled the truck in a bar ditch beside the road?

"Ring, damn it!" Nick burst out.

It rang.

Nick snatched up the receiver. "Hello?"

"Hello, Thorn, it's Mother. We just got back from our marvelous cruise to the Caribbean. Daddy and I were treated like royalty the entire time."

Nick rolled his eyes. Damn, what a time for Mother to call. "I hate to cut you off, but—" Nick discovered that *he* was the one cut off when Mother started yammering ninety miles a minute.

"You wouldn't believe the elegant meals served on those cruise lines," Mother carried on—and on. "We ate in grand style, serenaded by an orchestra, waited on hand and foot. And you should have seen the flames shooting up from the bobbaloo and baked Alaska! It was fantastic, absolutely wonderful!"

"Mother—"

"And those islands, with their palm trees swaying in the breeze, the rolling waves of crystal clear water. It was like being in heaven—"

To Nick's surprise, Pops hobbled over, jerked the phone from his fist and slammed it down.

"If you haven't learned by now, the only way to shut that woman up is to hang up on her."

Nick glanced at his watch. He couldn't wait any longer. Adrenaline was shooting through him, making his blood cells crackle like popcorn. "If the phone rings again, tell Gib I'm headed back to my truck—"

"What?" Pops questioned when Nick made the mistake of wheeling away while he was still talking. Pops hadn't been able to read his lips.

Nick snatched up the hearing aids sitting on the end table and thrust them at Pops. "Lock the door behind me! I'll be back to pick you up in a few minutes!"

"I can't lock the door. You broke it."

"Then use your walker as a weapon if somebody shows up while I'm gone."

Nick hit the door running and he didn't slow down until exhaustion forced him to pause to catch his breath. He would have to use the two-way radio in the truck to contact Gib, he decided. Hopefully, Hazard had arrived and had received the order to stay put.

Nick charged toward his four-wheel drive truck. The biggest drug bust of the decade was going down and here he was, sprinting across a pasture instead of scrunching down beside the dirt runway to reel in the cartel's big fish. Hazard better not have gotten herself in trouble. He'd kill her—if somebody else didn't do it first.

Amanda put the pedal to the metal, demanding the old jalopy give her all the power it had—which wasn't much. The engine sputtered, missed several vital beats, and then settled into its top speed of fifty-four miles an hour. Hands clamped to the steering wheel, eyes on the road, Amanda swerved to avoid as many ruts as possible as she raced toward Thorn's farmhouse.

She really should have seen through the murderer's ploy, she chastised herself. But, she rationalized, she had been distracted by Thorn's betrayal, her grandfather's arrival, and a hectic two weeks at the office. She had fallen for the oldest trick in the book. The ploy of your-friend-is-your-worst-enemy applied in this case. Amanda should have been more suspicious, and she mentally kicked herself a few times because she hadn't been.

It was the absence of the cigar and strength of the expensive cologne that had thrown her off course. *And let's not forget that calm, casual air, either,* Amanda silently added.

While applying the brake to make a left turn, Amanda told herself she should have remembered that scenario about trained killers being the most polite, self-controlled individuals on the planet. Why shouldn't they be? They were nothing more than lethal robots without consciences, ethics, or regard for human life. They were mercenaries who considered extermination nothing more than a high-paying profession.

Amanda was more disappointed in herself than startled when the passenger door of the truck flew open and a man dressed in black hurled himself into the cab— from his hiding place in the bed of her pickup. Neither was she surprised to see the semiautomatic weapon that rammed against her ribs immediately before the passenger door slammed shut.

Even with his face camouflaged by grease and his head covered by a black stocking cap, Amanda knew who had made his dramatic entrance. She could also guess the man's background. Too bad she hadn't paid attention earlier.

Now it was too late.

The man she needed desperately to avoid—the highly dangerous professional, the ex-commando soldier with his clean-cut appearance and unshakable self-discipline—was sitting beside her, holding a weapon she was absolutely certain he knew how to use and had done so on numerous occasions.

Amanda had committed the crucial mistake of over-looking the obvious clues that would have alerted her to impending danger. The perfectly executed about-face hinted at military training. The heavy-handed application of cologne and breath mints concealed the odor of smoke. The killer had deliberately misled Amanda into believing he didn't smoke cigars.

"Pull over, Amanda. Nice and easy."

Amanda noted he didn't add that she wouldn't get hurt if she did. That, Amanda knew, had no bearing on the situation. She had joined the ranks of those who knew too much—and death was the only cure.

When Amanda tried to jerk the wheel to throw her assailant off-balance, he poked the weapon between her ribs and grabbed the wheel with a gloved hand. The man was thorough, she would give him that. No incriminating fingerprints in the vehicle to lead authorities to her murderer.

Amanda found herself wedged between a steel-hard body and the door of the truck. Jim Johnson—or whatever his real name was—had taken control of the vehicle, applying the brake to bring it to a grinding halt.

Anticipating that Amanda would attempt to bolt and run, Jim snaked a muscled arm around her neck, cutting off her air supply. Amanda managed to snatch a quick breath before her throat closed.

With experienced ease, Jim braced the deadly weapon between his hip and Amanda's ribs. Then he reached into the pocket of his black leather jacket for the roll of duct tape.

"You are entirely too curious and intelligent for your

own good," he said, as calmly as ever. "You aren't the least bit surprised to see me, are you?"

Strong fingers clamped her wrists together like a vise grip. Tape whirled around her hands, practically fusing them together. Amanda attempted her own version of tae kwon do when Jim grabbed her leg. Unfortunately, the painful jab of his elbow against her chin discouraged her escape attempt and momentarily stunned her brain. Amanda struggled to remain semialert as Jim taped her ankles and knees so she couldn't walk.

"Can I expect to receive the same treatment you dished out to Will Bloom and Jayme Black? The death-blow with the lethal whack of your hand, perhaps?" Amanda questioned when she regained the use of her vocal apparatus.

Jim never changed expression. Robots usually didn't. "No, actually we have a more dramatic scheme in mind for you, Amanda."

"We?" she chirped.

Jim didn't elaborate. He simply clamped his arm around her waist, making her ribs crack like peanut hulls. After he had thrust her onto the passenger side of the truck, he taped Amanda to the open door of the glove compartment, discouraging further escape attempts.

Jim scooted beneath the steering wheel, put the truck in gear, and mashed on the accelerator. Amanda studied his shadowed profile as he changed direction. "Did you plan to haul Bloom's body off the farm after you broke his neck? Surely you didn't intend to leave him there."

"Of course not," Jim replied blandly. "But the farm became a hubbub of activity. I had to take cover before I was spotted. The Hampton woman showed up, discovered the body, and lit out. Then her husband arrived to drag Bloom into the corral. When you drove in, I decided to leave Bloom where Hampton put him. But then you started poking around and asking questions. I had to keep an eye on you. Sure enough, you made several dangerous discoveries. I could sense it when I came by your house earlier. You couldn't get rid of me fast enough, so you could rush off to investigate."

"There's one thing I can't figure out. Why were you given the order to dispose of Bloom, when the undetected drug ring was operating at peak efficiency?"

"Bloom became too assertive," Jim explained in his usual, nonchalant manner. "He ventured out on his own by selling merchandise on the side. Mr. Big doesn't approve of traffickers making local distributions and lining up their own pushers. He expects to be given the majority of the profit. I was called in to threaten Bloom. Instead of cooperating, Bloom made arrangements to extort money so he could bail out."

"So you took Bloom out because he blackmailed Bobbie Sue Hampton and hired Jayme Black to peddle dope to the high school crowd," Amanda speculated as Jim veered down the gravel road toward Bloom Farm.

Jim nodded slightly. "He also peddled the goods to a few of his lady friends."

Georgina Green for one, Amanda reminded herself. "And, of course, Jayme had to go, because she tried to make a little extra money for herself by blackmailing the aspiring senatorial candidate, Daniel Green."

"I found the second extortion note for Hampton in an envelope on her dining room table," Jim said as he glanced up to see the small aircraft circling overhead. "The woman was a born troublemaker, and so is her deadbeat ex-husband who dropped by, wanting a piece of the action. Jayme had to be stopped before Blake got involved and someone other than you started asking questions."

"Lucky thing you were exceptionally chummy with Jayme. I'm sure you led her to believe you had arrived to guard against the discovery of the crime ring in Vamoose and let her think you would put in a good word for her with the big boss," Amanda muttered. "Unlucky for me that you used breath mints and cologne after snuffing out your imported cigars. I would have figured this out days ago, if you hadn't."

The sarcastic remark didn't faze Jim. He reached for the two-way radio in his pocket and sent a coded signal to the pilot of the plane.

"Mr. Big and company, I presume? Will I have the grand distinction of meeting him?"

"Very shortly. Or should I say very briefly," Jim amended.

Amanda suspected the comment carried a double meaning. *Briefly* also applied to her life expectancy.

She wondered if Thorn would miss her when she was gone. She also wondered if her chance of survival carried the same odds as Pops's chance of winning his grand prize sweepstakes—one in a zillion.

"I suppose the unsuspecting community of Vamoose will have another low-profile operative installed at Bloom Farm when the property is placed on the auction block," Amanda predicted.

"Yours truly," Jim replied.

Amanda wasn't surprised. "That's why you acquainted yourself with the citizens of town. I suppose you also plan to quit your job with the nonexistent oil company.

I wish I had thought to double check the legitimacy of Petro Fuel with the Better Business Bureau."

"It wouldn't have mattered," Jim assured her. "The company is in legitimate operation—at least on paper. Mr. Big's oil company allows him to maintain his plane to check on the geological areas of potential wells. It also gives him an outlet for laundered money. I will be purchasing the Bloom Farm for Petro Fuel and managing the property."

"I suppose the money from various business interests are deposited in the Swiss bank account that Bloom recorded in his ledger," Amanda mused aloud.

Jim nodded. "And by the way, the contract for surface damages for a well site is null and void. The only contract out is on *you*."

Amanda rather thought that would prove to be the case.

Nick gunned his four-wheel drive truck and took the shortest route to Hazard's house. He had made contact with Gib, receiving the frustrating news that Hazard still had not arrived and that Nancy Shore had called from Miz MacAdo's house to say she had a flat tire on the country road.

Damn it! What else could go wrong?

Nick decided not to speculate on the answer to that question. He simply wanted to find Hazard.

Pops was standing in the driveway by the time Nick whizzed around the corral. Hopping out, Nick folded Pops's walker and tossed it in the back of the truck. With Pops belted to his seat, Nick shot off, driving like a maniac to compensate for lost time—and a missing ex-girlfriend.

Following his hunch, Nick headed for Bloom Farm. He wondered how the devil he was going to approach the place without the circling plane catching sight of his truck.

Nick was faced with a difficult dilemma. If he called in the special agent teams to nab Mr. Big when he touched down on the dirt runway, Hazard might become the human sacrifice. The fact that she had gone missing lent testimony to the fact that she had run into trouble.

If Nick concentrated his efforts on rescuing Hazard, Mr. Big would become suspicious and soar off into the night, free as a damned bird. It always seemed to come to this where Mr. Big was concerned, Nick mused in frustration. The man was as slippery as an eel. Mr. Big never had qualms about sacrificing others' lives to save himself from indictment and prison sentences.

"What's going on here?" Pops demanded. "And don't give me the runaround again, Thorn. I want a straight answer."

"A drug bust," Nick replied reluctantly.

"And my granddaughter is in serious danger, I suppose."

"Possibly."

"Then she must have found valuable information in that accounting ledger she was studying before she left the house with it in such a rush," Pops observed.

If that ledger contained incriminating evidence, then Mr. Big would naturally want to get his hands on it. There would be no ledger as evidence, not if Mr. Big had his way—and he usually did.

"Hold on to your hat, Pops," Nick advised as he topped the hill at excessive speed and plunged down the washboard road. "This low-water bridge is a little rough."

Pops braced his arms against the dashboard when the truck bounced on its shocks and bobbled on the uneven ruts. When the truck swerved toward the ditch, Nick spun the wheel, fishtailing in loose gravel.

"What are Amanda's chances of survival?" Pops asked grimly.

"I don't think you want to know."

"That bad?" Pops wheezed.

"Not good."

Nick clenched his fists around the steering wheel, thinking of the other times Hazard had suffered near brushes with disaster. Those other cases were mere child's play compared to the caliber of hardened criminals she was about to encounter.

Hazard might learn—firsthand—how truly vicious some people could be. Nick had dealt with plenty of hard-core villains while serving on the OKCPD and the narc squad. Too bad Hazard hadn't taken his advice and backed off. Now she was involved—up to her neck!

Nick's mind reeled, trying to devise Plan B, in case Plan A had to be abandoned. If, by chance, Hazard did wind up in Mr. Big's private plane—which had yet to be traced by authorities—she could kiss her fabulous fanny good-bye. Mr. Big only offered one-way tours. There would be no special FBI agents waiting when Mr. Big reached his final destination, because no one knew where his private hangar and airstrip were located.

In short, Nick thought grimly, Hazard was probably in the worst of all possible trouble.

* * *

Amanda's mind raced, conjuring up and then discarding possible escape plans. She tried to remain as calm as Jim Johnson, but it was difficult, since she wasn't holding the upper hand—or the semiautomatic. When Jim reached into his pocket to retrieve a lighter and a Cuban cigar, Amanda wondered if that was customary procedure before he disposed of his victims.

Pungent smoke filled the cab of the truck. Amanda wrinkled her nose distastefully . . .

Then an ingenious thought occurred to her and she acted on it.

"Would you please extinguish that stogie. I'm allergic to smoke."

Obviously, Jim didn't care. He puffed away. Amanda figured he would.

Amanda burst into theatrical coughing spasms—which Jim ignored. While he kept his gaze trained on the road, she swiveled on the seat to kick at the flaming cigar with her booted feet. Her unexpected blow sent glowing ashes showering onto his legs. The stogie dropped to the crotch of his pants, causing him to roar in outrage.

Grueling military training prompted Jim to strike out with the back of his hand—the same kind of blow that probably broke Will Bloom's and Jayme Black's necks, she suspected.

Amanda ducked. The karate chop struck the side window. Glass shattered.

Damn, Amanda thought as she strained to pick up a shard of broken glass. She could imagine how fast this trained assailant ended lives!

While Jim scrambled to retrieve the cigar that was burning a hole in his pants, Amanda sawed at the leash of tape anchoring her to the glove compartment. Hoping to keep Jim distracted, she kicked at the gun beside his hip. When it clanked on the floorboard, he reflexively slowed down and groped to retrieve it.

Amanda took full advantage of the situation. When she yanked fiercely on the sliced tape it gave way. In one fluid movement she flung open the door, grabbed the ledger, and plunged toward the ditch.

Gravel bit into the sleeves of her jacket as she skidded across the road and then tumbled into the ditch. Ignoring the pain, Amanda curled herself into a ball to slash at the tape that secured her ankles. She heard the truck grind to a halt and knew she didn't have much time to free herself. Jim would be on her in the space of a heartbeat, armed with a weapon that would fill her with so many holes she'd leak like a colander.

Frantically, Amanda cut the tape, her gaze glued to the ominous shadow that bounded from the truck and dashed toward her. Jim reminded her of a guerrila fighter answering the signal to charge. She knew she was out of her league, but her self-preservation instinct had kicked into high gear.

Quick as Amanda tried to be, she was way too slow to outdistance this well-conditioned ex-soldier. He was standing over her in the blink of an eye, shoving his loaded weapon in her face.

"Nice try, Tinker Bell."

Amanda noted that Jim didn't sound the least bit out of breath, while she was panting like a Kentucky Derby winner. Next time she decided to investigate a murder that involved wild chases and exhausting escape attempts, she vowed to get herself in better shape.

If there was a next time. . . .

Amanda was jerked, none too gently, to her feet and

carried to the idling truck. When Jim had repeated his tape routine, he snatched up the cigar he had tossed on the road and puffed away.

In grim resignation, Amanda watched the circling plane swoop toward Bloom's pasture.

"Have you ever been skydiving, Tinker Bell?" Jim asked in that infuriatingly calm voice.

"No, I have an aversion to heights."

"Mr. Big and I have decided you should try the daring sport."

"Do I get a parachute?" Amanda asked hopefully.

Jim's greased face turned toward hers. The dashboard lights illuminated his insidious smile and the flaming stogie clamped between his teeth. "What do you think?"

Amanda thought, when push came to shove, she would be free-falling without a parachute.

When Jim swerved through the cattle guard and bounced across the rough pasture, Amanda inhaled the fresh air swirling through the broken window. It was time for her to make peace with the world, just in case. This incident—provided her last remains were recovered and identified—was going to ruin Mother's homecoming from the Caribbean cruise. It didn't look as if Amanda was going to be around to see if Pops won his sweepstakes, either.

And Thorn . . . Amanda sighed inwardly. She was going to miss the big lug, even if she was still so furious with him that she could spit nails. She hoped he felt guilty about not taking her suspicions seriously. If he had opened an official investigation, she wouldn't have been on the fact-finding mission that had led to calamity.

* * *

Nick swore inventively when he saw the aircraft set down on the dirt landing strip. He had been unable to overtake the speeding truck before it turned into the pasture gate. Now Nick had a crucial decision to make. The special teams were in place, awaiting the command to simultaneously storm the City warehouse and Texas grain mill. The agents who had moved into position to overtake the plane before it left the runway had been hiding in the windrow of cedar trees for an hour. But if Hazard was on that plane, she would become a hostage when the special agents attacked.

The grim thought caused Nick to hesitate. If he gave the signal to charge the plane, he was all but signing Hazard's death certificate. He would wait as long as he could, in hopes of saving her—somehow . . .

When the plane touched down, a cloud of dirt billowed around it. Amanda swallowed hard when Jim brought the truck to a halt. She had given her escape attempt its best shot, and failed. No other brilliant schemes popped to mind as she watched the door of the plane open, revealing the silhouette that was surrounded by the golden glow of interior lights.

"Come on, Tinker Bell," Jim said as he slid off the seat. "Mr. Big is anxious to make the acquaintance of the woman who complicated what should have been a simple transition—"

Jim suddenly realized that the incriminating ledger which had been lying on the seat was missing. His menacing gaze drilled into Amanda.

It was her turn to smile wickedly. "Oops, during all

the commotion, I must have dropped the darned thing somewhere."

Jim muttered a string of foul oaths at his captive. Leaving her tied in the truck, he executed a perfect about-face and stalked off to report the missing ledger to Mr. Big. Obviously Mr. Big was no more pleased about the inconvenience and delay than Jim was. Through the broken window Amanda heard another round of curses filling the air.

"All right then," Mr. Big said gruffly. "Bring Hazard into the plane and then go find that damned ledger."

Amanda was promptly cut loose from the glove compartment by the nasty-looking knife Jim had strapped to his shin. He tossed her over his shoulder like a feed sack and toted her onto the aircraft. Amanda got an upside-down view of Mr. Big's face and emotionless blue eyes as she was carted inside.

"Mr. Big, meet Tinker Bell," Jim introduced while he secured Amanda to her seat. "The two of you can get acquainted while I'm gone."

After Jim scrambled down the steps Mr. Big sat down in the seat across the aisle from Amanda. "You, Ms. Hazard, have proved to be an annoying nuisance. I can understand why Thorn washed his hands of you."

Amanda forced herself not to react to the unexpected comment. "You're a friend of Thorn's?"

"Friend?" Mr. Big chuckled, reminding Amanda of a nickering horse. "No, we are arch enemies. He came uncomfortably close to pinning down my hide a few years ago, when he was an undercover agent in the City. That was one of the reasons I chose this rinky-dink town of his for my operation. He has no idea how I have amused myself by trafficking my products, right under his unsuspecting nose. It would have proved even more amusing to me if the two of you were still on friendly terms."

Amanda distinctly remembered Thorn telling her that his girlfriend had been mowed down in a violent act of revenge by some kingpin in the drug world. Obviously Mr. Big was that particular kingpin. She expected Mr. Big would have derived excessive pleasure in disposing of her, if she and Thorn had still been an item. Mr. Big wasn't going to enjoy more vindictive delight at her expense!

"I hate to spoil your fun, but there is nothing between me and Thorn, except bitter memories. We don't even speak to each other these days."

Mr. Big shrugged an Armani-clad shoulder. "Ah, well, love comes and goes, Ms. Hazard. Money is the only constant."

"I suppose it comes in handy when you have to pay somebody like Jim Johnson to do your dirty work for you. What is he? Ex-CIA or FBI?"

"He was previously affiliated with CIA's special forces," Mr. Big said with a sad shake of his head. "Such a pity the American government expects patriotism to be compensation in itself and cannot afford to pay such highly trained men their worth." His teeth gleamed. "Fortunately, I can."

Johnson was all mercenary, Amanda mused. She, on the other hand, investigated murder cases for nothing. She wondered if there was some twisted moral to this story about working too cheap.

"My right-hand man has handled unpleasant matters that have cropped up in my extensive operation the past several years," Mr. Big continued. "His first job entailed getting that pesky Thorn to back off when he got too close for comfort. Thorn used to be as relentless as you are, until I crushed his enthusiasm. Now I'm taking delightful enjoyment in beating Thorn at his own game, in his own sleepy little hometown.

"I have applied his agricultural practices to my business and have made considerable more money at it than Thorn has with his farm crops. It's a shame Thorn is unaware of how creative I've become. He's too busy fooling around with that floozy of his. If he had a clue what's going on, I think he would have appreciated the irony as much as I do."

Mr. Big lifted a beefy hand to comb his windblown black hair into place. Huge, diamond-studded rings sparkled in the light. "Haskell had better hurry along before he misses his ride," he grumbled, squirming impatiently in his seat.

"Haskell?"

"Alias Jim Johnson," he informed her. "He goes by many names, depending on his special assignments." Mr. Big glanced at his Rolex and then at the open hatch. His gaze swung to the pilot. "If Haskell isn't back in five more minutes, we'll leave without him. We're already fifteen minutes behind schedule."

The pilot nodded without glancing back. Of course, Amanda probably wouldn't have the chance to identify Mr. Big's personal pilot in a police lineup anyway. Not if her first skydiving lesson was everything "Jim" had promised it would be.

Reluctantly, Nick plucked up his two-way radio to contact his brother, who was in charge of the raid on the landing strip. Nick felt the overwhelming impulse to stall for more time, to pray for a few more minutes. He could use a miracle right about then. He'd even settle for a slight edge, one slim chance of saving Hazard from certain death.

"Send out the dancing bears," Nick ordered, giving the coded signal for the agents to storm the drug warehouses in the City and in Texas.

Static sizzled over the airwaves. "What about Robin Hood and his band of merry men in Sherwood Forest?" Rich came back.

"Sit tight, Robin."

"You sure about that?"

Nick knew Mr. Big would receive word the instant the special forces swarmed in. Nick also knew Mr. Big would take to his wings if Rich's strike force delayed for even a minute. But Hazard's life was hanging in the balance. What was he supposed to do? Let her become Mr. Big's shield of defense? The latest human sacrifice?

"You're going to let the Sheriff of Nottingham bolt and run?" Rich came back a few seconds later.

Nick cursed under his breath and then said, "He's carrying extra baggage."

"Damn. Well, maybe we can get lucky."

"Maybe, maybe not. Give me a few minutes before you start shooting your arrows, Robin."

Nick signed off. He would wait until Mr. Big received the news of the strikes. His next move would depend on Mr. Big, Nick decided. He preferred to act on Mr. Big's mistake—provided the slippery bastard made one.

Mr. Big checked his watch again. His stubby fingers drummed against his knee. "Call Haskell," he ordered the pilot. "Tell him to dispose of Hazard's vehicle. We'll pick him up on our way back from Texas."

Amanda suspected the phone number and fax number she had seen in the ledger were linked to Mr. Big's headquarters and supply house in Texas. It seemed Bloom had gathered all sorts of incriminating information against Mr. Big. Bloom had hoped to have his own brand of revenge, if he couldn't escape the crime ring.

The pilot's hand shot out to clasp the microphone, but a voice—crackling with alarm—blared over the radio. "Invasion at Uni-Comp! The cops have found the goods!"

Mr. Big launched from his seat and stormed toward the cockpit. "Get this goddamn plane in the air—now!" he roared.

Amanda's bound hands knotted into fists when the pilot grabbed the throttle. Her heart pounded like hailstones against her rib cage. Amanda had never been fond of flying, especially when she would be taking the short way down from the airlanes.

As the plane taxied down the runway, Amanda braced herself for the worst ride, and biggest fall, of her life.

Nick saw the pickup headlights coming toward him and heard the sound of bad muffler pipes. Hazard's truck! This was the opportunity he needed.

The truck fishtailed to a halt. Nick didn't recognize the man who jogged through the beam of headlights like a shadow in a fog of dust. The dark-clad man seemed to be searching for something in the ditch.

Without switching on his own headlights, Nick mashed the accelerator through the floorboard. The man dressed in black spun around to take cover in Hazard's jalopy, but Nick cut him off at the pass. The man tried to leap over the hood of Nick's truck and roll away, but the pickup's forward momentum sent him cartwheeling across the windshield. He collapsed in the gravel with a thud and a groan.

In a flash, Nick leaped out to crack the butt of his pistol over the man's skull and then frisked him for weapons. Nick came up with a Crocodile Dundee-sized knife.

"Holy smoke, it's Jim Johnson!" Pops croaked when the interiors lights shone on the man's greased face. "Why, that sneaky son of a bitch! What did he do with my granddaughter!"

"Pops, take my truck to my farm," Nick ordered hurriedly.

Nick stripped Johnson out of his leather jacket, stocking cap, and lethal hardware. Reaching into the bed of his truck, Nick grabbed a lariat to bind Johnson up tighter than a mummy. When he had hoisted him into the truck bed and secured him to the protruding hay fork, Nick charged toward Hazard's jalopy.

"The plane is turning around, as if it intends to take off!" Pops hollered out the window. "Do you think Amanda is in it?"

Nick sprinted toward Hazard's vehicle, whipped through the ditch to reverse direction, and floorboarded the old truck, praying he could reach the plane before it went airborne.

The forgotten weapon that lay on the seat bumped against his thigh. Nick pulled the gun onto his lap as he swerved around the corner, throwing gravel on the herd of cattle that had bedded down by the fence. The cattle, spooked by headlights and flying gravel, stampeded across the pasture, charging toward the safety of Bloom's barn and the corrals.

"Come in, Robin Hood," Nick called to his brother.

"Where the hell are you?"

"On my way to the damned plane. Where the hell do you think?"

"By yourself?" Rich growled. "Jeezus! Are you nuts!"

"Contact Gib and have him call every farmer and rancher in the area. I need every tractor, swather, and combine in this field as fast as they can get here. If that plane takes off, Hazard's a goner. And call Velma," he added in afterthought. "I want a convoy of cars descending on Bloom Farm—PDQ. Mr. Big won't elude us again. He's going to regret setting up operations in our hometown."

As Nick had hoped—prayed, actually—the taxiing plane slowed down when the pilot recognized the jalopy truck that bounced across the pasture behind the stampeding cattle. Cattle were scattered everywhere, startled by the lights of the aircraft and roar of the truck's mufflers.

Nick was thankful he had the foresight to exchange clothes with Johnson—or whoever the son of a bitch really was—who had deviously toyed with Hazard's affection. With any luck, Mr. Big wouldn't realize Nick was on to him until he had a foothold in the plane.

Nothing would make Nick happier than confronting Mr. Big face-to-face, eye-to-eye for the first time in almost seven years. And if Mr. Big had harmed one shorn hair on Hazard's head—

Nick stifled the bitter thought. He couldn't let emotion interfere. Mr. Big was as ruthless and clever as they came, and this was no time for careless mistakes and misguided fury. It was a time for swift, rational action.

"What's going on!" Mr. Big roared to the world at large.

From the partially open door of the plane he could see distant lights appearing from all directions at once. Farm tractors, like lumbering monsters, crawled through the darkness. A stream of traffic descended on the countryside in a fog of dust. Mr. Big glowered at the rattletrap truck that had pulled alongside the taxiing plane.

"Damn it, Haskell, what have you done—?"

It took a moment for Mr. Big to recognize the man dressed in Haskell's jacket and stocking cap. When he did, a furious roar exploded from his lips. When Nick Thorn—the strap of the semiautomatic weapon slung across his broad chest—leaped from the truck, Mr. Big hastily pulled up the folding steps, refusing to let his arch enemy board the plane.

"Take off, damn it!" Mr. Big snarled at the pilot.

"But there are cattle—"

"I don't give a damn if buffalos are thundering across the prairie in front of us. Get this bird in the air!"

The pilot revved the engine and sped across the dirt runway while Mr. Big struggled to fold up the steps so he could secure the door.

Amanda's stunned gaze fastened on the blazing black eyes and scruffy beard of the man who had leaped from her jalopy truck and was now giving chase on foot. Despite the futility of the situation, she did give Thorn an

A for effort. He was making a spectacular attempt to rescue her. For that, she would try to remember him fondly, even if he had turned into the biggest louse on the face of the earth.

No daring and dramatic act of valor would redeem him, of course, but she would remember not to curse Thorn quite so soundly when she was shoved out the door of the plane.

Dear Readers,

In many cultures, thirteen is considered an unlucky number. Given the precarious circumstances of my situation, I respectfully request—I hope it isn't my final request!—that the last chapter of *Dead in the Dirt* be entitled: *FINALE.* At this critical point in the story it is inadvisable to thumb my nose at superstition and scoff at the darker elements of fate.

Thank you, dear readers, for your indulgence.

        Yours truly,
        Amanda Hazard, CPA

P.S.

        HELP!!!!

~~Thirteen~~

Finale

The pilot was forced to slam on the brakes to dodge the cattle that were frozen to the spot, blinded by the lights. Nick took advantage by hurling himself toward the door of the plane. He managed to thrust his upper torso through the narrow opening before Mr. Big could lock the hatch.

Nick's fingers itched to squeeze the trigger of the semi-automatic, but he didn't trust his luck. If he missed Mr. Big and hit Hazard, he would have defeated his purpose.

Hazard's eyes were as wide as salad plates. Nick couldn't tell if she was surprised to see that he had squeezed himself through the opening or if she was simply scared speechless. At any rate, she didn't move, couldn't move. She was taped to her seat.

"I'll take her out," Mr. Big hissed as he snatched the pistol from his jacket and aimed it at Amanda's head. "You know I'll do it if I have to, Thorn. You may kill me, but she's going with me. Never doubt it."

"You underestimate me if you think it's going to matter what happens to her," Nick growled back. "Diana was the only one I ever cared about. Every other woman since Diana has been the time I was killing. Hazard and I were playmates in the bedroom. No more, no less. If she is the price I have to pay to avenge Diana's death and put you away until you rot, then so be it. I sure as hell can live without Hazard. If you haven't found out for yourself yet, she's a royal pain in the ass—"

Nick thanked the powers that be when the pilot, for whatever reason, was forced to apply the brakes once again. Mr. Big was tossed off-balance—his pistol swinging away from Hazard's fuming face. Nick registered the fact that his damning comment had hurt her feelings and ignited her temper, but his absolute concentration was fixed on Mr. Big.

"You were always a pain in the ass yourself, Thorn," Mr. Big sneered as the barrel of his pistol swerved toward Nick. "Maybe I'll just take *you* with me instead."

To Nick's amazement, Hazard nearly turned herself upside down, despite the restraining tape. He hadn't realized Hazard was so flexible or acrobatic. Before Mr. Big could fill Nick full of bullets, Hazard's bootheel slammed against Mr. Big's Rolex watch. The misdirected bullet ricocheted off the wall.

Nick instinctively dived for cover.

Grabbing the semiautomatic with both hands, Nick pounced on his worst enemy. The side of the weapon clanked against Mr. Big's nose, leveling it against his right cheek. When blood spurted down the front of his Armani suit, he let out a scream to raise the dead.

With brute force, Nick shoved the butt of the weapon into the man's soft belly. The kingpin pitched forward into the aisle. Nick slammed his foot down on Mr. Big's neck—hard—and then half turned to see if the pilot was planning a heroic attempt to rescue his employer.

No attack came. The pilot had his own problems, trying to dodge the convoy of vehicles and special agents swarming around the plane like a multitude of avenging angels.

When Nick heard the collapsible steps snap into position, he didn't bother glancing over his shoulder. He knew Robin Hood and his band of merry men were coming aboard.

"Shit, Nick," Rich grumbled at his brother's back. "You scared ten years off my life. What the hell were you thinking?"

"Revenge—pure, sweet revenge," Nick murmured as he stared down at the man pinned beneath his boot.

"Come on, boys, let's clear the garbage out of the plane," Rich ordered. He wheeled to see Amanda half-sprawled in her seat. "You okay, Hazard?"

"Take me home—*now!*" Amanda demanded.

"Will do, Hazard, as soon as we slap on the cuffs," Rich promised.

Nick noted that Hazard made a grand display of ignoring him. She uttered not so much as a thank-you as she drew herself up to proud stature in the seat and waited to be freed.

When Roger Proctor cuffed Mr. Big, Nick strode over to loose Hazard. Despite her objection, Nick scooped her out of her seat and carried her to the door of the plane.

Headlights shone on Nick and Hazard like spotlights. A round of cheers resounded, praising Hazard's bravery. Once an outsider from the big city, Hazard had been accepted by the rural community and had become one of their own. The citizens of Vamoose had eagerly responded to Nick's call for assistance, doing their part to rescue Hazard from disaster. Their collective contribution had prevented Mr. Big from taking to the air.

"My God, Nicky looks just like Rambo, doesn't he?" Velma Hertzog bugled.

With Hazard still cradled in his arms, Nick glanced down to see that his shirt was gaping open, having lost several buttons during the challenging feat of boarding the plane. The strap of the weapon lay diagonally across his bare chest and the gun dangled beside his hip. He didn't know where the hell his stocking cap had gotten to, but his shaggy hair was waving in the breeze.

"Sly Stallone, eat your heart out. We've got our great American hero, right here in Vamoose!" Velma announced before she struck up another round of applause.

"Put me down, Thorn," Hazard hissed in his ear. "I wouldn't want to strain your *injured* arm."

When Hazard squirmed for release, Nick set her to her feet and then cut the tape loose from her knees and ankles, allowing her to descend the steps.

The moment her feet hit the dirt, Hazard was surrounded by enthusiastic well-wishers who demanded a full account of the events leading up to her kidnapping.

After the crowd swept Hazard away, Rich glanced curiously at his brother. "What did you say to get snubbed by Vamoose's most popular and best-loved citizen?"

"I assured Mr. Big that she meant absolutely nothing to me."

Rich smothered a grin. "That would do it, I guess. You saved the day and lost the dame, Rambo. Better luck next time."

While Rich led the pilot away, Nick strode back to

Mr. Big, who was pinned down by Roger Proctor. It felt good to see his broken nose being rubbed into the carpet of his private jet, one bought and paid for with innocent lives and illegal drugs.

In supreme satisfaction, Nick squatted down on his haunches to confront Mr. Big. "Gotcha," he said with a grin. "We have enough evidence against you that even O.J's. high-priced lawyers couldn't get you off. And I've got one witness who will eat you alive when I turn her loose on the stand. Hazard is going to be unmerciful. And so will the judge."

Rising, Nick stared at his arch enemy. "See you in court, asshole," he smirked before he turned and walked away.

Amanda assured herself that the excessive tears she had shed the past twenty-four hours were the direct result of her traumatic experiences. She told herself that the emotions she had valiantly kept under control in the face of danger had simply come pouring out. It was a normal side effect of plunging down from her adrenaline high.

Discovering that she had never meant more to Thorn than the place he came for recreational sex, that he had built a shrine to his lost girlfriend's memory, had nothing whatsoever to do with this outpouring of tears—she told herself.

Amanda was overwhelmed by the support of Vamoosians who banded together to save her from catastrophe. Dozens of flower arrangements had arrived at her house, in appreciation of her efforts in solving the murder case and saving small-town America from syndicated crime. Amanda had pitched out only one flower bouquet—the one from Thorn. She didn't care if he had looked like Rambo and had rescued her. He had lied to her, purposely misled her, and then dragged her feelings through the dirt.

The time Thorn was killing, was she? The big louse!

The jingling phone interrupted Amanda's mutinous thoughts. She snatched up the receiver, striving for a pleasant tone.

"Hello?"

"Hi, doll. It's Mother. What's going on out there in Podunk City? When I called last night Thorn hung up on me. I wish you'd dump that inconsiderate, disrespectful jerk. He isn't good enough for you."

Mother cleared her throat and plunged into another topic of conversation. "Now, about your grandfather. I've been thinking—"

Amanda didn't have to be clairvoyant to know what Mother was thinking.

"—since you have all that extra space out in the boondocks, why don't you let Pops stay awhile longer? The change of scenery will do him a world of good. He was going stir-crazy in town."

The phone beeped, indicating there was a call waiting. Amanda leaped at the excuse to cut Mother off. She wasn't in the mood to listen to her yammer for a half hour.

"Sorry, Mother, there's another call coming in. I'll talk to you later."

"But I'm family!" Mother yowled. "If you hang up on me, then you can keep Pops at your place for the next month, maybe two."

"Fine, I'll keep him. Good-bye, Mother."

Amanda punched the flash button on the phone to

take the incoming call. "Hello. Hazard's Retirement Center."

"Hazard, I'm on my way over."

It was Thorn's sexy, baritone voice. Amanda snarled into the receiver. "Don't waste a trip."

"I have something to say to you, damn it!"

"I have something to say to you, too. Go to hell, Thorn!" Amanda shouted over the line.

"Okay, whatever you say, but I'm detouring by your place on my way to hell."

The line went dead and Amanda cursed extensively. He hadn't even given her the satisfaction of hanging up on him, the jerk.

So Thorn was coming over, was he? Well, fine and dandy, thought Amanda. She would dress accordingly. Since Thorn had taken an interest in bimbos, then she wouldn't think of disappointing him.

Good thing Pops had gone to bed at his usual time, Amanda thought as she careened down the hall. Her grandfather wouldn't recognize the floozy Amanda intended to turn herself into for Thorn's benefit.

Nick Thorn, freshly showered, shaved, and his hair neatly clipped, climbed down from his truck. He was gussied up in his Western finery for this monumental occasion. He glanced back to see the carload of agents who had accompanied him—reinforcements, as it were. Each agent was fashionably dressed, walking quietly behind Nick as he approached Hazard's door.

Nick clutched the bouquet of red roses in one hand and knocked on the door. A few seconds later, Hazard appeared.

Nick's dark eyes bulged in incredulous disbelief. Hazard stood before him, her curvy body clad in a revealing black negligee, her silky legs wrapped in garters and hose. She had applied so much makeup that her face resembled a mask. Her short blond hair was so thick with hair spray and mousse that it stood up in pointed spikes. She looked like a second-rate slut!

"Hot damn! A fantasy come true," Gib Cooper hooted as he peered around Nick's broad shoulder to get a better view.

Hazard shrieked in humiliation, turned tail, and streaked down the hall to grab a robe—Nick hoped. He didn't appreciate his sidekicks getting their eyes full of Hazard.

When snickers broke out behind him, Nick swiveled his head on his shoulders to give his coworkers a scowl. "Clam up."

They clammed up. Or at least they tried. Nick could still hear his brother struggling to stifle his amusement.

When Hazard reappeared, clutching her terry cloth robe, she glowered at Nick. "You could have told me you were bringing guests."

Nick surged into the living room to offer the bouquet of roses. "I want to explain what has been going on."

Hazard took the flowers and tossed them into the recliner—without so much as a thank-you. "Don't you think I've figured out that you had set up a sting?" she hissed at him. "I'm not entirely stupid . . ." Her voice trailed off when she noticed Nancy Shore, minus the Dolly Parton wig, standing behind Nick. "She was in on this, too?"

Hoping to defuse the situation, Richard Thorn stepped front and center. "Nancy is a special agent from ATF," he explained. "Her kid sister spent a year in drug rehab after Mr. Big's pushers got her hooked."

Rich gestured to Roger Proctor. "Roger was in charge of electronic surveillance at the farm. He served with Nick and me on the City narc squad. So did Gib Cooper. We were all involved in the investigation seven years ago that cost an innocent life and sent Mr. Big into hiding.

"I know you're furious with my brother, but he did what he felt he had to do to lure Mr. Big out in the open so we could convict him."

Nick couldn't tell if his brother's efforts had influenced Hazard. She simply stood there, staring at all of them.

"Richard will need a statement from you," Nick requested. "All the information you gathered will help us put Mr. Big behind bars—permanently."

Amanda organized her thoughts and then proceeded to give a precise, detailed account of how, when, and why Bloom had fallen from the drug lord's favor. She also included the Hamptons' involvement and extortion attempts. By the time she finished, Richard had a notebook full of information and cramped fingers.

Nick muttered under his breath when he noticed the expressions on his coworkers' faces. It went without saying that Hazard had impressed the hell out of them. She knew it, too. Nick could see her gloating.

"We appreciate your help in wrapping up this case," Rich said as he ushered the agents through the door. He halted on the threshold to fling Amanda a cajoling grin. "I have one request."

"What's that?" Amanda inquired.

"Go easy on Rambo, will you? He's the only brother I've got."

Nick held his position until the troops had filed out.

When the door clicked shut, Nick took advantage of Amanda's silence. "I didn't mean a word I said about you, Hazard," he gushed. "I was trying to save you from Mr. Big. I lied up one side and down the other, and I'd do it again if I had to."

Her reply was an unladylike snort.

Since Hazard didn't seem receptive, Nick began phase two of his return to grace. He reached into his shirt pocket to retrieve a box containing the jewelry she had put on sale at the flea market.

"I bought these back, because they are a symbol of my affection for you."

One perfectly arched brow lifted to a skeptical angle. Hazard wasn't buying that explanation, either.

Nick reached into his pocket again, retrieving the velvet case. He opened the box to unveil the engagement ring. "I had planned to give this to you two weeks ago, but circumstances beyond my control prevented it."

Hazard didn't move, didn't bat a thickly caked eyelash.

"I want you to be my wife, Hazard," he murmured softly, sincerely.

"Why?"

"Why?" he repeated stupidly. "Well, because I'm crazy about you."

"Crazy? Yes. About me? Ha!" she all but shouted at him.

"Damn it, Hazard," he growled, nearing the end of his patience. "I'm proposing to you. Cut me some slack, will you?"

"I'm not playing second fiddle to anybody, Thorn," she scowled at him. "I refuse to be a substitute for another woman. And furthermore, I'm not sure I can trust anything you say, ever again."

"I told you I was playacting for Mr. Big's benefit," Nick muttered, frustrated. "What the hell did you want me to say? That I was so damned scared that he'd blow your head off that my hands were shaking? That if I lost you I'd go as nuts as I let everyone in Vamoose believe I was? Hell, Hazard, I was trying to save your life any way I could. And this is the thanks I get!"

"Thank you for saving my life," she said begrudgingly.

"Are you grateful enough to marry me?"

"No."

"Why the hell not?" he yelled, totally exasperated.

"Because you don't trust me," she yelled back. "This entire fiasco hinged around the fact that you didn't trust me enough to tell me what was going on."

Nick had her now. Smiling wryly, he reached for the thick file of papers he had stuffed inside the back of his belt. "Here, Hazard. If the engagement ring doesn't reassure you that I trust you, that I care about nobody but you, maybe this will convince you."

Amanda's legs wobbled beneath her when she realized what Thorn had presented to her—his income tax forms and expense vouchers.

Although most of Vamoose had placed their financial records in her care and trusted her discretion, Thorn had been holding out on her. At last, Amanda knew Thorn was sincere in his proposal. His tax records said it all.

"Oh, Thorn!" Amanda flung herself into his arms and kissed him right smack on the lips.

"Is that a yes?" he whispered, searching for—and finding—that ultrasensitive spot beneath her ear.

Amanda shivered. There was no doubt about it. Furious though she had been with Thorn, he was still the only man for Amanda Hazard. If Bobbie Sue Hampton could turn her back on fame and fortune in country music to stay down on the farm with Buddy, Amanda could forgive Thorn's shortcomings. She would dedicate her life to perfecting his imperfections and making sure Uncle Sam had no complaints about Thorn's tax statements.

"Yes, I'll marry you," she whispered back to him.

Thorn scooped her up in his brawny arms, grinning wickedly as he headed for her bedroom. His face fell when he remembered Pops. Disappointed, he glanced between Pops's bedroom door and Amanda.

"Is Pops going to throw a ring-tailed fit if he finds out we're in bed together?"

Amanda graced him with a blinding smile and snuggled closer. "Pops's hearing aids are lying on the kitchen table beside the stickers for the latest phase of his sweepstakes contest. He won't even know you've come and gone, Thorn."

Thorn flashed that rakish smile that Amanda had never been able to resist. "Maybe he won't, but you will . . ."

The evening proved to be a tantalizing, fulfilling celebration of their engagement. Amanda was pleased to note that her short hairdo didn't stifle Thorn's seductive techniques one bit. In fact, the inventive way he slid the diamond ring on her finger would have sizzled the pages off a romance novel.

Thorn, Amanda concluded several hours later, was every bit the great American hero—brave, courageous, and bold. Of course, she had known it all along. Her infallible feminine intuition had told her so.

MAKE SURE YOUR DOORS AND
WINDOWS ARE LOCKED!
SPINE-TINGLING SUSPENSE FROM PINNACLE

SILENT WITNESS (677, $4.50)
by Mary Germano

Katherine Hansen had been with The Information Warehouse too long to stand by and watch it be destroyed by sabotage. At first there were breaches in security, as well as computer malfunctions and unexplained power failures. But soon Katherine started receiving sinister phone calls, and she realized someone was stalking her, willing her to make one fatal mistake. And all Katherine could do was wait. . . .

BLOOD SECRETS (695, $4.50)
by Dale Ludwig

When orphaned Kirsten Walker turned thirty, she inherited her mother's secret diary—learning the shattering truth about her past. A deranged serial killer has been locked away for years but will soon be free. He knows all of Kirsten's secrets and will follow her to a house on the storm-tossed cape. Now she is trapped alone with a madman who wants something only Kirsten can give him!

CIRCLE OF FEAR (721, $4.50)
by Jim Norman

Psychiatrist Sarah Johnson has a new patient, Diana Smith. And something is very wrong with Diana . . . something Sarah has never seen before. For in the haunted recesses of Diana's tormented psyche a horrible secret is buried. As compassion turns into obsession, Sarah is drawn into Diana's chilling nightmare world. And now Sarah must fight with every weapon she possesses to save them both from the deadly danger that is closing in fast!

SUMMER OF FEAR (741, $4.50)
by Carolyn Haines

Connor Tremaine moves back east to take a dream job as a riding instructor. Soon she has fallen in love with and marries Clay Sumner, a local politician. Beginning with shocking stories about his first wife's death and culminating with a near-fatal attack on Connor, she realizes that someone most definitely does not want her in Clay's life. And now, Connor has two things to fear: a deranged killer, and the fact that her husband's winning charm may mask a most murderous nature . . .

Available wherever paperbacks are sold, or order direct from the Publisher. Send cover price plus 50¢ per copy for mailing and handling to Penguin USA, P.O. Box 999, c/o Dept. 17109, Bergenfield, NJ 07621. Residents of New York and Tennessee must include sales tax. DO NOT SEND CASH.

**NOWHERE TO RUN . . . NOWHERE TO HIDE . . .
ZEBRA'S SUSPENSE WILL *GET* YOU—
AND WILL MAKE YOU BEG FOR MORE!**

NOWHERE TO HIDE (4035, $4.50)
by Joan Hall Hovey

After Ellen Morgan's younger sister has been brutally murdered, the highly respected psychologist appears on the evening news and dares the killer to come after her. After a flood of leads that go nowhere, it happens. A note slipped under her windshield states, "YOU'RE IT." Ellen has woken the hunter from its lair . . . and she is his prey!

SHADOW VENGEANCE (4097, $4.50)
by Wendy Haley

Recently widowed Maris learns that she was adopted. Desperate to find her birth parents, she places "personals" in all the Texas newspapers. She receives a horrible response: "You weren't wanted then, and you aren't wanted now." Not to be daunted, her search for her birth mother—and her only chance to save her dangerously ill child—brings her closer and closer to the truth . . . and to death!

RUN FOR YOUR LIFE (4193, $4.50)
by Ann Brahms

Annik Miller is being stalked by Gibson Spencer, a man she once loved. When Annik inherits a wilderness cabin in Maine, she finally feels free from his constant threats. But then, a note under her windshield wiper, and shadowy form, and a horrific nighttime attack tell Annik that she is still the object of this lovesick madman's obsession . . .

EDGE OF TERROR (4224, $4.50)
by Michael Hammonds

Jessie thought that moving to the peaceful Blue Ridge Mountains would help her recover from her bitter divorce. But instead of providing the tranquility she desires, they cast a shadow of terror. There is a madman out there—and he knows where Jessie lives—and what he has seen . . .

NOWHERE TO RUN (4132, $4.50)
by Pat Warren

Socialite Carly Weston leads a charmed life. Then her father, a celebrated prosecutor, is murdered at the hands of a vengeance-seeking killer. Now he is after Carly . . . watching and waiting and planning. And Carly is running for her life from a crazed murderer who's become judge, jury—and executioner!

Available wherever paperbacks are sold, or order direct from the Publisher. Send cover price plus 50¢ per copy for mailing and handling to Penguin USA, P.O. Box 999, c/o Dept. 17109, Bergenfield, NJ 07621. Residents of New York and Tennessee must include sales tax. DO NOT SEND CASH.